THE WEIGHT

a novel

JEFF BOYD

SIMON & SCHUSTER

New York London Toronto Sydney New Delhi

Simon & Schuster
1230 Avenue of the Americas
New York, NY 10020

This book is a work of fiction. Any references to historical events, real people, or real places are used fictitiously. Other names, characters, places, and events are products of the author's imagination, and any resemblance to actual events or places or persons, living or dead, is entirely coincidental.

First Simon & Schuster hardcover edition April 2023

SIMON & SCHUSTER and colophon are registered trademarks of Simon & Schuster, Inc.

For information about special discounts for bulk purchases, please contact Simon & Schuster Special Sales at 1-866-506-1949 or business@simonandschuster.com.

The Simon & Schuster Speakers Bureau can bring authors to your live event. For more information or to book an event, contact the Simon & Schuster Speakers Bureau at 1-866-248-3049 or visit our website at www.simonspeakers.com.

Interior design by Wendy Blum

Manufactured in the United States of America

10 9 8 7 6 5 4 3 2 1

Library of Congress Cataloging-in-Publication Data has been applied for.

ISBN 978-1-6680-0725-9
ISBN 978-1-6680-0727-3 (ebook)

For Cece

No free negro or mulatto, not residing in this State at the time of the adoption of this constitution, shall ever come, reside, or be within this State, or hold any real estate, or make any contract, or maintain any suit therein; and the Legislative Assembly shall provide by penal laws for the removal by public officers of all such free negroes and mulattoes, and for their effectual exclusion from the State, and for the punishment of persons who shall bring them into the State, or employ or harbor them therein.

—Article 1, Section 35 of the Oregon Constitution, 1857

Who will speak these days,
if not I,
if not you?

—Muriel Rukeyser, "The Speed of Darkness"

PART ONE

1

THE PLACE WAS A RUIN. Painted blue so many years ago, its primary color was now dirt brown. William walked up to the house's front landing. I stayed on the sidewalk. It was a beautiful day, but if anyone was inside the house, they didn't seem to care. There was a window to the right of the door and the blinds were drawn. The doorbell didn't work. The screen door was locked. William hit it a couple times. The frame rattled violently, and still no one came to the door.

"Can't you just call the guy?" I asked him.

He turned to me and shook his head no. "I don't have his number," he said.

Two houses down, a white woman was standing by a street-side mailbox. She was watching us.

"Let's get out of here," I said.

"Hold on a minute. Maybe we should ask those guys across the street."

On the front porch of the house across the street there were two sketchy white dudes sitting on lawn chairs smoking cigarettes. When we first pulled up, William had waved to them, and they'd acted like we didn't exist, eyes not focused on anything in this world. I took a quick glance behind me. Nothing about them had changed. I turned back to William.

"No way," I said.

"Then we should head around back and see if it's still there."

"I'm not trying to get shot over a damn fire pit," I said.

William smiled.

"Good buddy," he said. "Don't be silly. No one's going to shoot us."

He acted like I was being absurd. Well, I'd never heard of a white guy like him getting shot in a stranger's backyard for no good reason. For people like me, that kind of shit happened all the time. Despite that fact, I followed him anyway, refusing to let him believe that he was brave and I was a coward.

We walked across the empty driveway to the left side of the house where a string slipped through a hole in a wooden fence. William pulled the string and yanked the handle. The gate didn't budge. He threw up his hands in defeat. He was the kind of guy who got surprised when a door didn't open for him almost automatically. He was lucky to have me with him. Standing on my toes, I reached over the fence and pulled up the latch.

We entered the backyard. The blinds on the back of the house were closed just like the front. The sliding glass windows were covered with paper bags so you couldn't see inside. The wooden deck was rotten, big holes, missing panels. No signs of life. No outside furniture. Only the fire pit standing alone amid high grass and weeds, like bait to a trap.

William walked up to the fire pit without concern, but I approached cautiously. When I stepped on a twig and it snapped, my body braced for an explosion. Seconds slowly passed and, somehow, I was still alive.

The risks I took for my friends. I was a friendship soldier sometimes. I kept marching ahead until I stood next to William.

The fire pit was about three feet in diameter, a big black metal bowl with slanted legs. The bottom of the iron cylinder contained ash, burnt wood, and a carton's worth of cigarette butts.

"Let's dump this shit out and bounce," I said.

"That's not how I roll," William said.

I thought he might take it as an admission of my fear if I followed him to his car just for him to grab a trash bag, so I stayed in the backyard, trespassing by myself. I looked over the low wooden fence to the neighbor's backyard. An out-of-commission refrigerator was toppled over in the grass. Two rusted cars without wheels sat on cinder blocks underneath a giant tree. I didn't see a soul, and somehow that only made me feel worse, like I could be shot at any moment without knowing it was coming. Every second alone felt like an eternity. I wished I still believed in the power of prayer.

William came back with a paper sack and held it open. I tilted the fire pit. A lot of shit missed the bag. He bent down to grab a chunk of burnt wood and it turned into ash and fell through his fingers. Undeterred, he kept picking up little pieces. He picked up a couple of cigarette butts and tossed them into the bag.

"This is going to take forever," I said.

He looked up at me from his crouched position.

"Then how about you help instead of just standing there?"

"Fine," I said. "Get out of my way."

He stood up and moved aside. I stomped at the debris until everything disappeared into the grass. William sighed as if he didn't like my method of cleaning, but he didn't tell me to stop. We picked up the fire pit and headed out front. It was heavy and I was walking backwards. I tried to move faster.

"What's wrong with you today?" William asked.

"My fingers are getting numb," I said.

"You want to take a break?"

"No," I said. "I want you to hurry up."

The woman who'd been watching us from a mailbox now stood behind William's Subaru, blocking our access to the trunk. She wore a white sweatshirt with a large screen print of Minnie Mouse driving a red convertible down a scenic cartoon highway. Her wispy white hair was the sons of Noah after the flood—wild in every direction. She had a flip phone flipped open with her thumb over the call button like any false move and *boom!* she'd call the cops.

We set the fire pit down in front of her.

"You boys moving in?" she asked.

"We're just here for the pit," I said.

"How'd you know it was back there?"

"It was listed for free on Craigslist," William said.

"That's peculiar," she said. "Last tenants moved out about a month ago. And good riddance to those godforsaken meth heads." She put her phone in her pocket but didn't move away. Instead of moving, she told us the last tenants used to pack the garage with stolen bikes and spray-paint them with the door opened only a smidge. "The fumes almost killed me from all the way across the street. I don't know how they survived. Must have been all the drugs. They were invincible, like cockroaches. Unwanted just the same."

She spoke so loudly I got the impression she was also addressing the dudes across the street. Letting them know she had an eye on them as well. She went on and on about the transgressions of the last tenants. William kept nodding like he understood this lady's troubles, like he hadn't grown up a San Diego surfer kid with adolescent memories of being stoned and playing guitar on the beach with his friends as the sun disappeared into the ocean. Fine for him. But what if the zombies across the street woke up and decided to cause trouble for the Black man? I wanted to tell her to get the hell out of our way. Yet I didn't want to do anything to make her call the cops.

Once she finally moved, we put the fire pit in the trunk and headed for home. From the safety of the car, I waved to the zombies as we drove away. They waved back. Maybe they weren't so murderous after all, but how was I to know until it was too late?

Finally out of Gresham, back in Portland, William rolled the windows down. He was enjoying the drive. He took the tree-lined route home instead of the fast one.

"Thanks for helping me out," he said.

"My pleasure," I said.

And even with the danger, I was being sincere. I was happy to help him because I missed him. We used to be the kind of roommates who did everything together. We used to sit in our living room and get stoned and listen to music and drink and talk until the sun came up. A few times we'd pissed in the toilet at the same time so there'd be no interruption in the conversation we were having. But not anymore, not since things got serious with him and Skyler. Now, except for band stuff, we barely saw each other. Which is why I'd agreed to help him with the fire pit in the first place, so we could spend some time together just the two of us. But our errand had taken longer than I'd thought it would. It was close to three o'clock and I had somewhere else to be.

"Mind speeding up a little?"

"What's the hurry?"

"I'm supposed to meet up with Anne."

"Why?"

"Why not?"

"Because she's engaged."

"Exactly," I said. "That's why we need to talk."

"But what's there to talk about?"

"Just speed the hell up, man."

"Jesus," he said. "Fine. It's your funeral."

He rolled up the windows and pressed on the gas. I sat in the passenger seat and hoped I wasn't headed for the end.

2

ON A SATURDAY AFTERNOON LIKE this one, our neighborhood, St. James, felt like a refuge from all things evil and hard. It was home to one of the oldest amusement parks in the country. And if you took a ride on the park's ancient Ferris wheel and looked around once your car rose above the oak trees, you'd see charming single-family homes, the public swimming pool, the cat hospital, the middle school, antique shops, bars, restaurants, coffee shops, small businesses of every kind, a wildlife refuge, two sprawling public parks, beachfront, boat docks, the Willamette River, houseboats, the sailing club, and a stucco mausoleum with a terra cotta roof that made death seem far off and peaceful. Cars slowed. Walks became strolls. Pain and suffering ceased or was greatly reduced.

By the time we got back to our bungalow it was already ten past three. I helped William drop the fire pit in our backyard and then went inside the house to change. Anne was a punctual person. I imagined her sitting at the bar waiting for me impatiently. Riding my bike would have been faster, but I couldn't risk the sweat. I needed her to find me irresistible. I put on a fresh T-shirt and walked as fast as tranquility would allow.

Almost everyone in the neighborhood was white except for me. I'd just finalized my divorce and was living in my parents' basement in suburban Illinois, feeling washed up at twenty-four years old, when I got the idea to move somewhere far away. Maybe Portland, why not? I went online and found William's Craigslist ad looking for a roommate who'd be interested in starting a band. The ad said he was a singer and guitar player originally from California. He listed some of his favorite artists. Mentioned the Velvet Underground. No pictures of the house, but the rent was cheap. Two weeks later I shipped a few boxes and my drum set and flew out of Midway with a backpack and a duffel bag.

That was almost two years ago. St. James felt more like my home now than anywhere else, but I never felt settled.

I crossed the busy street. I just started going and cars stopped for me to pass, a phenomenon that had taken some getting used to. The first time I jaywalked in this neighborhood and a driver slammed on his brakes and stopped his car in the middle of the street just for me to pass, I thought maybe it was because he'd made a personal oath to no longer impede a Black man's journey. But that wasn't the case. Drivers letting pedestrians cross the street whenever and wherever they wanted was understood within the community as an outpouring of the love and compassion that lived inside the hearts and minds of all St. James residents.

The glory of the day vanished as soon as I walked into Klay's Cosmopolitan. A holdover from the neighborhood's grungier past. The barroom was long and narrow, as was the bar counter. Booths with vinyl-upholstered benches lined the opposite wall. Tinted windows blocked out the sun. The glass orb lights hanging from chains on the ceiling were always kept dim, concealing whatever it was that made the floor so sticky, accomodating my depression, and complementing the posters on the wall. Posters of topless Black women from the 1970s, Bob Marley, Billy Dee Williams, a velvet black panther with a cub in her mouth, and a velvet Elvis. Indoor smoking had been banned for a year, but the smell of stale smoke remained. Even in the dimness you could see the walls were tinted yellow like stained tobacco teeth.

I stood at the bar and didn't see Anne. Something was wrong. She was never late. Four middle-aged white women who sat at the opposite end of the bar counter, likely on an antiquing respite, smiled at me like they were oh so glad to have a Black man in their midsts. David Bowie played from the jukebox. I ordered a beer from a bartender I didn't recognize, which was strange because I thought I knew them all. I looked around the bar again to see if maybe Anne was hiding in a corner.

I was beginning to think I'd been stood up or something horrible had happened, when I heard the front door creak open behind me. I turned my head. Light poured in the room, and as the door closed, a shadowy figure materialized into Anne. I finished my Pabst in one long gulp and met her at the door. Her face was damp with sweat. She wore Teva sandals, rolled-up jeans, and a dirty T-shirt. Her dark blond hair was in a ponytail under a green Yellowstone National Park baseball cap. She wasn't wearing an engagement ring. We hugged and it felt so good just to touch her.

Once we got our drinks, we sat across from each other in a booth and clinked glasses.

"Why'd you pick this place?"

"We always come here," I said.

"Sure," she said. "But only at night. It feels awful during the day."

"We can leave," I said.

"Too late. We're already here."

When I'd called Anne the night before, I was drunk and upset about what William had told me. I told her I needed to see her as soon as possible. Asked her if I could come over to her place. She'd said we should meet somewhere during the day. Probably because she didn't trust us not to mess around if we met in private. I didn't trust us either. That was part of the appeal of seeing her. But to honor her intentions, I suggested we meet the next day at the finest dive bar in our neighborhood.

"So you finally did it," I said.

"Yes. I did. I told you it could happen at any time, remember?"

"Where's the ring?"

"At home. I didn't want to mess it up earlier when I was gardening, and then in my rush to get here I guess I just forgot, it's going to take some getting used to."

It was hard to believe. I needed to see that ring. I needed proof. All those nights she'd whispered so many things. We both did.

"But I don't understand. We slept together the night before you left."

Anne's cheeks puffed out like I'd made a charming little joke.

"I guess that was our last hurrah."

She always knew how to cut me.

"Are you moving back to Denver?"

"Not until I finish school. We're not in a rush."

"So why get engaged?"

"It's a matter of commitment."

"So that's it. It's over?"

"We can still be friends, Julian. We just can't sleep together anymore."

"But we were never friends."

"Don't be silly. Of course we're friends."

"But I don't want to be just friends."

"That's all we ever were. I thought you knew that."

I felt like I was going to burst. I wanted to scream. Maybe rip the velvet Elvis poster off the wall and break it over my knee. I never told her because I knew she'd think it was strange, but I'd only been with two people in my entire life: my ex-wife and her. Was that kind of weird? Yeah. It probably was.

"But I love you," I said.

"What do you love about me?"

"You're so beautiful."

"Yeah right," she said. "I'm the plainest woman you ever saw."

I looked at her in her weekend gardening clothes and her oversized eyeglasses and considered the owl tattoo she had above her left elbow and decided she was probably right. She looked like a lot of women in Portland. And that was part of the attraction. She belonged in this world just by her being herself.

"I think we have something special," I said.

"That's nice," she said. "But friendship is all I can offer you."

We got up and went to the bar. Anne stood beside me and patted my back like she was consoling a child. Already the way she touched me had changed and I just couldn't stand it. We ordered another round of tequila with beer backs. The bartender had a pack of smokes in his shirt pocket. If Jackie, our favorite bartender, was there I would have bummed one, but since we didn't know this guy, I got Anne to offer him a dollar for one. We went outside the bar to split it. I lit it with a match. Took a big drag. Held the smoke in my lungs for as long as I could.

When I was growing up, my pastor condemned Disney, but never J. D. Salinger. The days of book burning were over. No one read for pleasure anymore, so the Evangelicals had all but forgotten about the temptation that dwells in literature. My mother used to take me and my sister to the library multiple times a week. I read all the Hardy Boys books. I read all the Nancy Drew. I read all the books where they teamed up together.

I borrowed art history books just for the nudes—the closest I could get to pornography. Maybe all those years of pining for adventures with someone like Nancy and imagining those paintings of pale white women from centuries past as real flesh and blood, full of desire for a love that only I could give, even though I had no idea how to give it, had messed me up real good.

3

I OPENED THE CUPBOARD WHERE I kept a bottle of bourbon. The bottle was empty, so I went for the vodka bottle William kept in the freezer. Grabbed a bag of potato chips and plopped down on the living room couch. I wished I could talk to someone about my new misery. William wasn't home, of course, and since we didn't have band practice that night, there was a good chance he wouldn't be home until tomorrow at the earliest. Anne and his girlfriend, Skyler, were roommates. I imagined he was with them, talking about me.

The front door opened.

"Hey man," William said.

"Wow," I said. "What a pleasant surprise."

"Just got back from yoga," he said. "And speaking of surprises, are you drinking my vodka straight from the bottle?"

He turned on a lamp and sat on the easy chair across from me.

"Anne," I said. "You want some?"

"No thanks, the bottle's yours. I told you seeing Anne wouldn't do you any good."

"No Skyler tonight?"

"She's got a lot of school stuff, so I'm giving her space. Here, hand me the bottle. I'll pour some in a glass for you."

William wasn't in the mood for getting drunk, but he was down for hanging out and getting stoned. We didn't talk about Anne for the rest of the night. We got baked and listened to records. Ordered pizza. We watched a movie called *Jules et Jim*. He'd seen it, I hadn't. It was a great movie. We decided to use the fire pit. Got in William's car and drove the few blocks to the late-night grocery store to buy wood, ice cream, and beer. We sat around the blazing fire having bursts of conversation about unimportant things, followed by contented bouts of silence, just looking at the flames and appreciating the smell of the crackling wood and the heat and the companionship.

Since that night, I hadn't seen him in three days. I spent every night alone trying not to drink too much or call Anne.

4

THREE NIGHTS ALONE WAS ENOUGH. I practiced drums for a while but then started feeling too lousy to concentrate on anything. I had to go out and find my friends and I knew they'd be at the Woods. Before it was a music venue, the Woods was a funeral home, and still looked like one too. Inside and out, from the wallpaper to the furniture. And when it was crowded, the fact that it had been built to service the deceased and aggrieved only added to its charm. But not tonight. Tonight it was raining hard and the streets were empty, and from the outside, the Woods's white church-like building, surrounded by violently wavering trees, looked so creepy I hesitated to enter. Until the weather forced me in.

Wednesday nights were free, so no one was working the door. I went in undetected. I hung my rain jacket on the coatrack in the entryway, then sat on an orange velvet couch against a wall in the foyer where I could see both the stage and the bar. The stage was filled to the brim with an absurd amount of instruments and antique lamps that the band had brought in themselves. One guy had three keyboards and he wasn't using any of them. For the current song, he only played tambourine. Softly, but without finesse. On the downbeat every time. The band's name was Vestiges. They put me half to sleep, but I really wanted to like them because of my buddy Liesel. She was standing stage right, playing an acoustic guitar, looking lovely as ever. The drummer was playing a triangle. There was a violinist. There was a French horn player. An upright bassist. And the lead singer, whose name I should've known but could never remember, was singing about a tree losing its leaves, a flower blooming in the snow, and a soldier's love letter to his high school sweetheart.

These kinds of bands were all over the Northwest. Groups that seemed to be having an unspoken competition for who should be the house band on the next *Titanic*. Even when this kind of band played loud or fast it sounded like a sea shanty or a swashbuckling hoedown. Irish jig stuff or mournful shit with the violin wailing like the song Vestiges was playing now. Band members swayed and played with their eyes closed.

When the song was over, Vestiges opened their eyes, and the twenty or so people in attendance clapped twice as loud as the music had been.

"Thanks so much," the lead singer said. "That song was called 'Over the Pacific to Be Specific,' about the eternal love between my grandfather, who was just a scared kid from Corvallis when he stormed Normandy, and my grandmother, who had her funeral here last week."

People chuckled. Not me. I didn't think death was anything to laugh about.

William was working behind the bar, talking to Richmond, who was sitting at the bar counter. I got off the couch and walked over to them.

Richmond stood up and gave me a hug. He was sturdy and liked to slap his friends on the back when he hugged them. He was a New Jersey all-state wrestling champion in high school. The only friend I had who I didn't think I could take in a fight. One time when we got super stoned, he told me the only reason he'd wrestled growing up was because his father had never missed a match. We were the only guys in the band who'd played sports in high school. I sat on the barstool next to him.

"We're talking about practice," he said. "You cool with Friday night?"

"Hell yeah," I said. "Keith on board?"

"No doubt. Talked to him earlier."

"Where is he?" William asked.

"He's with a lady friend."

"Is he still seeing Isabel?" I asked.

"Somebody new."

"Jesus," William said. "That guy has a problem. Skyler thinks he's a sex addict."

"Well, do *you* think Keith's a sex addict?" Richmond asked. He was on to something. When William shared Skyler's opinion instead of his own, it was annoying as hell.

"No," William said. "But clearly he's got issues."

He poured three shots of whiskey. We nodded at one another before we took them down.

"Speaking of love," Richmond said to me. "Anne's engaged. That mean you two are done?"

"That's what she told me," I said. "But I don't want to believe her."

"Believe her," William said.

"Why are you against my happiness?"

"What happiness? All Anne seems to do is mess up your head."

"Yo. Shut up," Richmond said. "My girl's about to sing."

He didn't need to tell us to shut up. When Liesel took the front of the stage, you paid attention. Her curly brown hair in the soft yellow light was a dream. She began to play her guitar, and no one in the room dared to breathe. The song was about losing hold of someone you loved. And if I didn't know who she was singing about, it might have made me think about Anne, but when I first met Liesel and Richmond, about a year and half ago, they'd just gotten over a rough patch in their relationship.

After the final note and a breath of space, everyone in attendance applauded. Richmond put fingers in his mouth and whistled. I always thought it was corny when guys did stuff like that, but he made it seem cool.

The show was over. People came to the bar to close their tabs. Richmond and I grabbed our beers and walked outside to the covered patio. It was too cold to feel good about sitting. Raindrops smacked the tin roof over our heads. We stood next to a Ping-Pong table and lit cigarettes. Richmond took a small ziplock bag out of his shirt pocket. He licked his pinky, dipped it into the bag, put the pinky in his mouth. He did that twice.

"You want any?" he asked.

"Is it cocaine?"

"Nah, it's Molly."

"Sure," I said.

I'd never tried it before, and I had to work in the morning, so I should have said no, but I was still upset about Anne and tired of being alone, and I didn't want Richmond to think I was lame. He angled over the bag, I put out a pinky and repeated what I'd seen him do. It tasted like the laundry detergent a cousin had dared me to eat when I was a kid.

With Richmond, I felt like I was running a long con. He seemed to think I was as cool as he was. But that wasn't true at all. I was a former homeschooler. My older sister was my only classmate from kindergarten to sixth grade—until she left me for the Christian high school affiliated with our church. Seventh and eighth grade I was alone. Fortunately, my parents let me go to our town's public high school so I could follow my father's footsteps and play basketball for the Cardinals. But every morning before school my mother would hold my hand as she prayed for my protection. She wrote Bible verses on my paper sack lunches. She made the school promise I wouldn't be exposed to the big bang or sex education. I was a member of the Future Educators of America and the Bible Club. I would sit in the high school library while my classmates learned about Darwin, STDs, and birth control. All through high school, I didn't smoke, I didn't drink, and I never got blow jobs under the bleachers like some of my fellow jocks claimed to be getting. I didn't date, kiss, hold hands, or fondle. Only side hugs. I wasn't cool at all, not like Richmond. He was such a serious guitar player that any musician who saw him walking down the street could tell he had chops just by his stride.

Richmond told me he read some of the poems in the collection I'd given him for his birthday. He said the poems were beautiful, but they didn't make much sense. I told him most of the time if you read a poem looking for its meaning then you probably wouldn't find it. A poem was good if it hit you in the gut. Took you somewhere else. It could act as a mirror. Utter the unspeakable. Somehow embrace you. Just like good music. It was art, so the possibilities were endless. I didn't mention the only poem I'd ever gotten published was about a plastic cup of orange juice that wished it were a glass of milk, and ended with the lines, "and the sneaking suspicion that if I was made of glass / this would have been different." Or that the only reason I started writing poetry in college in the first place was because creative writing seemed like an easy enough major. And I didn't tell him his lack of interest in books of any kind was somewhat disturbing to me. Instead, we talked about New York City and Chicago and how Portlanders were shitty drivers with no aggression. We agreed our band could be dope if we just worked our asses off. In three weeks, at the end of April, we were opening for a big-time indie rock band at a swanky mid-sized venue called the Spruce, our biggest show ever. Label reps would be there, booking agents, too.

He tossed his cigarette in the ashtray sitting on the Ping-Pong table. "I'm going inside to find Liesel."

"All good, man," I said. "See you in there."

I stood alone on the patio and took stock of myself. When were the drugs supposed to kick in? I didn't feel much different than I usually did. The only Black person I'd seen all day was my own reflection. Earlier, at the grocery store, I thought I saw a Black man, but when I stopped to take a closer look, it was my reflection in a mirror in the cosmetics aisle. I wanted to see that man again. I went to the restroom and got a look at myself in the mirror above the sink. I made all the faces I could think of. Moved my eyebrows up and down. Put my index fingers in my mouth and pulled at the corners. Closed one eye, kept the other one open, did the reverse. Tugged on the tops of my ears. Stuck out my tongue, whirled it around. After I was done with silly faces, I pulled up my striped sweater and grabbed my gut. I squeezed and released the flesh so my stomach looked like it was talking. I made it say, "Hello, Julian. I'm your fat Black tummy and I love you. Silly to think you're alone. You have me." And I felt better, like I'd actually gotten some good words from my gut.

I opened the restroom door. "Pusherman" by Curtis Mayfield blasted out of speakers and into my bloodstream. Bringing a pleasant memory from the past. Growing up, my mother didn't allow secular music in the house, so my sister and I would borrow CDs from the library and keep them hidden. I'd mostly only listen through headphones, but when my parents were both out of the house I'd go to the basement, sit behind my set, and blast library songs on my boom box. I'd try to play along like I was in the band, a real band, not a church worship group. One time my father came home and heard me playing "Pusherman." I'd had it on repeat. That snare, the entire groove, I just couldn't get enough. And my father, police detective, member of the church board, and a teetotaler, walked down the stairs in his suit and tie, bobbing his head and singing along. He knew every word . . . *I'm your mama, I'm your daddy, I'm that nigga in the alley* . . . And when the song ended, all he said was, "What you know about Curtis, Son? That track was the cut back in the day." And that was the power of music: father and son grooving to Curtis Mayfield together.

I found William and Richmond and Liesel sitting at a table and drinking with members of Vestiges. Liesel got up and gave me a big hug.

"We thought maybe you left without saying goodbye," she said.

"Never," I said. "You were great tonight."

She stepped back and smiled. Reached for my face. Pinched my left cheek. I loved when she did that. I could feel myself grinning.

"Where were you?" she asked.

"In the bathroom," I said.

"Shit," Richmond said. "That whole time? You okay?"

"God is in heaven, and all is right with the world," I said.

I sat next to William. "You see?" he said. He elbowed me in the stomach. "You're a drummer and a poet; you're going to be okay."

"I haven't written a poem since you've known me," I said. "Where's Skyler?"

"Working late," William said. "But don't worry. I told her I was going to get loose with my friends, and all she told me was to be careful."

William only bartended when he felt like it, which wasn't very often. Sometimes he would lock up the Woods after closing time and throw a small after-party for the bands that had played that night and not make them pay for anything. I wasn't 100 percent sure, but based on the amount of mail William received from financial institutions and law offices, I was pretty sure he was a trust fund kid. He owned our bungalow, which meant he was technically my landlord, but aside from the pesky matter of my monthly rent payment, we tried not to talk about it; we only referred to each other as roommates.

No one in our Portland circle talked about money in a way in which you could determine their actual wealth. Everyone had roommates and lived in shabby homes. Everyone drank cheap except for special occasions or when things were free. Sometimes I wondered if I was the only one around who wasn't playing pretend poverty.

It was all very confusing. William got his hair cut once a month at a fancy salon in the Pearl District and only purchased organic food, yet he just had to have that free fire pit. Liesel worked for a catering company, sometimes. Richmond had professionally printed business cards that simply said *Richmond: All Around Man* with his phone number and email address. He dabbled in commercial painting, web design, construction, carpentry, and guitar lessons. He had a shitty car and always wore the same pair of jeans, but he owned at least thirty thousand dollars' worth of musical equipment. I was the only person in our crew who worked a nine-to-five and I assumed that was because I was the only one in our crew who needed to work those kinds of hours to survive.

At some point in the night, we ended up in the basement. There was a rusty metal grate over a drain on the floor where William told us they washed away the blood.

"Look," he said. "You can see dried blood on the corners of the drain."

"That's rust," Liesel said. "This is a funeral home, not a coroner's office."

"Yeah," Richmond said. "There are rules to human waste."

"What do you think?" William asked me.

"This doesn't look like a place for draining blood," I said.

"Thank you, Julian," Liesel said.

Richmond winked at me.

William shook his head. "You guys are all wrong."

The drugs were taking over. In the dim and creepy basement, I looked at my three closest friends. William was a beautiful guy with great hair, but when he was silent, his best qualities were hidden.

People didn't understand how powerful he was until he got onstage and opened his mouth. Liesel had that quality too. The way her voice could take you by surprise, especially when she sang quietly, could knock you over. Richmond was different. Even silent and drugged, his power permeated as if it were a scent. And I wanted to tell him that I hoped to gain that same kind of power, to become fiercely human, but after hitting the joint Liesel passed me, my mouth became too jumbled for speech.

We went back upstairs. Across the covered patio there was a small building where they kept the body incinerator. Richmond wanted to see it. William unlocked the door and let us in. The light switch on the wall didn't work. Liesel turned on her phone light. The incinerator looked like a big metal oven. Normally I would have been too scared, but I was feeling indestructible thanks to the Molly. I walked up and lifted the hatch to the oven. We huddled together and looked inside, Liesel's phone our only source of light. Inside, the oven was eerie and dark and dusty with human ash. Richmond got some on his finger and snorted it. William laughed and looked like a ghost with the low light and his paleness. Liesel too; she cackled. I shuddered.

Things got hazy after the body incinerator. I remember lighting cigarettes and putting them out. I don't remember smoking them. I know I went behind the bar a couple of times to get more beer and whiskey. Eventually switched to water. William and Liesel played guitars and sang duets. Richmond played piano. The woman who played French horn for Vestiges cried in my arms as we sat on the bathroom floor and talked about how God used to feel as real as anything we could see or touch, how we used to speak to him every day, and now we couldn't feel his presence no matter how hard we tried.

5

I AWOKE IN MY BED—an old mattress against the right corner of the carpeted floor of my bedroom—and saw Anne at the doorway holding a vase full of flowers she'd probably picked from her garden. She put the vase on the dresser. Went to the window. Pulled back the curtains and lifted the frame. Light, children's voices, fresh air, and the sound of rattling wagon wheels wafted into the room.

"You look terrible," Anne said.

"Thanks," I said. "What time is it?"

"One in the afternoon. Shouldn't you be at work?"

Anne stood close, but not close enough for me to touch her. I reached for my cell phone on the floor next to the mattress. My head was pounding. I looked through my email.

"At seven in the morning, out-of-his-mind Julian sent his boss a coherent message about severe stomach pain."

"Congratulations," she said.

"I'm responsible," I said.

Anne rolled her eyes. But I was serious. I almost never missed work. Last winter I'd worked through the flu. Typical hangovers were alleviated by coffee and a breakfast burrito. My sick days were saved for days like this one.

I tossed my phone back onto the carpet. My head on my pillow, I looked up at her.

"Why are you here?" I asked. "I thought you were done with me."

"I'm here because I knew you were hurting and I didn't want you to suffer alone."

"Hurting how?"

"From debauchery."

"No other reason?" I asked. "Not my hurting from you?"

"I'm just here as a friend who'd like to see you live," she said. "Why are you being an asshole about it?"

"Because I'm dead inside," I said. "Thanks for coming."

"That's more like it," she said. "Can I sit?"

Naked, I sat up and leaned against the wall that touched the long side of my bed. Anne sat down next to me. She opened her backpack and handed me a bottle of coconut water, a smidge of relief for my body, but my brain needed something stronger. I leaned forward to grab the half-smoked bowl and the lighter that were on top of the cardboard box I used as a nightstand. The box was the only furniture I'd contributed to the house. It was sturdy enough to hold a lamp and a glass of water. It was packed tight with the stuff I didn't want to lose but didn't care to think about.

The tokes were nice for my head, but I didn't feel like being naked anymore, not if Anne didn't want me. I took the blanket and wrapped it around me. I turned my head to look at her.

"How'd you know I'd be hurting?"

"Skyler. She stopped by the Woods last night after she hadn't heard from William. She said you guys were pretty much incoherent. She said William and Richmond had to practically lift you into her car."

"William picked *me* up? I doubt it. Is he here?"

"He's at my place," she said.

"You should charge him rent," I said. "He practically lives there."

Anne said she'd come over to keep me company, but I couldn't remember a time she'd come into my bedroom and we hadn't had sex.

She took out her laptop to work on a paper. She was in a graduate program at Portland State, something to do with public policy. She'd told me about it many times, but I could never get the details to stick in my head. After I finished the coconut water, I put my head back on my pillow and pressed my feet against her right hip.

I fell asleep and had a terrible dream where Anne creeped behind me and knifed me to death in the foyer of the Woods. She took me to the basement. Tied a rope around my legs. Threw one end of the rope over a hook connected to the ceiling and pulled until my body was hanging upside down and my blood flowed down the rusty drain. Once I was bloodless, she cut the rope and I fell to the floor. William helped her pick me up and throw me into a wheelbarrow. He pushed me into an elevator. The elevator door opened, and we were in the crematorium. Liesel and Richmond were there. They lifted me onto a metal table and started sawing away. Piece by piece they threw me into the blazing-hot oven.

Anne was shaking my ankle. She told me there was a pepperoni pizza in the oven and it was probably done. Especially nice of her because she didn't eat pork or dairy or gluten. My head was pounding, and the dream had me shook. Before I could find the energy to sit up, the cat jumped on the blanket I was wrapped in and kneaded my stomach.

Olympia was William's cat, but she loved me best. I scratched under her chin. She purred and purred, and as I lay there scratching her, it became clear to me somehow that though I felt like shit in a way I'd never felt like shit before, closer to death than I'd felt in some time, I wasn't going to die due to last night's activities. Permanent damage, maybe. But not death.

"The pizza is going to burn," Anne said.

"Okay," I said. "It's just hard to get up when I'm getting all this love."

"Love from who? The cat?"

"Yeah," I said. "She's the only black friend I have."

Anne snorted with laughter. I pushed off the cat and the blanket. I got up unsteadily. My body was tight. I tried to touch my toes but couldn't get past my shins. I reached up and touched the ceiling with my fingertips. Put my arms out sideways. Rotated my neck. Joints cracked like crazy. I could feel Anne watching me.

"Maybe you should put some clothes on," she said.

"Why?" I asked. I turned around to face her. Hands on my hips. "Too tempting?"

"Oh please," she said. "You're not naked like a man, you're naked like a baby."

I moved closer to her.

"Are you proposing some kind of role-play?"

Anne threw a pillow at me.

"Go."

I walked out of my bedroom, through the recording studio set up in the alcove, down the treacherous carpeted stairs, onto the cool and creaky wooden floor of the secondhand-furnished living room, then onto the cracked tile floor of the kitchen; the crumbs and dirt felt unpleasant on my bare feet, and it was all my fault. It was my turn to clean the kitchen, but I couldn't get motivated.

All the curtains downstairs were wide open. Anyone looking through the right window at the right time would have seen a big, naked Black man pulling a pizza out of the oven, cutting it up, burning his mouth, and gulping down a Mexican Coke.

Back in bed, I tried to read a collection of James Baldwin essays my brother-in-law had given me for Christmas. But my brain was too cracked for retention. I couldn't make a connection from one word to the next. Anne played Edith Piaf from her laptop's speakers. Edith sounded like a kazoo. The clack of Anne's keyboard rhythmless castanets. I would have preferred silence, but she was hard at work, and she never looked more beautiful than she did when she was deep in concentration. I watched her blue eyes dart back and forth behind her eyeglasses.

Back when we used to sleep together, before she got engaged and ruined our arrangement, I'd wake up and find her next to me, naked, except for her big glasses, writing in the forest-green journal she took with her everywhere, and I'd feel so lucky to be with her. I felt a little of that warm emotion being with her now. I fell asleep again and didn't dream about anything I could remember; it was a peaceful rest.

Five o'clock and Anne was hungry. She shook me awake and told me she wanted to go out to dinner. I put on my bathrobe and slippers and went downstairs to take a shower. To get to the bathroom you had to walk through the kitchen. There was a window opposite the breakfast nook that faced the neighbors' window. In their window was an intricate wooden lectern with a large leather-bound Bible opened to the middle. Probably in Psalms. Maybe on the page where it's says it's better to trust in the Lord than anyone else, because he's got all the power and he always has your back.

For all the times I'd passed that window, I'd never seen anyone standing there and reading that Bible. My own Bible was sitting on my desk at work as a prop to appease the boss. Like my neighbors, I didn't see any point in reading it anymore.

Anne and I went to a Thai place down the street and split coconut pumpkin soup, tofu, and vegetable spring rolls. I told her about the body incinerator.

"Richmond snorted some of the ashes."

"I doubt it was human. It was probably just dust."

"Either way. He had the intent."

"What made you guys decide to go crazy last night?"

"You know how it goes. It just happened."

"I get the drinking, but what about the drugs? Do you guys think it helps your music? It was a work night for you."

"Who knows about them. I got fucked up because of you."

"What does that mean?"

"I wanted to forget you."

"Did it work?"

"It worked until you walked into my room with those flowers."

"But why would you want to forget me?"

"You know why. You dumped me."

"That's not true, Julian. How could I dump you if we never dated?"

I didn't know how to answer that question. We both stopped talking. She slurped her soup loudly, I hated that. We put our credit cards on the table. We shook our heads yes when the waiter asked if we wanted to split the check down the middle. I tipped the same as she did, even though I needed every penny I had. We left the restaurant and walked around aimlessly. The sun was almost set. The sky was turning gold. And our neighborhood was freshly flooded with cherry blossoms. Pink and white petals blanketed lawns, driveways, sidewalks, and cars. Instead of talking, we anticipated each other's thoughts and feelings through body language. Almost everything I appreciated about nature I'd learned from Anne. We stopped for moss on the ground, lichens on trees, hydrangeas, daphne. We looked at kitschy mailboxes. Stopped for sidewalk hopscotch. Took turns hopping. My headache was vanquished by the beauty of the neighborhood. Signs said, SLOW DOWN. KIDS AT PLAY. And there were kids at play, and we were slow, walking in step, but not touching like we used to. There was a family of four eating dinner at a wooden picnic table sitting under a tree in their front yard. Glasses of beer for the adults. Juice for the kids. The father stood over the table and carved a chicken. He looked happy. The mother looked content. The children had good table manners. They sat up straight. Napkins in their laps. An advertisement for strivers who desired a nuclear family.

We passed a neighborhood watch sign, the silhouette of a burglar slashed out in red. We kept walking. A little dog barked and nipped at me. The owner jerked the dog's leash and apologized. I smiled to let the owner know I didn't think they'd trained their dog to be racist. Anne gave the owner a glare that was easy to decipher: take care of your dog or I'll take care of it for you. Anne was great at the terrifying stare. That was the bulk of her violence. Or so I thought. In my dream, she'd killed me.

As we approached the public swimming pool at the foot of the park, I thought about the night last summer when I first met Anne, about a month after Skyler and William had started dating. A bunch of us jumped the swimming pool fence at one o'clock in the morning. Everyone else scaled the fence with ease. But I wasn't so lucky. I made attempt after attempt while everyone watched me struggle from the other side of the fence. It was embarrassing. The fence stamped my palms with excruciating hexagons. Every unsuccessful climb put me further in despair. William tried to encourage me by saying stuff like *that's okay, dude, you got this . . . focus, man, just focus . . . oh so close . . . oh, dude!* And it was great motivation. I wanted desperately to get over the fence and punch William's beautiful face in, but once I made it over, there wasn't any violence; instead, I took off my clothes and got in the water. Anne and I had just met, yet we ended up kissing in a dark corner of the pool, and as night slipped into early morning, we passed out on my mattress, sticky from sex and chlorine. Maybe Anne was thinking about our first time together as well. She grabbed my arm as we passed the pool. It was covered with blue tarp, still closed for the season but opening soon. We walked around the park on a concrete path. We sat on a bench under a walnut tree, our backs to the busy playground. There was a field of grass in front of us, and beyond that a tennis court where two teenage boys kicked a soccer ball back and forth over the net.

"Anne, you and I are like two pearls locked in a safe hidden behind a Manet."

She put her head on my shoulder. Had she really never loved me at all?

"Whatever that means," she said. "Tell me this."

"Tell you what?"

"If you knew I was hurting like you were this morning, would you actually come to my place just to help me?"

"Of course I would. I love you."

She sat up and looked at me.

"I don't think that word means the same to you as it does to me."

"Don't get married," I said. "It sucks. Believe me."

"I bet you were a terrible husband."

"I was."

We held hands and stopped talking. Our bodies pressed together. Last summer in the pool, the only light in the darkness had come from just beneath her skin, steam rose from the water surrounding her, and her bra was so much sexier than any kind my ex-wife had ever worn. When I'd looked into Anne's eyes that night, I was sure I'd seen an answer to my loneliness, but eight months later, she was engaged to someone else.

We sat on the bench until the golden hour ended. We went back to my room. Sometimes our sex would be over in minutes, but this time it was long and thoughtful, all our greatest hits, a proper goodbye. I fell asleep with her next to me. Sometime later, Olympia's hungry meows woke me up. Anne was gone. It was dark outside.

But I knew I wouldn't be able to fall back asleep. My phone said it was five in the morning. A no-good time for anything I could think of. I got up to feed the cat. I drank coffee and read Baldwin at the kitchen table until the sun came up and it was time to get ready for work.

6

"SUNSET ROLL. DRAGON ROLL. TUNA belly sashimi. Unagi . . ."

On Friday mornings before he got on the phone to sell the benefits of our company's email marketing system, the guy in the cubicle closest to me, John, liked to warm up his deep sales-executive voice by reciting what he planned to eat for dinner that night. John was Korean, not a white guy like everybody else in the office, so when I first started working at Marketing Monkey, I tried to be his friend, but he was sober, conservative, and a super-duper Christian, and I was none of those things, at least not anymore. I was still out of sorts from the drugs and the fact that after Anne and I had sex last night, she'd said it could never happen again.

Maybe she was right. Maybe I didn't know what love was at all. But what about love? I'd had chances to sleep with other women between my divorce and before meeting Anne, but I hadn't. Probably due to my upbringing. I'd been taught to bundle sex with love and marriage. And the truth was, that night in the pool when Anne had touched me under the water and leaned in to kiss me, I thought maybe I could marry her. But she never thought she could marry me, and that hurt.

John was doing his warm-up, Trenton entered my cubicle and sat in the chair in the back corner. I swiveled my chair around and scooted close to him. We tried to talk quietly so no one could snoop.

“Missed you yesterday,” Trenton said. “Everything okay?”

“Rough night,” I said.

“Partying?”

“Yeah.”

“Good for you.”

Trenton was the only guy in the office I could relate to. My only work friend. For us, this was a hostile workplace environment. He was gay and often on uppers and had to work hard to hide it.

He whispered in my ear.

“I still need those call-in leads.”

“Of course,” I said.

“Good,” he said. He got up to leave. “Lunch today? Barbecue?”

“Perfect,” I said.

Trenton was on a cold streak. For the last two weeks, he’d stood next to me during our Monday-morning prayer meetings with a grip on my hand like I was the only person who could save him. So instead of doling out incoming new business calls in rotation like I was supposed to, I sent them all his way, and as a reward he took me out to lunch sometimes.

Free lunch, sneaking calls to Trenton, and doing as little work as I could get away with were all I had to look forward to until quitting time. I’d been at Marketing Monkey for a year. Even though, less than a week into the job, I realized I should have never applied for the gig.

My first week of work was on a Tuesday during the company’s five-year anniversary celebration. We were given stress balls with the company’s logo on them. The boss provided grocery store doughnuts and watery coffee all week. The office buzzed with anticipation of the work party the boss was throwing on his yacht that Friday. John was pumped. He boomed about it relentlessly. I was pumped too, first week on the job and I was going on a yacht.

We boarded the boat on a brisk afternoon. The yacht was a good size for the boss and his wife and their two teenage daughters, but cramped for eight grown men with no intention of swimming or sunbathing. While our coworkers bundled up in heavy jackets and stayed in places protected from the wind, Trenton and I sat on the top deck, loving it. He was from Michigan. For us, this type of weather was nothing at all. The voyage started out well, the boss blasted Michael McDonald Motown covers on the boat's powerful sound system, and as the yacht picked up speed, crisp wind blew across my face. I felt wonderful. Then I got thirsty.

"I know there's going to be food," I yelled to Trenton. "But what about booze?"

Trenton's graying brown hair blew in the wind, he looked up at the overcast sky, he turned to me, shook his head in bafflement, then yelled, "Oh God, you don't know?"

"Know what?" I yelled back.

The only way we could hear each other over the motor and wind was if we yelled. Trenton looked around to make sure no one was lurking before he replied.

"I believe we're the only two non-recovering alcoholics on this boat."

"Damn! Are you serious?"

"I'd also advise you not to swear around them either. These guys are very religious. Jesus is very personal to them. He keeps them off the bottle or whatever."

"They're born-again?"

"Something like that," Trenton yelled. "No booze, but I bet you could find a gun or two. The boss loves them."

Turns out everyone else who worked in our office were guys the boss had met in the Christian AA group he led. Trenton and I had been hired under unique circumstances. Trenton had cold-called the boss two years ago to sell him on the high-speed internet business package he was peddling, and the boss had been so blown away by Trenton's skills, he'd convinced him to join the sales team at Marketing Monkey. My job was the only one the boss had ever put out an ad for. Before this job, I'd only worked in retail. My résumé was light. I think he hired me because I graduated from a Christian college.

But escaping a Christian environment was part of the reason I'd left Illinois in the first place. I should have quit when we got back to shore. I should have quit the moment I found out the boss had the whole company pray together every Monday. But over a year later, I was still on the job because I couldn't afford to miss a paycheck. I had so much student loan debt that the total balance seemed like an error. My two credit cards were close to maxed out.

After Trenton left my cubicle, I spun my chair back to my computer and tried to figure out how I was going to make myself look busy. I scrolled through my work emails looking for something hard to respond to so if the boss walked by my desk and asked what I was doing, I could tell him I was providing customer service. I was the only Marketing Monkey employee paid hourly. I was the only one who wasn't in sales. I received about three phone calls an hour. The company's website and email marketing system were built and maintained by independent contractors. I made sixteen dollars an hour with limited benefits. Nine to five. Monday through Friday. I answered the phone, reluctantly replied to emails, and co-wrote and edited the boss's weekly newsletter. I thought about the Baldwin I'd read before work. I thought about what he said about Black people being born in the ghetto, destined to die in the ghetto. But that wasn't me. I was born in the suburbs, I was supposed to be able to make something of myself, and here I was making shit pay and being poor.

My desk phone lit up right before lunch. The boss said he needed to see me immediately. He reminded me of a megachurch youth pastor I used to know. Especially on casual Fridays, when he wore jeans and shirts that were too tight, distressed, and European for his age, body, and worldview. His thinning hair was meticulously styled and colored. His slang felt forced. He was condescending, loud, self-righteous, muscular only in the arms and chest.

I walked into his office.

"Julian," the boss said. "My homie. Shut the door and sit down."

With his hands out of sight, I thought maybe he was holding the handgun I'd heard he kept in a locked desk drawer and that he was deciding whether to pull the trigger. I could never tell what he was thinking, and he never let on until he was ready for the reveal. He looked sort of happy to see me, but also like he'd somehow found out that Trenton and I had pounded vodka energy drinks at the park across the street during lunch break on Monday. Or maybe he'd caught me staring at his eldest daughter's butt when she came in on Tuesday to surprise him for his birthday. I tried not to look at her framed high school graduation photo sitting on the shelf behind him.

"Feeling better?" he asked.

He put his meaty hands on the top of his desk. They were empty. He was a maniac. I sat on the chair across from him.

"It was a nasty bug." I said. "But I'm feeling much better."

He scowled.

"I hear Trenton's getting all the call-in leads."

"Says who?"

"A little birdie told me."

I figured it must have been John. Despite his big booming voice, he had somehow managed to eavesdrop on my conversation with Trenton. He was the boss's lead disciple.

"Just the Seattle calls," I said. "Trenton's head of sales there, right?"

The boss didn't like to talk about our fictitious Seattle office listed on the website to make the company seem larger than it was. If someone called the number with the 206 area code, the call would come to me on line 3, and I'd say, "It's a beautiful day in Emerald City and a beautiful day at Marketing Monkey, how may I direct your call?" And if the person was interested in using our fun templates and marketing system to create enticing spam for potential customers, I sent them over to Trenton.

The boss leaned back in his chair. Pushed it away from his desk. Put his hands on his head and flexed his tanned biceps. A bit of his non–beer belly hung out of his luxe polo shirt. "If it's giving you trouble, I can take that Seattle number off your hands."

"That's okay," I said. "I don't mind at all."

"Good," he said. "Keep on doing great work."

I got up and walked toward the door.

"Yo," the boss said. "Check it." I stopped at the door and turned to look at him. "I'd like to see you take on more of a leadership role at this company. Strong faith is essential. How would you like to lead us in prayer next Monday?"

I wanted to tell him *no way, I'm done with that game*.

"Sure," I said.

"Praise God," the boss said. "Have a good lunch."

7

OUR BAND PRACTICED IN THE basement of me and William's bungalow. I was exhausted, but not without belief. I knew if my kick drum got sluggish, Richmond's guitar too dissonant, or William forgot to play altogether, Keith would hold it down. He was our glue. A natural-born bass player. A weirdo with a big bushy beard. Almost everything he wore could have been featured in a Sears catalogue during my grandfather's tenure as the first Black shoe salesman in the company. He was the shortest guy in the band by five inches and the only native Portlander.

Practice went well, too well. You could feel it in the room; we all knew our parts, but no one had pushed the envelope. Everyone had played it safe. The songs hadn't improved, and neither had we. It was one of the most unsettling and least-satisfying practices we'd ever had. Afterwards we passed around a joint and tried to finalize our setlist for our big show at the Spruce. Problem was, we didn't have enough original material to fill our hour-long time slot, so we needed to play a cover. Keith suggested "Don't Talk (Put Your Head on My Shoulder)."

Before we'd had any originals, when we first started playing together, we came up with a great version of that song. We'd sped up the tempo, punched up the dynamics, crunched up the guitars, gave Richmond room to rip, and let William's voice do the rest. The night we got that song right we just knew we were going to be a great band. But I didn't want to play it.

"The song's too short," I said. "Besides, we haven't played it in months."

"Well excuse me for wanting to get laid," Keith said.

"How about that Television song," Richmond said. "Bass line is sexy as fuck."

"Not sexier than the Beach Boys," Keith said. He was wearing a cream-colored short-sleeve button-down shirt with pearl snap buttons, big tweed pants, loafers without socks. He was holding a bottle of beer, leaning on his amp with his bass still strapped to his body.

William bent down to pick up Olympia. He held her in his arms and scratched her back. "I agree with Julian. The song is too short." When he looked at me, Olympia turned to look at me too. "But dude, be honest, you don't want to play it because it's Anne's favorite."

"She ruined a great song," I said.

Keith looked disgusted.

"Do you think Brian Wilson is still having sex with whoever he wrote that song about? I don't. And I bet he plays it every show."

"That's got nothing to do with me, man," I said.

"Sure it does. Putting women on a pedestal is anti-feminist."

"I'm not an anti-feminist."

"You're not? Well, you could have fooled me."

"Oh, stop it, you horny bastard," Richmond said.

"No Beach Boys," William said. "Let's honor Julian's wishes."

"Fucking cockblockers," Keith said.

"You'll just have to use your natural charm," I said.

"Screw you," Keith said. "Holly from French Navy is the baddest bitch in the northwest music scene, and you're no help at all because you can't be Brian Wilson."

It was stuffy in the basement and there was no more beer. The Woods had bingo night. No thank you. We decided to go to Klay's Cosmopolitan. We piled into Richmond's Volvo 740. His car was as sunburned and cracked as an old white sea captain. I sat in the front passenger seat. Richmond got the car started on the third attempt. Once we were on our way, he pushed in the cigarette lighter, and when it popped out red hot, he lit a cigarette. We rolled down the windows. The smoke stayed in the car. William started to cough.

"Jesus Christ," he said.

"Hold on a sec," Richmond said.

He turned left and the smoke cloud vanished.

"I was at Hollywood Vintage yesterday," Keith said. "They had these awesome Native American bolo ties. I think it'd be slick if we wore them at our show."

Richmond laughed. "Are you serious, dude? I thought you were trying to get laid."

"Ever think about finding a woman you could see yourself with long term?" William asked.

"Always," Keith said. "Believe me, I try. I just haven't found her yet."

Plaid Parenthood was the first real band I'd ever been part of. Keith came up with our name during a walk of shame. He loved to tell the story. He'd been doing a walk of shame, thinking about setting up an appointment at Planned Parenthood for an STD screening, when he came across a man wearing the same plaid shirt as him. The man was standing outside of a Plaid Pantry convenience store holding a baby. Keith said the guy looked exactly like him. Like he was seeing himself in an alternate universe. So he did what felt right. He ran away from himself as fast as he could.

Every time I hung out with these guys, even through bad practices and dumb arguments, I always had the feeling I was right where I was supposed to be. If I still believed in predestination, I would have called our coming together fate. This band was my refuge. The first time I ever smoked weed was with William my first night living in Portland and I was surprised to wake up the next day feeling great. After twenty-four years of believing marijuana would ruin my life. Theses guys were my guides to another way of living. The way I grew up, I was Christian before I was Black or American or anything else. With these guys the band came first, and that made us brothers.

Richmond parked on a side street a block from the bar. You could go days without seeing a cop in St. James, but could never be too careful. Just picture it: A cop sees you walk out of a bar and trip over a rock and now he thinks he's caught a drunk driver, so as soon as you start the engine, he turns on his lights and makes you do a Breathalyzer when all that could have been avoided by just parking around the corner. These were the type of life-changing solutions we came up with sometimes during band practice breaks and at bars.

We walked into Klay's Cosmopolitan. Friday night, so they had table service. We sat at a booth and ordered drinks, it was the same booth I'd shared with Anne when she'd confirmed her engagement. I still hadn't seen the ring. I mentally checked out of the conversation the guys were having and took out my phone to look at old texts. In the first message she ever sent me, the day after we first hooked up, Anne told me she had a serious boyfriend, and that when she decided to move to Portland for graduate school, they'd agreed that fooling around with other people was fine as long as it didn't turn into a relationship. But if what we had wasn't a *relationship*, what do you call having sex multiple times a week and texting almost every day?

I put away the phone. Picked up my drink and listened as Keith lamented the struggles of being a vegetarian and working part-time at a doughnut shop. He said the bakers never washed their hands after handling and frying the massive amounts of bacon needed to make tons of batches of the shop's signature Porkland Trail Glazer doughnut. "I gotta shower and scrub bacon grease out of my pores after every shift."

"Have you talked to your boss about it?" William asked.

"Yeah. I told her we're selling contaminated vegan doughnuts and it's unethical."

"What did she say?"

"She pretty much told me to go fuck myself. She thanked me for expressing my concerns, but I know she won't do a damn thing about it. I think I might have to contact an investigative reporter I know at the *Willamette Week*."

"You'll get fired," I said.

"You'll be a whistleblower," William said. "That's a heavy position."

"And the vegan doughnuts will start tasting like shit," Richmond said.

"Why is that?" Keith asked.

"Because they'll *actually* be vegan," I said.

Richmond and I laughed and high-fived. William laughed too. He was a vegetarian also, but not religious about it like Keith was. When we decided to go outside to smoke, William stayed in. He detested smoking. And for good reason. He lost his father to cancer when he was in middle school. I didn't smoke as much as Keith and Richmond, but when I was drinking, or out of sorts for one reason or another, nothing sounded better than a Camel. Keith had to run to the bathroom. Richmond and I got outside first.

"Hey man," he said. "You doing okay? You look tired."

"I'm alright," I said.

"It's okay to be bummed about the end of a relationship. It's natural. But you're going to be okay, man. You're the coolest dude around."

"Yeah?"

He put his cigarette in his mouth and put his hands on my shoulders. He could play the guitar with a lit cig in his mouth without coughing or getting watery eyes.

"The coolest," he said.

I wished I could believe him. Keith came outside to join us. We were still smoking when Anne and Skyler walked up.

"Gentlemen," Skyler said. "Still trying your luck with cancer, I see."

William had first met Skylar in a yoga class. She was elegant and tall. Sharp features and long hair. Full lips. From Idaho originally, although you'd never guess. Always dressed Portland chic. Tonight a tan and soft black patterned dress underneath a dark blue blazer. Pearl earrings.

"Well hello to you too," Keith said.

"Two more years," Richmond said. "I'm quitting when I'm thirty."

"Mind if I have a drag before you put it out?" Anne asked.

"Sure," Richmond said.

Anne with her eyeglasses and her granola fleece. Why hadn't she asked me for a drag?

We went inside. Scrunched together so we could all fit in one booth. I shoved my ass next to Skyler, who was practically sitting in William's lap, but half of my left butt cheek still hung off the side of the bench. Anne was sitting across from me now, next to Keith. She once told me I had the biggest ass of any man she'd ever slept with. I hadn't slept with enough people to have a list like that.

Jackie came to our table. She was my favorite bartender. A big woman in her forties who dressed like a punk.

"Hello, lovelies. Drinks?"

"Whatever IPA is on tap," Anne said.

"Same," William said.

"Me three," Skyler said.

"Tall whiskey soda," I said.

"Two of those," Richmond said.

"Make it three, Jackie," Keith said. "And a round of Jell-O shots. We have an engagement to celebrate."

"Fantastic. And who's the lucky couple?"

Anne raised her hand. It was the first time I'd seen the ring. It was huge. Jackie took her hand to get a closer look.

"Gorgeous! Congratulations. And who's the lucky guy? Is it . . ." Jackie looked at me.

"The lucky guy is in Colorado," Anne said.

"Well, congratulations."

C'mon, Jackie, I thought. *Be on my side; tell her she's making a mistake.*

Once the Jell-O shots arrived we loosened them up by circling the inside edges of the tiny plastic cups with toothpicks. The Jell-O shots only cost a buck, and the unofficial bar rule was that if someone offered you a shot, you couldn't turn it down.

Keith gave the toast.

"To Anne and her fiancé, who I've never met. Here's to your engagement."

"Aren't you big spender," Skyler said.

"Only the best for Anne and her man."

"His name is Ryan," Anne said.

"I would have bought a bottle of Dom, but they don't have it here. To Anne and to Ryan: the luckiest guy in the world," Keith said. He looked at me and winked. "Bottoms up."

The shots were awful. I downed my whiskey soda to wash out the taste. What a jerk. I didn't want to play the Beach Boys song, so now he was rubbing Anne's engagement in my face. It was so dumb.

Richmond said he was headed to the Liberty Glass to meet up with Liesel. He asked me if I wanted to go and was disappointed when I declined, like he knew why I was staying and thought that was a bad decision. Keith decided to leave with him. I got up and sat next to Anne.

William, Skyler, Anne, and me, just the four of us together, had been a common enough occurrence before the engagement, but now it felt weird.

"So, Julian," Skyler said. "How's basketball with the boy across the street?"

"His name is Reggie, and he's away for spring break," I said.

"I think it's great you guys play together," she said. "He probably doesn't get the opportunity to interact with a lot of other Black men."

Skyler thought she knew everything about everything.

"Wow, Skyler, I never thought about it like that," I said.

William sat up straight and narrowed his eyes at me like he thought I might be talking shit to his girlfriend and he wasn't sure what to do about it. Anne took my hand under the table and squeezed it with her nails going into my skin. Skyler laughed.

"I'm not calling you a role model," she said. "I'm just saying kudos."

When Jackie came by, I bummed an American Spirit; not a Camel, but it would do. Anne got up to go with me. And I knew as soon as we were out of sight, Skyler and her boyfriend were going to talk shit about us.

Outside, Anne lit the cigarette. Someone started singing "You Send Me" by Sam Cooke. Undoubtedly drunk. He held out the *you* in fluctuating tones for as long as he could, before saying *send me* in a trail of dying breath. I looked around and couldn't figure out where the voice was coming from. Anne figured it out and pointed toward an unlit alcove between the St. James Theatre and a bar called Limelight. She handed me the cigarette. Her diamond ring a cruel reminder of what had been lost. I took a drag of the cig and didn't like it at all.

Anne looked at me gravely.

"I only held your hand in there because you got angry."

"Thanks for the clarification."

"Why does Skyler always put you on edge?"

"She doesn't always," I said. "I just hate when she acts like she knows shit about Black people."

"Well, she *is* a psychologist."

"No, she's not, not yet anyway, she's still in grad school. She's got a long way to go, and besides, she'll never be a Black psychologist."

"You're impossible," Anne said.

"You are," I said. "I'm surprised you're here."

"It's not like I'm trying to avoid you."

"Well maybe you should," I said. "Maybe we both should for a while."

"Why?"

"That ring. It's weird. I don't know how to act around you."

"Just act the same as always."

"But you don't actually mean that," I said.

"We'll always have a history."

"Fuck history. History is dead."

"Isn't it better than if nothing had ever happened? And now we can be friends."

She took the last drag and tossed the spent cig in the bucket filled with sand. She opened the door to the bar and held it open for me to walk in before she did. I couldn't take her stoicism. I decided to go home and get stoned out of my mind. I gave Jackie a healthy tip using my last good credit card. I gave my goodbyes. When we hugged, Anne acted like everything was cool between us, and that was the cruelest thing she could have done.

I crossed the street and walked toward the alcove, hoping to get a look at the man who'd been singing. He was white, sat on top of a sleeping bag holding a forty in a paper sack.

"Hey man, help a brother out."

I put my hands in my front pockets like I was looking for money.

"Sorry," I said. "Don't have any cash."

"You got cigarettes?"

I shook my head no.

"Bullshit. I saw you smoking."

"I bummed it off the bartender."

I felt bad for using the word *bum*.

"Can you get another one?"

"I wish I could, but I have to go home now."

I started down the street

"Worthless damn nigger."

I kept moving like I hadn't heard him. I went along the winding road. Passed closed stores and the ancient mausoleum. Got off the sidewalk where the road curved and aligned with the bluff and sat on a bench that overlooked the wildlife refuge, the marsh, and the park. I looked across the dark river to the downtown buildings and the lights and the hills covered with trees and the giant houses hiding in the hills and the radio tower with the flashing red light at the top of the highest hill and I wept.

8

A BASKETBALL BOUNCED OUTSIDE THE window. I sat up and looked at my phone. Almost noon. I had no new messages. I got out of bed. Put on my gym clothes, scarfed down a granola bar, and guzzled the half-consumed energy drink I found in the back of the refrigerator before heading outside.

For the first year I lived in Portland, the house across the street was almost a mirror image of the bungalow I shared with William. An old couple had lived there, hippies. The guy wore Grateful Dead T-shirts and sandals almost year-round. The lady spent a lot of time tending to her garden and baking. She baked a batch of bran muffins as a welcome-to-the-neighborhood gift and had her husband deliver them. They were chill people, I liked them. But I never got a chance to say goodbye because I never saw them move out. I came home from work one day and their garden was gone. Soon after that, the house was demolished and all that remained was a hole in the ground. Then out of all the dust and the madness-inducing commotions of construction, a new home slowly emerged. It was massive, took up most of the lot. There was no front yard. Only a row of bushes along the walkway and a small patch of grass between the street and the sidewalk. A basketball hoop was installed at the edge of the grass. It hung over the street.

Though I didn't talk to the new neighbors for the first few months they lived there, I paid close attention. The man and the woman were white. I'd often see them going for or coming back from a run. She stayed home. He went to work. They had a son, clearly adopted because he was darker than I was. He was always shooting hoops by himself. Training, not just playing around.

I wanted to know who these people were. I wanted to make sure the kid was being treated okay—I mean, who knew what these white people were telling him about who he was. But I never spoke to them. Then one evening around four months ago when I was about to hop on my bike, the new neighbor lady walked up my driveway and introduced herself. She shook my hand and said her name was Claire. Her hair was cut short. She was wearing cold-weather running gear: black tights and a lavender-colored jacket. No one could have worn it better. She invited me over for a glass of wine. I was supposed to meet Anne at a party, but that could wait. We entered the house through a side door that opened into the kitchen. The kitchen was large and full of light. Everything clean and top-of-the-line.

"Mind if we finish the red I opened last night?" Claire asked.

"No problem," I said. "I'll take whatever you got."

I sat at the kitchen table. She went to the island and poured the wine. Her family had moved from Palo Alto to Portland for her husband's new job at Nike. She said the move was a good reason to quit her job at a law firm she hated. The wine was fantastic. She sat down across from me.

"It's so nice to finally meet you," she said. "I was about to go on a run but when I saw you alone, I couldn't pass up the opportunity."

"Your place is very nice," I said.

"Thanks," she said. "Where did you live before Portland? Or did you always live here."

"Chicago," I said.

"Great city. And what brought you to Portland?"

"I visited once and thought it was beautiful."

She nodded, then shook her head.

"Yes. It *is* beautiful, isn't it? Except for the big issue."

"What's the issue?"

"Portland is the whitest place I've ever lived," she said.

"Totally," I said.

I always thought it was funny when white people complained to me about whiteness as if there was something I could do about it.

Claire was older than me, but I couldn't tell by how much. Crow's-feet, but the subtle lines only made her more alluring and substantial, they didn't take away from her youthfulness. I remembered hearing somewhere that the best way to tell someone's age was by studying their hands, but all I could tell by looking at hers was that they were strong and well cared for. There was a tan line where her wedding ring usually was.

"Have you met my son Reggie?" she asked.

"I haven't. Is he here?"

I was more concerned about her husband.

"Peter took him camping. Would you like more wine?"

"Sure," I said. "Mind if I use your restroom?"

"Second door on the left once you're in the hallway," she said. "I'll open another bottle and make us a snack."

Once in the safety of the locked bathroom, I tried to determine if I was being seduced. Why else would this woman skip her run to invite me into her home and give me good wine while her husband and son were out of town? No ring on her finger. This had never happened to me before. I felt like I was in a movie. My moral hang-ups vanished. I wondered where the sex would occur. Kitchen table? Against the island? In this very bathroom? Surely not the master bedroom, but preferably somewhere soft.

When I got back, my wineglass was full. Cheese, crackers, and quince paste were laid out on a wooden cutting board shaped like the state of California. There was jazz playing softly. Claire said sometimes she heard our band practicing. I apologized. She said it was no big deal because her house was practically soundproof. She could only hear us playing if she stepped outside. She said it brought back good memories, her most serious college boyfriend had been a bass player in a ska band before he gave up music for medical school.

"It's a good thing, too," she said. "Ska was dead, and his family had no money."

"Where did you go to college?"

"New Haven. Sorry. I mean to say, Yale. What about you?"

Every time she spoke, I could tell she was a class or two above me.

"A Christian college right outside Chicago," I answered.

"Did you like it?" she asked.

I didn't like to talk about college. Everything had been so backwards. One day sophomore year, I went to breakfast in the dining hall and there were notices on the doors that said in order for students to better understand segregation, there would be a COLORED section and WHITE ONLY section in the dining room. But my college was so white, nothing had to change that day except for me. I ate all alone in the mostly empty colored section; and the rest of the day I drank from colored water fountains and used the empty colored bathrooms and elevators.

"If I could change the past, I'd have gone somewhere else," I said.

College talk soured my mood, but I was tipsy and loose, and Claire kept looking at me, so the sorrow went away real fast. She made the first move. Leaned in. Put her elbows on the table. Rested her face on her hands. It looked like she was about to say something important. I held my breath. This was it.

"So, you're probably wondering why my husband took my son camping on a school night in the winter."

Was that supposed to be her pickup line?

"I hear cold weather camping is nice if you have the right gear," I said.

"That's true, but this was a special circumstance. Reggie was suspended from school yesterday because he stood up for himself after a white classmate called him the N-word. He was so upset he just wanted to get out of town. Peter took him camping."

"A white kid called your son a nigger?" I asked

Claire grimaced.

"It's a horrible word. I've never uttered it. Reggie punched him."

"Good," I said. "Sounds like that kid had it coming."

Claire sat up and pounded the table lightly.

"Yes! Thank you. Exactly. I'd like to walk over to that kid's house and punch his parents. But Peter doesn't want any trouble." Her eyes opened wide like she had an epiphany. "You should hang out with him."

"With who? Your husband?"

"My son."

"Oh," I said. "Sure."

"Awesome. This is good. It's going to be so great."

When my wineglass was empty, I knew it was time to leave. We shook hands at the door, and right before I walked out, Claire said, "Next time you see him shooting hoops, ask him if you can play. Just don't let him think I had anything to do with it."

Reggie and I had been playing basketball for months now. He was good, starting shooting guard on his middle school team. But I wasn't too bad either. Out of shape, but my jump shot had been molded by my father's hand. I could still get buckets. Me and Reggie's record was marked on a sheet of legal paper attached to a clipboard he kept in his garage. We usually played twice a week, even in the cold and light rain. Last week he'd been on spring break and had gone to Martha's Vineyard to visit his grandparents, so we hadn't been able to play. Our all-time record was twenty-nine to twenty-nine. Before he left for break, we'd decided that our next game would be our first championship. Loser buys ice cream.

Reggie passed me the ball. I took warm-up shots. He rebounded.

"How was Martha's Vineyard?"

"It was okay. You ever been there?"

"Never," I said.

"It's kind of boring. My favorite part was flying by myself."

"I heard you got a date for eighth-grade formal."

"Oh my God. How'd you know that?"

"Your mom told me."

"Geez. She's always telling people my business," he said.

She never invited me over again, but Claire and I had friendly neighborly chats just about anytime we saw each other alone. She told me about Reggie's date when I saw her at the grocery store last Wednesday, right before I thought I saw a Black man in the cosmetic aisle.

Once the championship game had begun, Reggie used every skill he practiced: pivots, pump fakes, dekes, fadeaways, he used his body to protect the ball, was right-handed but could dribble left with ease, his jump shot looked great—he stayed square with the basket, kept his elbow in, full extension to release. He was tall for his age and athletic. Better than all that, he was smart. I saw it in his eyes; he was dead set on winning. So was I.

We were playing to twenty-one. We battled until we were tied at nineteen. He was quick and hard to guard. I got exhausted. My jump shots stopped falling. A car came down the street and we moved out of the way to let it pass. I put my hands on my knees and tried to catch my breath. There was nothing left in the tank.

I knew it was cheap and unsportsmanlike, but the only way I could hope to win was by utilizing my adult strength. Reggie checked me the ball. I backed his bony ass toward the basket until we were right under it and all I had to do was flip the ball in. I scored. One more point and the game was mine. I was ready to end it. I tried to back him down again, but this time he stole the ball from me. He scored and I checked the basketball back to him. Determined to stop him from scoring again, I guarded him close. He jab-stepped to his left, then dribbled to his right. I thought I saw an opening, I tried to steal the ball from him, he crossed to his left, I lost my balance and almost went headfirst into the pavement, he blew right by me. It was beautiful what he did, but then he made a mistake. On his way to the basket, he turned around and said, "Did I just break your ankles? Do you need to see a doctor?"

Up until this point in our relationship I'd been on my best behavior. Poor Reggie didn't know about the tossed monopoly boards, the broken video game controllers, the fistfights with neighborhood kids, or that girl who broke her arm when we were playing king of the hill and I pushed her off the monkey bars. When Reggie decided to turn and talk some shit before his layup, he didn't know who he was really dealing with. I regained my footing, set him as my target, and in the greatest athletic achievement of my life, I sprinted at him, jumped higher than I knew I still could, and swatted the basketball out of the air. His eyes got big. Utter shock. I felt fantastic. I got in his face and wagged my finger and said, "No, no, no. Not today, nigga. Not today. Not in my house."

9

MY OLD PASTOR ALWAYS SAID faith without works is dead, so when I was thirteen, I joined the youth worship band. I wanted my drums to be so powerful that people in the congregation would fall to their knees and be healed, blessed, touched, and spoken to by God. Even when I was married and miserable and full of doubt, even when I was pretty sure he didn't exist, I saved my most tasteful licks for alter calls, trying to aide in the conversion of lost souls. Lying in bed on Sunday night, I decided I was going to pray at work. Either I'd be playing lead idiot in a room full of idiots or talking to the most powerful person in the universe for the first time since my divorce; either way, I'd be getting it over with. I walked into work ready to speak directly to God.

We held hands and bowed our heads.

"Dear Lord," I said.

"Yes God," John said.

"Thank you for blessing us with this beautiful day," I said.

"Thank you for your love, Lord," John said.

I lifted my head and took a quick glance at him: his eyes were shut tight as if in pain. I hoped that meant he was now having an intense silent communication with God. I took a deep breath before I continued: "Lord, we ask that you protect us and give us a pure heart. We pray for our families and for all those in need of your grace. We pray that everything we do will be to glorify you. We know that we are sinners unworthy of your love."

"Thank you, Jesus." It was the boss. A relevant ad-lib, Jesus was essential.

"Lord, thank you for our salvation through the blood of your son, Jesus Christ. Dear God, we pray that you continue to bless us and watch over us. And we pray these things in Jesus's name. Amen."

"Amen," John said.

"Amen," the boss said.

To celebrate my successful prayer, Trenton insisted we go to lunch at our favorite Chinese restaurant. They had great specials and you got your food quick. I ordered orange chicken. Trenton ordered Szechuan beef.

"This is a special occasion," Trenton said. "We'll have martinis too."

"Okay, what kind?" the waitress asked.

"Vodka," I said.

"Disregard him," Trenton said. "We'll both have Tanqueray, dry, up, three olives."

The waitress took our menus and walked away. I took a gulp of water and chomped on the brittle ice cubes. I was starving. Trenton was shaking his head at me.

"What's your problem?" I asked him.

"Martinis are made with gin," he said. "Vodka martinis, chocolate martinis, appletinis, those aren't martinis. A martini is London dry gin and a splash of vermouth stirred over ice and strained into a chilled glass. The only variation is no vermouth."

"Who cares. It's just a cocktail."

"Just a cocktail? You're the only person I know who reads for pleasure and yet you got no class."

"Hey man. I've got plenty of class," I said. "I just haven't read any books with martini instructions. Okay?"

"So what changed your mind? Friday you tell me you're going to call in sick, but this morning you sounded like a televangelist."

"I've had a lot of practice and I decided to put it to use."

The waitress brought us our martinis. Trenton held up his glass.

"To a man of God," he said.

"Cheers," I said. After a nice cold sip, I asked him, "How come the boss never asks you to pray?"

"He thinks I'm Jewish."

"Are you?"

"My dad was. But my mother isn't."

The restaurant had big bay windows that looked over Macadam Avenue. We drank our martinis and watched the cars drive by. Praying had really messed me up. I finished my martini, ate the olives. When the server came over with our food, I asked for another.

"Are you sure?" Trenton asked.

"Celebrating," I said.

That was a lie. I knew it was a bad idea to order the second drink, but I just didn't care. I was drinking to forget. When I prayed that morning it felt like there was nobody up there listening. Where did God go?

When I was a kid, I had faith the size of Mount Sinai. I believed that when I was weak, he would make me strong, and I never needed to fear, because I would never be alone. Every night before bed, I thanked Jesus for dying on the cross. I thanked God for his many blessings.

The day I was baptized had been the best and most magical day of my life. I was ten. Walking across the burgundy-carpeted stage toward those two great men of God: my pastor and my father. Both barefoot with their pants rolled up to their knees as they stood in the large baptistry pool waiting for me to join them. My mother standing on a riser in the alto section, fancy choir robe, ready to rejoice as soon as her son emerged from the water and was born again. Behind the choir, on the wall, a humongous wooden cross, lit from behind in a warm golden light, and as I moved across the stage, the lights behind the cross faded in and out in concert with my breathing. God was everywhere and in everything. I waded into the water. And when it was time, I fell back into the waiting arms of my father and pastor and held my breath as they led me down until I was completely submerged. Underwater, I felt a force of light wash over me and I knew it was the Holy Spirit. I arose from the water born again. The choir sang. The congregation rejoiced. My father shed tears. The only time I'd ever seen him cry.

I hadn't felt drunk when we were sitting down, but when it was time to stand up, I had to steady myself by putting a hand on the table. But that was okay. The rest of the day at work I'd just sit at my desk and do a job that I could almost do in my sleep. Once we got outside, Trenton offered me a smoke. I declined because I had a mint in my mouth. I swished it around to neutralize the smell of gin. We walked toward the parking lot to his car. My phone buzzed in my pocket.

"The boss is calling me," I said.

"Don't pick it up," Trenton said.

"Hey, Boss," I said into the phone.

"Julian, hey man. After lunch, can you swing by my office?"

"Umm, yeah, sure," I said.

I hung up the phone.

"Well, what did he want?" Trenton asked.

"He wants to see me after lunch," I said.

"Yikes."

"Smell my breath. Do I smell like booze?"

"You smell like peppermint schnapps," he said.

I spit the mint I'd been sucking on into the patch of grass next to Trenton's car.

"I'd rather get fired for gin than get fired for drinking fucking schnapps," I said. "What should I do? Skip out of work?"

"No, not that. I'll fix you right up. C'mon. I have energy pills in my truck."

Trenton gave me half a pill, took one and a half pills himself. We took sips of a warm, flat soda he had in the car to swallow the pills. We made it back to work with a few minutes to spare. Trenton was already wired. He shadowboxed as we walked from the parking lot to the office, bouncing from side to side. He kept his hands close to his face. Ducked to evade the punches no one was throwing; threw counterpunches. He knocked on the boss's window and yelled, "I'm ready to sell!" The boss gave him a big grin and two thumbs-up.

I stopped by Trenton's cubicle to grab the cologne from his desk. Went to the restroom and locked the door. Splashed water on my face and drank some too. Patted my face and dried my hands with paper towels. Grabbed the cologne I'd put on the counter. One spray under each arm and one at the chest. The chest spray got into my mouth and nostrils and made me cough. I opened the bathroom door, John was standing there waiting. I wanted to slam the door in his face and stay in the bathroom, but that's something a drunk person would do; I needed to act stone-cold sober.

"Whew," John said, waving away the strong smell of cologne.

"I might have overdone it," I said.

"Better than the smell of shit. Am I right?"

"You be the judge," I said.

John laughed as he walked into the bathroom. Since when did this guy say *shit*? I wanted to grab him by the collar and ask him if he'd really spoken to God during morning prayer. But I knew nothing he said would satisfy me.

I went back to Trenton's cubicle and put the cologne on his desk. He was already back to work. Standing and talking into a headset as he tossed a stress ball from hand to hand. He mouthed *good luck* to me. Then he rolled his eyes and said into his headset, "That's right, sir. We provide twenty-four-hour support. And I'll tell you what, I'll give you my personal number so you can reach me at home. Just try not to call after midnight unless its urgent because the wife gets . . . Ha! Yes, you're right about that, Jeremy. Happy wife, happy life. Now, when would you like to get started?"

When I walked into the boss's office, he looked up from his computer and beckoned.

The chair in front of his desk never looked so appealing. I knew my best chance at hiding intoxication was to keep my distance, and now he wanted me right next to him. I stood behind him, as far away as I could without seeming suspicious. He had dandruff on his distressed T-shirt, and I couldn't stand the sight of it. My hands itched to dust the flakes away. His computer monitor was tilted to the left. I fought the urge to adjust it. I put my hands in my pocket. Now I understood why Trenton was standing at his desk, tossing that stress ball back and forth incessantly and pretending to be married to a woman. The pill made it hard to stay calm and act natural.

"Which one do you like?" the boss asked.

On his monitor was a side-by-side comparison of two brand-new pickup trucks. One truck looked practical. The other one was gigantic. I didn't know anything about trucks, but when I spoke, I made sure to enunciate.

"What do you plan to do with it?" I asked.

"Drive it to work. Haul some stuff maybe."

"Then the big one," I said. "If you get the small one, you might wish you had the bigger one, but you're never going to wish you had a smaller truck."

"That's smart thinking," the boss said.

I backed away slowly. Sat in the chair in front of his desk. Tapped my feet to the rhythm pounding in my head. I patted my knees but refrained from hitting the imaginary cymbals and tom drum in front of me so the boss wouldn't think I was intoxicated.

"How you feeling?" the boss asked.

"Great," I said.

"That was a nice prayer this morning, Brother Julian."

"Thanks," I said.

"Got drums on the mind, I see."

I stopped tapping.

"Always a little bit," I said.

It was tough just sitting there. I felt a headache coming on. The boss put his hands on his head and leaned back in his office chair. The way his big old baby face was smiling, I got the impression he was happy with me.

"Julian, I'd like to give you a raise. Two more bucks an hour. How does that sound?"

I did the math; eighty dollars more a week. Not bad.

"Awesome," I said.

"The Lord is good to those who put their faith in him."

"You know. My mother likes to say that," I said.

"You've been here more than a year and you've been doing a great job. I want to expand your role. I'm thinking we might have you update the employee handbook. Also, my daughter is going to be home this summer. I'd like to see her do some actual work instead of hanging around the house like a princess. I'm going to have her come in someday soon and I'd like you to teach her how to answer the phones."

"A change might be nice," I said. My responses sounded sober;

the pill was working, I just needed to keep a handle on the spikes of abject fear, despair, and adrenaline.

We both stood up. The boss came from around his desk to shake my hand.

"That's quite a smell on you, Julian," he said.

"Sorry. I guess I overdid it with the cologne."

"Oh no, *mon frère*. No need to apologize. It's a great scent. Hey, I'm about to blast you our newsletter. Edit it for me, would ya?"

"I'll get right to it," I said.

Making sense of the boss's sentences was my favorite part of work, and the energy pill and the raise had me pumped to do it. But back at my desk, I thought about how the boss had said the Lord was good to those who put their faith in him, and how that had never really been my experience.

10

REGGIE WANTED FROZEN YOGURT INSTEAD of ice cream. He won the championship, so he got to choose. After riding the bus back from work, I met him in front of his house. We started walking away from our street, the only street we'd ever hung out on together. I was still feeling the remnants of the two-martini lunch, the energy pill, and the absence of God. Reggie moved through the neighborhood like it was as safe and secure as his fenced-in backyard.

The frozen yogurt place was next to the movie theater where the man in the alcove had called me a nigger. Yogurt machines lined two of the walls. Reggie grabbed the largest wax-lined paper bowl available and filled it with vanilla, Dutch chocolate, strawberry-lemonade sorbet, and carrot cake. He topped that with M&M's, gummy bears, kiwis, Nerds, maraschino cherries, and banana slices. I filled a medium bowl with Georgia peach, no toppings. We put our bowls on a scale in front of the teenage girl behind the counter. Reggie seemed to know her from previous visits to the yogurt place.

"Is this your uncle?" she asked.

"He's my friend," Reggie said.

"Cool," she said. "The total is $16.75."

I paid her reluctantly. For that much money I could purchase two or three beers at Klay's. We went outside and sat at a table close to the edge of the street. I didn't know him this way. With that cold mountain of uncomplimentary flavors and toppings in front of him, Reggie looked like a child. He told the cashier I was his friend, but before today, all we'd ever done was play basketball together. His eyes darted from passing cars to passersby. Then he began to talk about soccer. He seemed to know all there was to know about Manchester United and AC Milan. It was hard to keep up. My brain hurt and I didn't care about soccer. After he was done, I told him about a basketball game back in middle school when I grabbed five rebounds in the fourth quarter and scored eleven points, including a buzzer-beater three-point shot to win the game.

"I thought you homeschooled until you went to high school."

"My church had a school and they let homeschoolers play on their team."

"Wish I was homeschooled."

"No you don't. It was boring. I had no friends."

He looked down and played with his yogurt but didn't take a bite.

"Your parents are Black, right?"

"Yeah," I said.

"And you grew up with them in Chicago?"

"Not Chicago exactly, the suburbs."

"It's funny because you don't talk like your parents are Black."

"What's that supposed to mean?"

"My friend Imogene says I'm not really Black because I don't act Black and I don't talk Black."

"That's ridiculous," I said. "You can act however you'd like."

"Has anyone ever called you the N-word?" he asked.

"Someone called me a nigger last week. Right over there."

I pointed left to the alcove.

"Was he Black?"

"He was white."

"That's messed up. I don't understand why some people are racist."

"Everybody's racist."

"My parents aren't racist."

"Yeah they are," I said. "It's just society."

"That's not true," he said.

"Hey kid, I'm just telling you the truth. That's why the two of us need to stick together. We're the only Black dudes on the block."

"If we're supposed to stick together," he said. "Why did you call me the N-word when we were playing basketball last time?"

My frozen yogurt was melting fast. It was getting hard to make big spoonfuls. Reggie's frozen yogurt mountain was imploding.

"I said *nigga*."

"Same thing."

"Says who?"

"Says my parents."

"I meant it as a term of endearment."

"Endearment? Do you even know what endearment means? You were yelling at me."

He looked like he was about to cry. I wasn't prepared for this kind of discussion.

"Hey kid, I'm sorry if I offended you."

"You knew it was wrong when you said it. That's why you let me win the game."

"No I didn't."

"Yeah, you did. You stopped trying. And I hated to win that way. I wanted to beat you fair and square."

"C'mon, kid, that's not true. I ran out of energy."

"Stop calling me kid."

He was right, I did let him win, and why did I keep calling him kid?

"Okay, I'll stop," I said.

"Whatever," he said.

"How old were you when you were adopted?"

"I was a baby. But I met my birth mother once. Because my parents thought I should."

"What was that like?"

"I was like eight or something and we met her in this random parking lot. I think it was the grocery store where she worked or something. I remember it was a long drive to get there. And she just looked like a random person. Didn't look anything like me. We said some words to each other, but she mostly just talked to my parents. She asked if she could hug me, and I remember I wanted it to feel different, but it just felt like hugging a stranger."

"I'm sorry to hear that."

"My dad says she had to give me up because she was on drugs and too poor to raise me on her own. I guess she just didn't care enough about me to change."

"That's not fair, Reggie," I said. "Life is hard to control once the ball gets rolling. I'm sure she'd change if she could."

"Whatever," he said. "You don't know anything about her. I'm done with this stupid yogurt."

He stood up, picked up his bowl, threw it in the trash, and headed toward home. I followed behind and never caught up with him. If I sped up, he sped up. The whole time he stayed about three feet ahead of me. He acted like I was chasing him or something.

The first time someone called me a nigger I was around eight years old. Alone at the park. I don't know why I was alone, but that's what I remember, being by myself sitting on the bottom of a slide when these white boys rolled up on their bikes and one of them called me a nigger. They all started to laugh. Before my young brain could register what had happened, the posse rode off. I went home and told my father what happened. He held me in his arms until I got hold of myself. He told me being Black was something to be proud of. The next day he came home from work and surprised me and my sister with a Super Nintendo. My father always did what he could to ease the burden. I had to give him that. Sometimes he strengthened me, my father. But I was fucking it up with Reggie; I was failing him in every way.

11

WHEN I GOT HOME FROM work the next day, there was an envelope in the mailbox addressed to me in cursive. No address or stamp. Inside there was a neatly folded letter written on a yellow sheet of legal paper.

Dear Julian,

We cannot thank you enough for all the time you have spent playing basketball with our son. We believe it has been of some benefit to him. And hopefully to you as well.

After a family conversation, we have decided that you and Reggie should take time apart. We feel that you have tried to undermine our parental authority by telling our son that because we are white, we are racist. We know we aren't perfect, and that we could never fully understand what it's like to be a black man in this country, but we do our best to understand and support him every day.

We know that you are a good person coming from a good place, but we don't think you and Reggie should spend any more time together.

We know that this may seem harsh, but this is our decision. We have informed Reggie of our decision, and he agrees it's for the best. We are his parents and we love him. We hope you can understand.

All the best,
Claire and Peter

PART TWO

12

AFTER READING THE LETTER FROM Claire and Peter, I decided I had two choices: more booze or more health. The next day after work I took the bus straight to the gym. I used my only non-maxed-out credit card to sign up for a membership and a same-day consultation with a personal trainer named Muhammad. He was ripped, ex-military. Seemed like a serious guy. First, he asked me lifestyle questions. His eyes got big when I told him what I ate. Mouth agape when I told him how much I drank. He told me to count my calories, to drink more water, to get eight hours of sleep, to eat chicken breasts and vegetables.

"But the big thing is all the alcohol, bro. That shit needs to go."

"How much of my drinking?" I asked.

"All of it, bro. Only way for you to reach your goals."

"But you don't know my goals."

"You want to look and feel your best?"

"Of course," I said.

"Smash hot chicks?"

"Sure."

"Then quit drinking and get yourself a haircut, bro. Believe me."

"All of my drinking?"

"All of it," he said.

I did what I could. I did burpees, bear-crawls, squats, push-ups, and lunges, tried to eat healthy, drank plenty of water, gave up on beer, drank liquor only in moderation, went to bed at reasonable hours, and worked up the guts to make a barber appointment—a big deal because I hadn't had a haircut since I moved to Portland two years ago. A lot of white people liked my hair, but I knew most Black people didn't find it respectable. When I went to Illinois last Christmas, Grandma Strickland asked me why I chose to look homeless, and my sister laughed like she used to when we were kids and I'd done something embarrassing.

All these life changes I'd made since that letter, five days ago. And now here I was on Martin Luther King Jr. Boulevard in Northeast Portland, pretty much the Blackest area you could find in this white city, walking into a barbershop.

I took an empty seat in a corner and waited for my turn. There was a kid getting his hair cut who couldn't stop crying. His mother stood beside him and tried to keep him still as the barber put all his concentration into not nicking the kid in the ear with his clippers. A middle-aged man who didn't have much hair to work with in the first place was getting his hair buzzed down to microscopic levels, just a touch above baldness. Everyone was Black except for a white guy in a Jordan jersey talking to one of the barbers like he was a regular.

I pulled down the brim of my White Sox baseball cap and leafed through a two-month-old celebrity magazine. It felt like half the people in the barbershop were staring at me. I thought being in a room full of Black people would allow me to enjoy the rare feeling of anonymity, but there must have been something wrong with me that I couldn't see that was clear to every other Black person. Like maybe my whole demeanor was that fucking wack. It was a horrible feeling. I wanted answers. The guy with no hair pointed above me and laughed. I looked up and realized I was sitting under a television. The only person actually watching me was the crying kid. His face was still covered in tears, but he was no longer crying. I smiled at him. He pouted and crossed his arms. I pulled down my baseball cap and went back to reading about the "rough lives" of celebrities. Everyone had problems, but it seemed more fun to have problems as a millionaire.

The barber who'd been cutting the crying kid's hair called out my name. His name was Quentin, he had the best online reviews for Black barbers in the area. Luckily, I'd called to set up my appointment right after he'd had a cancelation, or I would have had to wait another week. We shook hands and said nice to meet you. He told me to take a seat. Draped my body with a cutting cape and closed it at the back. I took off my baseball cap and braced myself for public shaming. None came.

"What are we doing here, boss?"

Quentin stood behind me. I looked at his reflection in his barber station mirror. He looked to be in his mid-thirties. His hair was impeccably wavy.

"Whatever you think is best," I said.

"For real? You want it short? Trying to keep it long? All the same length? Some kind of fade? C'mon man. You gotta give me something."

"Short I think."

"Tapered? All one length? Ahh shit. Never mind. I got you."

He took out a pair of scissors and started chopping away. A copy of Janet Jackson's *Rolling Stone* cover, the one with her arms up and someone else's hands covering her bare breasts, was taped to the bottom left corner of the mirror. I remember seeing that issue in a grocery store aisle when I was a kid and being mesmerized. Maybe if my parents hadn't been so strict about what we could bring in the house, I would never have gotten so mixed up with white girls.

On the bottom right corner of the mirror was a picture of Quentin and presumably his wife and two daughters at a Blazers game. A beautiful Black family, smiling and holding foam fingers that said RIP CITY.

Years of my life were being removed; in the mirror I recognized the matted afro that I had in college. Quentin put away the scissors and started using clippers. The vibration of the motor as the blades swept over my head felt relaxing until I noticed the dandruff. I could feel it on my ears and my neck before I could see it collecting on the cutting cape I wore.

"Sorry about my scalp."

"It's all good, brother, you just need to moisturize. Think about it like this: dandruff is just dead skin, right? Which means you're shedding your past life. When I finish this shit up, you're going to be a brand-new man."

The barber next to us laughed. "Quentin, I swear, you say some wild shit, bro."

"But it's true, nigga. You can't say what I say because your cuts aren't transformative."

Quentin swiveled my chair to the window to show me a white couple walking down the street pushing a stroller that looked like a luxury vehicle. "There goes the neighborhood right there. A place opened a block from my house that sells crystals and ten-dollar juices. My girl's been talking about having another kid. I told her what we need to be doing is saving up to buy a house while we still got a chance."

"Real estate is how you build generational wealth," I said. I'd read that somewhere. I didn't think I'd ever own a home.

"My nigga, that's exactly what I'm saying."

Quentin turned my chair back to the mirror. He kept switching clippers and going at different angles. My hair was getting shorter and gaining better texture. My face was getting sharper, more defined. Quentin stood in front of me and pushed up my chin. He lined me up. He brushed away all the dandruff. Put in some moisturizer. In the mirror I hardly recognized myself, I looked like a guy who had his shit together. Quentin was a man of his word. I paid him and dapped him and gave him a brief hug.

"My man," he said.

I left the barbershop feeling energized. I walked over to the bike rack outside. Although I'd taken the bus to my appointment, I'd brought my bike along so I could ride it to Mississippi Avenue. I liked the idea of pulling up to the coffee shop I was headed to as if I'd biked all the way from home. Richmond would be impressed. I unlocked my bike and hopped on.

Instant fatigue. Legs on fire from squats the day before. I rode down Martin Luther King Jr. Boulevard. Took a left on Fremont.

I stopped to wipe my brow. It was Saturday evening. Around six o'clock. The hottest day of the year so far. A few feet away, an old Black woman struggled to carry a cardboard box up her front steps. She needed to hold on to the railing to climb, but the box was too big to carry with one hand. I laid my bike on the grass and met her at the bottom of the steps.

"Mind if I help?"

"Phew. Oh, would you? I don't know what I was thinking."

She handed me the open box. Inside there were ceramic figurines of Black angels in various positions of prayer and jubilation. The lady told me to leave the box on the porch next to the busted recliner. I put it where she said and walked back down the stairs. She patted my shoulder and grinned. Her head bobbed slightly, involuntarily. She reminded me of my Grandma Strickland.

"Thank you, young man."

"It was nothing."

"Boy I wish I was as strong as you. Always good to be strong."

"I know that's right," I said.

I got on my bike and rode away. The old lady started up the steps to her house. If only Black angels existed. What a world we would live in. If there was a God, he was a white man and so were his angels, that was pretty clear. Maybe the old lady's husband was inside taking a nap on the couch, but probably not.

As I rode and sweat my ass off heading down to Mississippi Avenue, I thought about my namesake, Julian James Strickland. His funeral was held at Victory Baptist Church, the church my father was raised in, not the one my family attended due to my father's dissatisfaction with their doctrine. My grandfather was born in the summer of 1930 and died four years ago, a few months after my honeymoon, back when I was still happily married.

When I stood with Lauren, my wife, in front of Grandpa Strickland's open casket, it was the first time in my life that I realized death might be the absolute end of everything, that what you got in this life might be all you were ever going to get. Because even in death, my grandfather wore his signature smirk, and if that expression was a part of his body, and not his soul, then the soul didn't exist.

13

I TURNED ONTO MISSISSIPPI AVENUE, where hip-looking white people moved in and out of shops, bars, and restaurants, and coasted until I reached my destination: an old house that had been turned into a coffee shop. I locked up my bike. Walked in. Mismatched tables and chairs. Worn-out couches and area rugs. Richmond was behind a table, untangling a mess of wires. We'd spent a lot of time together, but before he told me about this gig, I had no idea he spun records.

There was a Black woman behind the bar counter punching buttons on a vintage cash register, clearly frustrated with it. She wore white overalls and a salmon-pink tank top. Her hair was almost as short as mine, but dyed blonde. I wiped the sweat from my forehead with the back of my hand. I stood in the doorway, frozen in place. She looked up at me.

"Sorry," she said. "We don't open again until eight."

I couldn't speak. The best I could do was smile in acknowledgment.

"Yes! Julian, what up, killa?" Richmond's voice brought me out of my stupor. For a moment I'd forgotten that he or anyone besides this woman behind the bar counter existed. We shook hands and hugged in front of the cash register. "I'm running behind. Do you mind helping me with my speakers?"

"Sure," I said.

"Liesel borrowed my car because hers is in the shop, so they're in Ida's truck." He turned to the woman behind the counter. "Hey Ida, this is Julian. He's a rad dude and the drummer in my band and he just got a fresh new haircut."

"Hey," Ida said.

"Hi," I said.

She had a gold hoop nose ring. Her nose was perfectly proportioned to her face, and it made me wonder if she wore the ring to distract from the perfection or to highlight it. I reached over the bar counter to shake her hand. One of her fingers scratched the webbing between my thumb and my index finger and it was the best jab of pain I'd felt in my life.

"Nice to meet you," she said.

"You too," I said.

"Mind showing Julian where the speakers are?" Richmond asked her.

"I'm busy," she said. "Can't you do it yourself?"

"I got too much left to do," Richmond said. "We're running out of time and this night won't work without music."

Ida rolled her eyes.

"Fine," she said. "But if someone comes in, tell them we don't open until eight."

She came from around the counter and headed toward the door. I followed her, would have followed her anywhere. We walked up to an old Ford truck in great condition parked across the street from the coffee shop. Body cherry red. Shiny chrome details. Roof painted white. Ida stepped onto the back bumper. Her powder-blue high-top Chuck Taylors were splattered with paint and dirt. She lifted up a tarp sitting inside the truck bed and looked underneath it.

"Speakers are still here," she said. "To be honest, I thought someone would be smart enough to steal them by now."

She hopped off the back bumper.

"Opportunity theft is the most common type of theft," I said.

"Are you an expert on crime?" she asked.

"I used to be in the mob."

"Somehow I doubt that. Do you smoke?"

"Yeah," I said.

I followed Ida to her driver's-side door, she unlocked it with a key kept in a tiny pocket of her overalls. She went inside the cab and leaned toward the passenger side. Even in overalls, she had a nice body. I got the feeling she knew I was checking her out. She took a metal cigarette case out of the glove box, closed up the car, and walked toward the coffee shop.

"Should I grab a speaker?" I asked.

She stopped and turned around to face me. She was standing in the middle of the street. I was still by the truck. A car passed between us.

"No," she said. "The speakers can wait."

I followed her through a narrow alley that led to the back of the coffee shop. Milk crates sat on the left and right side of the shop's back door. Ida sat on a black crate. I sat on a green one. We faced the brick wall of another building. I felt like a kid again—when simply being near the person I had a crush on was the height of my desire.

She opened her cigarette case. Six hand-rolled smokes were inside.

"They're spliffs. Want to split one or would you like your own? The weed is mellow."

"My own would be nice," I said.

"Good," she said. "I need all the help I can get before I go back in there and mess with that stupid cash register my boss thinks is charming and therefore won't replace."

She handed me a spliff and a lighter.

"Thanks," I said. "Here, I'll light yours first."

She put her smoke in her mouth and leaned forward so I could light it. Her eyes were big and brown. I would have given anything for a gust of wind, so she'd have to cup her hands over mine to keep the flame from going out, but the air was still, and the lighter worked flawlessly. After hers was lit, I lit my own, then handed back the lighter. She stood up and slid it into a pocket, sat back down and smiled at me. Her lipstick was the same cherry red as her truck.

"Are you thirsty?"

"A little," I said.

She handed me her spliff.

"Then hold this a second? I'll go get us something to drink."

The screen door hit my shoulder. To be hit by a door she'd just opened felt like a gift. I nuzzled the lucky shoulder with my chin, rested my cheek against it. I'd been drugged Shakespearean-style. Ten minutes ago, I didn't know Ida existed; now, I couldn't imagine life without her. I felt susceptible to doing or saying something foolish and irrevocable. Losing her before I'd ever had her. My pits were damp from biking. Thank God I only wore black T-shirts. To calm my nerves, I took a long drag of my spliff. The screen door opened but didn't hit me this time. Ida had two coffee mugs. She sat down and set a mug at my feet. I gave her back her spliff. We turned to face each other. She looked at me for a moment before taking a drag.

"What is it?" I asked.

"Oh, nothing," she said.

I took a sip of the drink in the mug.

"Whiskey Coke and a spliff," I said. "A stellar combination."

"Another key to dealing with the cash register is slight inebriation."

"Your truck is dope, by the way."

"Thanks. He's my baby. His name is Chuck. What's your car's name?"

What was I thinking bringing up cars?

"I don't have one," I said.

Ida smirked.

"Oh, so you're an environmentalist."

"Exactly. Money has nothing to do with it; I just don't believe in owning cars or private property."

"How Marxist of you. How'd you get here?"

"Bicycle."

"Cool. Where do you live?"

"St. James," I said.

She looked impressed.

"Damn. That's far. Does your bike have a name?"

"I've never considered it," I said.

"Well, I'm sorry. That just won't do." She put her head back and blew smoke into the air. There was a tiny scar at the bottom of her chin. "Every mode of transportation should have a name."

"That's your steadfast belief?"

"It's just the way it is," she said. "But don't worry, I'll help you. Come up with three names by the end of the night, and I'll help you pick the best one."

"Sounds fun," I said.

"It *is* fun, but it's also imperative. That said, my biggest advice is not to overthink it."

I couldn't believe what was happening. Usually if I was out somewhere, at a show, or a bar, or a house party, and there happened to be a Black woman—which was a rare occurrence in itself—and I also happened to be attracted to her, odds were, she was romantically involved with one of the white people she was there with. Now here was Ida, apparently as into me as I was into her, with no boyfriend in sight.

She told me the coffee shop was trying to expand their hours and become an evening destination. Tonight was their first attempt. I asked how she knew Richmond. She told me she'd worked with Liesel at a catering company before quitting to manage the coffee shop. When the owner asked her to find somebody to repaint the interior, she'd hired Richmond because he had given her his business card at a catering company happy hour that Liesel had dragged him to.

"He loves those damn business cards," I said.

"Too bad he's not a good painter," Ida said. "But he's cheap."

"But you paint, don't you," I said. "Not walls, canvases."

Ida sat up in surprise, increasing our distance.

"How'd you know?"

"The paint on your shoes looks like artist paint."

"Okay," Ida said. "That's both creepy and slightly hot. But wow, yes, you've got me; I'm a painter. I went to a fancy art school and everything. Unfortunately, I'd be starving if not for this job. What about you? Do you work for the man somewhere?"

"In an office."

"Do you like it?"

"I kind of hate it," I said.

"I understand," she said. "I tried an office job right after college and it almost killed me. I couldn't paint the whole time I worked there. A lot of artists have a hard time handling those kinds of jobs."

"Maybe, but I don't think of myself as an artist. I'm just a drummer."

"Do you take your drumming seriously?"

"I do."

"Then you're an artist," she said. "Embrace it."

The spliffs were gone and so were the drinks. Ida said she needed to get back to work. The screen door opened and hit me again. This time it hurt. Richmond stepped into the alleyway. Now here was an artist, no doubt about it, a whole life centered around making music. We stood up.

"There you guys are. Julian, I need those speakers, man."

"Fine, let's go grab them," I said.

"Great," he said. "But since we're here, I'll smoke a cig first."

"Make up your mind," Ida said.

Richmond lit his cigarette with a match. He put his hands on the sides of my face for a moment. He stepped back and took the cigarette out of his mouth.

"Julian, you look fantastic. Oh my God, Ida. You should have seen this dude with his old hairdo. I still can't get over it. He's a totally different person now."

"What did he look like before?"

"Like a Rastafarian," he said. "Like he only played dubstep."

"Jah's not spoken to me," I said. "I'm going for the disgraced Samson look to see if that gets him talking."

"I think you look great," Ida said.

"Me too," Richmond said. "You look tough as fuck."

The tables and chairs had been pushed to the corners to discourage their use, though people used them anyway. Others stood on the edge of the clearing that was meant to be the dance floor. Tapped their toes. Moved their heads. Sang along to the music. But no one danced. Richmond's DJ table was set up next to the bathrooms. He played strictly soul music. Motown. Stax. All vinyl. He combed through his crates of records with the same look of determination he had when he was trying to find the perfect riff, something undeniable, something you couldn't help but be moved by. But the music wasn't the problem. The vibe of the room was the problem. It was too dark with just the lamps, but the overhead lighting was no good either. We'd messed with the lights and found no great solution. We'd ended up with all the lamps on and all the overheads off except for the ones above the counter and the dance area. And to top it all off, the coffee shop had a limited liquor license, none of the hard stuff.

I sat on a stool at the bar to stay as close to Ida as I could. She had a bottle of whiskey hidden behind the counter that she was happy to share. An hour into the night and all hope for dancing seemed to be lost. She said she was afraid the night was a bust. Richmond looked defeated. I was having a pretty good time being around the two of them, but I also felt for them. I knew what it felt like to play to an empty room.

Liesel walked in and headed straight for the middle of the makeshift dance floor as if she were about to make a big announcement. But no words were spoken. She started dancing. She kicked like she was trying to kickstart a motorcycle, she spun around and moved her arms in big fast circles as if she were trying to steer through an obstacle course. She stopped and did the funky chicken. She did the twist. The sprinkler. The mashed potato. Her dancing was so fun and free, I got tired just watching. Ida took off her apron and asked me to stand behind the bar. She joined Liesel on the floor. They moved from side to side with the music, waved their arms in the air, got within inches of each other. Pretended like they didn't care if anyone was watching, even though they desperately wanted to be watched and, more importantly, imitated. It worked. People hit the floor and a proper dance party commenced.

The vibe was building. There were people who'd look in from the street and then come in to check it out. Another barista who worked there stopped in, and Ida convinced him to stay and help her. The place was getting packed. I stayed sitting at the bar. Liesel took the empty seat next to me. She leaned over and kissed my right temple.

"Love the new haircut. Ida must love it too. You guys set a date for the wedding yet?"

"Hey now," I said.

"Don't think just because I've been dancing my ass off, I haven't been watching you two."

"But somehow we just met."

"Why do you say that like it's my fault? You and Anne had that weird thing going on. Ida had a boyfriend until recently. But you're perfect for each other."

"You think?"

"Definitely," Liesel said.

We turned to survey the room. People were dancing.

"Look what you've done," I said.

"What can I say? When you got it, you got it. Plus, if this night was a failure, Richmond would bitch about it for a year."

"Richmond doesn't bitch," I said.

"Oh yes he does," Liesel said. "Constantly."

Ida came over and slid me a fresh mug of whiskey Coke.

"Ida, I miss you," Liesel said. "I wish we could dance all night."

"Me too," Ida said. "Julian, you should get out there."

"I'm not much of dancer," I said.

"That's nonsense," Ida said. "White wine, Liesel?"

"Perfect," Liesel said.

Ida turned around and grabbed the wine from the refrigerator. She poured some in a glass for Liesel. Left the bottle on the counter between us.

"What are you doing next Friday night?" Liesel asked her. "Actually, I'll tell you what you're doing, you're coming to Julian and Richmond's show."

"I haven't been to a show like that in years."

"No wonder I've never met you before," I said.

"My ex-boyfriend hated loud music."

"She's not joking," Liesel said. "I remember him flipping out at a party once over the volume."

"That was years ago," Ida said. "I'll go if Julian decides on a name for his bike."

"I'm thinking Elizabeth Bishop," I said.

"Like the writer?" Ida asked. The fact that she knew who I was talking about. Oh man, I was hit.

"Yeah," I said. "Sound good?"

"It's a keeper," Ida said.

She went to help a customer.

"You two are so hot," Liesel said. She downed the rest of her wine in one gulp. "I have an early day tomorrow. A wedding, and I'm the boss of all the servers. Join me while I say goodbye to Richmond?"

Richmond smiled and took off his headphones when he saw us approaching. Liesel put her hands on his shoulders. They kissed, then whispered to each other. I looked over at the bar. Ida saw me standing there awkwardly. She pointed toward the back door and put up five fingers. I gave her a thumbs-up.

Richmond and Liesel stopped kissing and turned to face me.

"Julian," Richmond said. "So nice of you to stop by."

"It's not you Richie, it's Ida," Liesel said.

"C'mon," I said.

"Your children are going be so fucking gorgeous."

Richmond put his arm around Liesel's waist.

"Babe, be easy," he said. "Don't jinx it."

"Oh stop. I'm not going to jinx anything."

"You're going to make him nervous."

"I'm fine," I said.

"You think you're fine until Liesel jinxes you. That's how it works. She doesn't know how to be chill. She makes a big deal out of everything. Don't you? Brought your car to the mechanic because you thought you heard a rattle, but what did they tell you? There was nothing wrong. Just like I told you. So believe me when I say that you should zip it about Julian and Ida."

Richmond winked at me. I hated when he gave Liesel shit in front of me just to prove that he could.

"You better watch your mouth, Richie," Liesel said. "I'll smash all your records."

"Hey man," I said. "This lady saved your ass tonight."

Richmond shook his head and smiled. "Fine. I know better than to take on the both of you. And you're right, dude. She saved me." He kissed Liesel on the cheek. "Thanks, babe."

"I love you, Richie," Liesel said. "You know I'd never hurt your records."

I gave Liesel a hug goodbye. I made it outside just in time to watch Ida lean against the back of the building and light a spliff. It was dark in the alley. The air was warm and pleasant. We stood close together. Ida offered me her spliff, and when I took it our fingers touched. My heart beat so loud I was sure she could hear it. I know I could; I could hear my heartbeats bouncing down the block until they faded out of range. For a while we just stood there and stole glances at each other.

She touched my arm.

"So why won't you dance?"

"I'm no good at it," I said.

"Nonsense. You just move your shoulders and bend your knees. Like this."

She started to dance. I followed her lead. When she laughed, it was loud and with her head flung back. I chuckled and grabbed her waist. She wrapped her arms around my neck. We kissed. She pushed me away playfully.

"Well, that was nice, wasn't it?"

"It was," I said. "Do we have to stop?"

"I have to go back to work, and to be honest, I don't even know you."

"But maybe you'd like to know me?" I asked.

"You can't tell? Or do you think I kiss strangers in alleys all the time?"

14

NOT LONG AFTER WE SAID goodbye, Ida sent a picture of my bicycle sitting in the bed of her truck in a garage, with a message that read, *Chuck and Elizabeth are safe. See you tomorrow.* I messaged that I thought it was cute our machines were having a sleepover. She responded with a wink. I was trying to decide if I should reply with something cute or let her wink be the final word, when Richmond pulled his car over to the side of the highway overpass and activated the emergency lights.

"We're out of fucking gas," he said.

"You're kidding me, right? How'd that happen?"

"The gas gauge doesn't work."

"Isn't that essential?"

"Not if you're paying attention. I told Liesel to gas up the car when she borrowed it, but clearly she forgot, because all she ever thinks about is herself. I swear to God." Richmond began to smack the shit out of the steering wheel. We needed his hands for next week's gig. I punched his right shoulder.

"Dude. C'mon. Calm down."

Richmond stopped smacking the steering.

"Fine," he said. "Okay, fine. Jesus."

"What do you think we should do?" I asked.

"Are you drunk?"

"Probably," I said. "You?"

He massaged his right wrist.

"I wouldn't bet against a Breathalyzer."

"Try starting the car again."

"It's fucking dead."

"It died while we were going uphill, right? Now we're flat."

"There's logic to that," he said.

The engine turned. For a moment it sounded like it was going to start, but it died again.

"What about Triple A?"

"Don't have it, do you?"

"I don't have a car," I said.

"You got any drugs on you?"

I told him I didn't. He did. He grabbed his backpack from the back seat and got out of the car to put it in the trunk. I thought about walking away, but even if I did find my way down the overpass, being Black and drunk and walking on the side of highway was probably a worse offense than being a passenger in the car of a drunk white guy. And abandoning that white guy when he was your friend and bandmate seemed like a shitty thing to do, so I stayed in the car.

A police car zoomed down the highway with its siren wailing and lights flashing. It flew right by us. Richmond got back in the car. He rolled down the windows and lit a cigarette; he took a few puffs then looked at me. "We gotta call nine-one-one." Before I could tell if he was joking or serious, he reached into his jeans and pulled out his phone. He punched in three numbers. I punched his arm. He took the phone from his ear and ended the call.

"Touch me again, see what happens."

"What are you doing?"

"What does it look like I'm doing? I'm calling the cops."

"But calling the cops on ourselves is stupid."

"I don't like it when people say I'm doing something stupid."

"Okay fine, then it's the whitest thing I ever heard," I said.

"No, it's not white. It's smart," he said. "The police car that passed us might have called dispatch. If we call this in before the cops get here, I bet they'll be less likely to treat this as a traffic stop and more likely to help us. But if you have a better idea, I'm listening."

I had nothing. Richmond made the call. The operator said someone would arrive in ten minutes or less. We got out of the car. We figured the police couldn't arrest us for drunk driving without being able to prove who'd been driving. The overpass lights were dim. We leaned against the trunk and split a cigarette. Richmond bit his fingernails between drags.

"You doing alright?" he asked.

"Hell no," I said. "Are you?"

"Fuck no," he said.

A squad car climbed up the desolate overpass. Richmond dropped the cig and stepped on it. The squad car stopped ten feet behind us. Its lights began to flash. There seemed to be only one officer in the car. I couldn't make out his face, I could only see his eyes, and his eyes never left us. He picked up his radio, said something, listened, talked again, listened, shook his head as if he'd lost all respect for the person he was speaking to. He put down the radio with eyes still trained on us, he never seemed to blink. He opened the door and got out of the car. Walked toward us slowly with his right hand hovered over his gun holster. He looked like the kind of cop who chose violence anytime he could. He had a short haircut and a trim beard.

"Evening. You the fellas out of gas?"

"That's us," Richmond said. "Thank you for helping us, Officer."

Richmond's easygoing whiteness seemed to soothe the cop. He moved his hand away from the gun holster.

"Officer Brainerd," the cop said. "James Brainerd. Call me Officer Jim."

When we told him our names, I was afraid he would try to shake our hands, but he didn't. He took his eyes off us for a moment to survey the surrounding area.

"I can help you guys," he said. "But I don't have a gas can. One of you is going to have to ride with me to a station. Whose car is this?"

"Mine," Richmond said.

"Then for your safety, sir, I'm going to need you to get back into the vehicle." He looked at me. "You ready to ride, Julian?"

"I'd planned to stay here," I said.

Officer Jim looked puzzled.

"Well now, you guys need gas, don't you? That's why you called us, right? Or did you call for something else?"

Richmond looked at me helplessly. He got back into his car.

I followed Officer Jim. Every step I took toward the squad car felt like a step in the wrong direction. He opened the back door to let me in.

"Do I really have to ride in the back?"

"Policy," he said. "Only authorized personnel can sit in the front. Now watch your head there, easy to bonk it if you're not being careful."

I got in the back of the car, he slammed the door shut. He opened the trunk, pulled out emergency road signs, and set them in a line behind Richmond's car. He got in the front seat and mumbled something in his radio before he put the car in gear. We started down the highway.

The back cab was sealed off from the front. The bench seat was made of hard plastic and set very low. No leg room at all, knees up to my chest. I was starting to freak out. It was getting hard to breathe.

I wanted to ask him to stop so I could get out of the car and stretch and find a place to pee, but I was afraid he'd find legal justification to shoot me with my pants down.

Officer Jim looked at my reflection in the rearview mirror. His voice filtered through the holes in the bulletproof glass that separated us. "You alright back there?"

"Uncomfortable," I said.

He laughed. He opened a container and put something in his mouth. "I don't think the people who designed this vehicle were all that concerned about comfort."

"How far is the gas station?" I asked.

"Further than I'd like."

Officer Jim spent more time looking at me than the road. His mustache bobbed up and down at the bottom of the mirror. He was chewing tobacco, kept spitting in a cup; it was disgusting.

"Hey, you know, my dad's a detective," I said.

"In Portland?" he asked.

"No. In Chicago."

"Good for him," he said.

My phone buzzed in my pocket. Maybe it was Ida.

"I have a message," I said. "Mind if I check my phone?"

Officer Jim laughed, then spit in his cup.

"You're a free man, Julian."

It was Richmond asking how things were going. I messaged him that I was trapped in the back of this car headed for seemingly nowhere. Officer Jim kept looking at me in the mirror. I put the phone away. When we got off the highway, the streets were empty. The moon was full in a clear black sky, as dark as it was going to be all night. We were driving in a part of Portland I'd never seen before. There were no houses or bars, only big industrial buildings surrounded by fences. I started to wonder if I was being taken somewhere to be tortured and disposed of.

The gas station appeared on the horizon. The glorious savior of cars and weary travelers. Officer Jim parked the squad car in front of the station store and let me out. I rushed inside and headed for the bathroom. It was locked. A clerk was standing behind the front counter.

"Did you just come out of that cop car?" he asked.

"Yeah," I said. "And I really need to use the restroom."

He held up a key attached to a huge wooden spoon. I walked over to the counter. When I got close, he said, "Are you under arrest?" He held back the key like he wasn't going to give it to me until I answered his question.

"I ran out of gas on the highway."

"Oh man, that's shitty," he said.

He handed me the key. I rushed to the restroom. While I washed my hands, I looked at myself in the mirror, but it was more like buffed metal than actual glass, and all I could see was a fun-house face. Dark, distorted, and pinched in the middle. Out of the restroom, I grabbed the only gas can the place sold and brought it to the front counter. I asked the clerk if I could prepay for the gas. He told me I had to pay at the pump. I walked outside. Officer Jim was leaning against his car. He spat onto the concrete. He put his hands by his neck and adjusted the bulletproof vest he had under his uniform.

"Let's get this thing moving," he said.

I walked up to the gas attendant who stood by a pump.

"How can I help you?" The gas attendant had one eye on me and the other on the cop. I wouldn't have been surprised if he was high or a little drunk, I know I'd be if I had his job.

"I need gas," I said.

"Are you sure?"

"Yeah."

"I have to ask you, though: Are you under duress?"

"No, man, I just ran out of gas," I said.

Maybe the gas attendant was afraid the gas he pumped would be used to burn me alive. I'd thought about that earlier in the bathroom, and decided Officer Jim would have done it earlier—if he was going to kill me, why would he bring me to a gas station to be seen by witnesses and captured by security cameras? Right?

The gas attendant was waiting for something.

"I need to swipe your card before I start," he said.

"Oh, sorry," I said.

"You alright there, Julian?" Officer Jim yelled.

"Yeah."

"Are you sure?" the gas attendant whispered.

I handed him my card. He swiped it and gave it back to me. Pushed some buttons and lifted the nozzle. Crouched down, unscrewed the cap, and started to pump. Officer Jim kept watching me, kept spitting on the ground. I was rocking on my heels. Hands in my pockets. My body told me to run. But running away seemed like a good way to get shot in the back. Maybe the gas attendant's fears were spot-on. Maybe the gas was necessary; maybe this cop came from a long line of white supremacists who preferred to kill Black people with fire; maybe that was the family way; some sort of fucked-up ritualistic racial cleansing. Take a nigger to an empty field next to a river, douse him with gasoline, light a match in front of his whimpering and pleading dark face, laugh at his pointless prayers to a white God before you toss the match and relish in the thrill of the ignition, the screams, the attempted run to the river, the collapse onto the grass, the smell of burning flesh, and the night becoming peaceful, the sun coming up on the white man's earth now made a little cleaner. If only I still believed that no weapon formed against me would prosper. I thought about Ida. There was never a good time to go, but dying before I got to know her seemed like a joke only a higher power could orchestrate.

The gas attendant took out the nozzle and put on the cap to the gas can. Gas dripped from the nozzle and made marks on the concrete. He stood up carefully and put the nozzle back into the holster. He turned to push some buttons. Once the receipt started to print, he whispered, "You don't have to get back into that car, man. We can figure this out."

"I'll be alright," I said. But maybe I wouldn't be.

"All set?" Officer Jim yelled. "Let's do this."

I picked up the gas can and took the receipt from the attendant's trembling hands. Officer Jim spit his chew on the ground then opened the back door. I handed him the can before I slid into the back seat. He slammed my door. Slammed the trunk after putting the can inside and got in the driver's seat. He rolled down his window.

"You have a good night now," he yelled to the gas attendant as we drove by him.

The gas attendant didn't say a word. He just stood there, head turning slowly to follow the car. Officer Jim looked at me in the rearview.

"That guy's not all there," he said.

I made it back to Richmond. The gas went in the tank and not on my head. Officer Jim sped past us, turned off his flashing lights. Once we were back on the highway, Richmond wanted to talk about what happened. I answered his questions but didn't offer my thoughts.

The car stopped under Reggie's basketball hoop. All the houses on the street were dark. Richmond and I shook hands. He held my hand tight and looked me in the eye.

"Are you sure you're okay?"

"It's not your fault," I said.

"You're right. It's fucking Liesel's, but still, man, I was scared for you."

"Nothing broken."

Richmond tightened his grip on my hand.

"Oh yeah, I forgot who I was talking to. A tough guy from the land of Al Capone. That must be why Ida digs you."

"How do you know she digs me?"

"She told me when we were packing up."

"Did she say anything else?"

He let go of my hand and shook his head.

"Nothing," he said. "I'll see you tomorrow."

15

INSIDE THE HOUSE IT WAS dark and William's bedroom door was wide open, which meant he wasn't home. This was the second night in a row. I turned on the lamp on the end table. I looked around the house for the cat but couldn't find her. No escape from my loneliness, so I set out to make it tolerable. I made a vodka soda and sat at the kitchen table. Dipped a finger in the drink and rubbed alcohol over the scratch mark Ida had made on the webbing between my fingers. It was three o'clock in the morning.

I thought about my parents. With the time difference, I thought my father might be getting up for work, but no, it was Easter Sunday, he was probably still sleeping. Later, he'd get up and get ready for church, and my mother would make them breakfast. I hadn't talked to them in over a month. I'd messaged here and there so they'd know I was alive, but I just couldn't get myself to take their calls. If I'd died that night, my relationship with my parents would have ended poorly, and they would have had to have held on to the belief that even though I'd refused to pray before dinner the previous Christmas, eventually breaking down and admitting I didn't know if I believed in God anymore, I wasn't burning in hell, because they'd witnessed and believed in my baptism.

I poured myself more vodka. When I was kid, I thought it was amazing my father was a policeman. Kids at church would ask if I'd ever seen his gun and if he ever arrested bad guys and if I ever rode in his police car and zoomed down the street with the sirens blaring and lights flashing, and I'd say, *yeah*, all nonchalant, like it was no big deal my dad was a cop, but I loved it, I really did, I was proud of him. And I was proud when he became a detective, too. But that was before I knew anything about the world. Nowadays, I didn't tell anybody my father was a cop unless I thought it would help me.

Toward the end of our marriage, I got in a fight with my ex-wife that landed me in the hospital. It all started with whose turn it was to do the dishes. It was her turn, but she wouldn't believe me. And instead of playing fair, she started to list my shortcomings. She said I should be doing the dishes every night because her job as a junior accountant was taxing, and I still worked at Trader Joe's like I had since our junior year of college. All I did was sit on my ass, tap sticks on my legs, drink whiskey, and write poems no one wanted to read. I wasn't a good husband. I didn't follow Christ. I lacked ambition. All that said over some dishes. I couldn't take it. I told her if she didn't shut up, I would find a tall building to jump off of. She started to cry and hit my chest. She told me to take it back. I refused. At the time I was serious, I wanted to die. We'd been drinking a little. She called a cab. We took it to Rush hospital.

Emergency rooms are notorious for their wait times, but Lauren convinced the lady at the check-in counter that I could die any moment. We were in a triage room within minutes of our arrival. The nurse checked my vitals and handed me a mental health questionnaire.

On our way to the hospital, I decided it wasn't that I wanted to kill myself, it was just that I wanted a divorce. When the doctor walked in, he slathered his hands with more hand sanitizer than his skin could absorb. He sat down and looked at the form I'd filled out. When he turned the form over, there were sanitizer fingerprints. I thought that was funny. He took my laughter as a sign of my derangement. Lauren burst into tears and told the doctor I was suicidal. He asked her if there were any weapons in the home. She told him my father had given me a handgun as a wedding present and that I kept it in a safe in our bedroom closest. "I honestly don't know what I was thinking, letting him bring that thing into our apartment." She walked into a corner with her face in her hands. I sat on the examining table feeling shitty. Neither of us were the person the other one wanted or needed. When we decided to get married, I'd only thought of the perks: living together, sex without sin, everything else pretty much the same. She'd thought marriage would fundamentally change us for the better. But she clearly believed that I was only getting worse, and I felt the same way about her.

The hospital was lit as if the sick and the lame could be healed from man-made versions of God's holy light. But all the harsh light did was make everything look washed-out and ugly. I told the doctor I was tired and drunk. That we got in a fight and I said something I shouldn't have. "Just look at the form I filled out," I told him. "All my answers are ones and twos. If I'd wanted to kill myself, I would have answered with fours or fives."

The doctor wasn't convinced. He started talking about a seventy-two-hour psychiatric hold. Lauren put a hand on my shoulder and said that sounded like a good idea. I shrugged her hand off me. I told the doctor my father was a cop. I asked if I could call him. An hour later we were sitting in the back of my father's unmarked police car. Lauren in the front. Me in the back. The car was silent. She'd told me before we left the hospital that if I didn't agree to the hold, I wouldn't be allowed back in the house. I told her that was fine with me. She got out in front of our Chicago apartment and headed toward the door. I got in the front seat. We headed for the suburbs. I thanked my father for coming to get me. I told him Lauren and I were having a hard time and that I wanted a divorce. I remember a clear image of his hands holding the steering wheel that night—at ten and two o'clock, just like he taught me. He had tremendous hands. Could palm a basketball with ease. When I was a kid, he rarely needed a belt to get his point across.

That night in the car, my father told me divorce wasn't an option for Strickland men. But here I was, three years later, divorced from so many things. I finished my vodka soda. Thought about making another one, but we had practice at noon. Not so long from now. I was going to see Ida later, too. I had to get myself together. And one thing I'd learned through the years is when it's late, and you're alone and thinking about death and all your failures, the best thing you can do for yourself is go to sleep. If nothing else, just lay down, close your eyes, and try to feel safe.

16

MY PHONE WAS ON THE ground next to the floor tom. It lit up with Ida's name while we were in the middle of a song. I couldn't stop playing to answer because the band was killing it. Richmond had already filled the guys in on the out-of-gas nightmare and my new love interest, so they didn't give me shit when I picked up my phone once the song ended and told them I had to go outside. I ran up the stairs of the basement. Hurried through the kitchen. Flung open the front door. Chuck was in the driveway. Elizabeth Bishop against a tree. A basketball bounced. I turned to the street. Reggie was under his hoop waiting for Ida to take a shot. She threw the ball at the basket with both hands like this was her first attempt at basketball ever. The ball bounced off the backboard and around the rim before falling through the net. She put her hands up in triumph. Reggie cheered, he ran up and gave her a high five.

It was cute to watch, but uncomfortable too. I didn't know how to insert myself into the situation. Reggie took a shot and missed. The ball rolled down the street. Here was my opportunity. I chased the ball down and passed it to Ida, who was right under the hoop. She hit another basket. But this time instead of cheering, Reggie stiffened as I approached. He turned to Ida.

"I have to get going."

"Yeah? Well, it was really great meeting you," she said. "Thanks for letting me play."

She tossed him the ball. He smiled at her. Didn't look at me once.

"It was nice meeting you too," he said.

He turned and headed toward his garage. I wanted to grab his arm, turn him around, and tell him I missed him. That I never meant to hurt him. That I'd wanted to make his life better, not worse. That I'd do anything to make things right. He went inside his garage, pushed a button on the wall, and the garage door started to close, making a very low hum. I hoped the door would malfunction and start going up instead of down. But the garage door kept on working as intended. Reggie's upper body went out of view. His legs disappeared. I saw his Nike basketball shoes step through the doorway into the house. The garage door whispered shut and we were further apart than we had ever been before.

"He's so adorable," Ida said. "Why'd he run away from you?"

"Oh man," I said. "It's a sad story."

"Will you tell me sometime?"

"Sure," I said.

We walked to Ida's truck. She sat on the tailgate. I wanted to sit next to her but was afraid my added weight would rip that old tailgate off its hinges.

"Thanks for dropping off Elizabeth," I said.

"It was a good excuse to see you again so soon."

"A great one. But maybe I should have biked home anyway." I told her about running out of gas. Freaking out in the back of the cop car. My fears of being shot or burned alive. "Or maybe shot and then burned," I said. "I thought I might never see you again."

She took my hands in hers.

"I'm so sorry that happened to you," she said.

"I'll be alright."

"But you don't have to be. Don't bury it. Let yourself feel everything."

"I appreciate that," I said.

Ida let go of my hands.

"How's practice going?"

"Great. The energy today is the reason I play music."

"Are you thinking about music right now?"

I was patting my thighs, didn't notice until she pointed it out. I put my hands in my pockets. With her and the music and my desire to fix things with Reggie, I felt like I was back on Trenton's energy pill.

"There's always a rhythm in my head," I said.

"I can relate," she said. "Even if I'm not consciously thinking about color or line, the signal is always on. When will you have time to hang out? Of course, only if you want to."

"Of course, I do," I said. "How about Thursday? We don't practice the day before shows."

"Perfect," she said.

We made plans to meet at the Hawthorne Food Carts on Thursday after I got off work. We hugged before she left. I kissed her cheek. I wondered if Reggie and Claire had watched us from a window, and if seeing me with Ida had helped my case somehow; I knew that was a strange thought, but I can't say that seeing a Black person with another Black person didn't influence my perception of who they were and what they were about.

Later I called my parents to say Happy Easter, and it only took two minutes with no drama and only proclamations of love and *I miss yous*, the unresolved issues unspoken.

17

THURSDAY AFTER WORK, ON THE bus headed for the Hawthorne Food Carts, I got a text from Ida saying that something urgent had come up and she wouldn't be able to meet me—*I'm so, so sorry! I was really looking forward to hanging. I'll explain the whole thing tomorrow night when I see you at your show.* I got off the bus. Sat on a bench in the food truck courtyard and cheated on my new diet with poutine and beer. Urgent matters involved other people. I wondered who she was with. I wondered if kissing her cheek when we said goodbye on Sunday had been a mistake, but no, she smiled when I did that.

I walked across the street to the liquor store. Picked up a pack of cigarettes and a pint of bourbon before taking the bus back home. At home, I sat on the old stone bench in the backyard. Smoked a bowl. Some cigarettes. Took pulls from the pint of bourbon while listening to Little Joy on my headphones—fitting because I possessed such little joy myself. I wondered if I was the first Black man to sit on this bench, live in this neighborhood, sleep in this bungalow, try to make a life here. I wondered if Ida ever asked herself the same kind of questions. At one point, I found the perfect balance of alcohol, weed, and nicotine, and reached a state of lo-fi bliss. The sun danced on my cheeks. Everywhere I looked, the leaves were rustling and I was at peace. It only lasted ten minutes. I knew if I tried to get back there again it would only end in inebriation. But I went for it anyway.

18

I WISHED I COULD SLEEP off my hangover to feel rested for our show at the Spruce. But I had to endure a day of work. I couldn't slack off, either, because the boss's daughter was shadowing me.

I showed Ailana how to put people on hold, transfer calls, answer the phone and say: *Thank you for calling Marketing Monkey. How may I help you on this fantastic day?*

"What else do you do?" she asked.

"Emails," I said. "And if someone walks into the office, I greet them. Although no one ever walks into the office."

"So you're a receptionist."

"No. I'm a customer service representative."

"But all you do is answer the phone and greet people."

"I can see how you would think that. But there are a lot of things I do that I didn't show you because your father didn't ask me to. Like all the tough-to-answer emails and working on the monthly newsletter."

"I thought my dad wrote the newsletter."

"I do all the editing," I said.

For the rest of the day, she was supposed to sit behind me and watch me do my job. But Fridays were slow. There wasn't much to see. I was a lowly receptionist at a lowly business. Most Fridays I'd sip coffee and read poems online or sometimes a short story until it lost my interest, go down internet rabbit holes, but since I was being watched, I made myself look busy by going through my inbox. Thousands of unread emails . . . 90 percent spam . . . Delete, delete, delete . . .

The boss stopped at my desk every thirty minutes or so to see how things were going. I still had a headache from last night's whiskey. Every time he popped his big fat head inside my cubicle, I wanted to throw my stress ball at him. Ailana had a fantasy novel on her lap but didn't seem interested in reading it. She started talking to me when her father wasn't lurking, about boys, sports, parties, and her dreams for the future, as if we were the same age and not six years apart. Her father had wanted her to major in business, but she was studying engineering. It was funny, the features they shared that made her father look like a giant baby made her very attractive. When I told her I was in a band, she got excited. She said if we ever played a gig in Corvallis, she'd bring all her friends and find us a place to stay. Every time we spoke, I stayed on high alert. I figured if the boss suspected I was flirting with his daughter, he would fire me at best and shoot me at worst. But really, he had nothing to worry about. I wasn't interested in a college girl who'd recently moved out of her dorm room and was dating a nineteen-year-old lacrosse player named Bradley. I only wanted Ida. And like that Marvin Gaye song. I wanted her to want me too. Because a one-way love is just a fantasy.

The boss once asked me if my band's name had anything to do with Planned Parenthood, and I'd assured him it did not.

Since Ailana was there to answer the phone, he let me leave at three o'clock.

Richmond picked me up. He had weed and a full tank of gas. We smoked a bowl and took in an awesome view of a snow-covered Mount Hood as we crossed the Willamette River by way of the Marquam Bridge. It was a beautiful late-spring day. We passed a large beer company mural painted on the side of a fifteen-story building. I was parched from the weed. I wished I could take a sip from the twenty-foot beer bottle that the racially ambiguous dude with freckles and a green mohawk was pouring into his gargantuan mouth. When the bowl was cashed, we rolled down the windows, lit cigarettes, and cranked up "Protect Ya Neck" by Wu-Tang Clan. Richmond knew every word but censored himself. He was the only guy in the band who knew anything about rap. Keith and William had a kind of whiteness that was incompatible with hip-hop.

The Spruce was a swanky compound on North Burnside. A hotel, restaurant, and music venue. I'd been to plenty of shows there but never had the honor of taking the stage—tonight that would change. We sat at the bar in the lounge. The place fashioned itself as an elk lodge from an alternate universe. A large glass moose head hung on the wall behind the bar. The carpet was zebra-patterned. Wood and white brick made up the bulk of the walls and the bar counter. The left side of the lounge opened up into the restaurant. The booths were plush and empty.

We didn't have much time before sound check. We looked around for the bartender. I saw workers refill napkins, count menus, check cellphones, talk in small groups, shake out fingers, and try to change the tired looks on their faces into something that would command respect and big tips. The working life was everywhere. I needed a drink to help me forget about the job I'd just left. I was about to make two hundred bucks to play in front of a crowd. I wanted to be *that* guy, the drummer in a band.

The bartender appeared and asked us what we wanted. We

hesitated, neither of us had thought about it. She closed her eyes and massaged her temples.

"I'll come back when you know what you want," she said.

We watched her walk away.

"Goddamn she's fine," Richmond said.

"Fine as hell," I said.

"When you were with Anne, you ever hook up with someone else?"

"Nope."

"What about Anne?"

"Only her boyfriend."

"No one-night stands? No make-out sessions? Nothing with no one?"

"I was happy with what I had."

"What a waste of an open relationship."

"You and Liesel ever try being open?"

He laughed and wrapped an arm around my neck.

"Hey now. What are you getting at? I'm no fool; I know she loves you. You'd probably be first in line. I wouldn't be able to take it. It would break up the band."

We ordered a large fry and two scotch highballs. Took our drinks and walked toward the sliding glass doors that opened to the patio. A large mirror hung on the wall above the doors. As we approached, I watched myself moving. I still had the pigeon-toe walk kids at church used to make fun of me for. I'd never grown up. My body had just expanded.

I was still a little stoned. We sat on a bench at the back of the empty patio next to a gas fire pit. Flames fought for relevance against the powerful sun—wisps of faded, wavering blue.

"You been talking to Ida?" Richmond asked.

"Yeah," I said. "She's coming to the show."

I never told him I was supposed to meet up with her the day before, so I didn't see the point in mentioning she stood me up.

"You really like her, don't you?"

"I do, man, I really do. Not only is she sexy amd cool, she's also a dope-ass artist."

"Have you seen her paintings?"

"No," I said. "But I don't have to see them to know that she's good."

"I've seen some of her paintings."

"What were they like?"

"They're okay," Richmond said. "To be honest, I prefer portraits and landscapes, and her stuff is abstract. But Liesel's roommate is a painter, and she thinks Ida is a genius."

"What were you going to tell me about her the night that I met her?"

"What do you mean?"

"After the cop shit, when you dropped me off at my house."

"I don't remember," he said.

He pushed his cigarette into the side of the bench, tossed it in the ashtray. The fries came. Two stories of hotel rooms flanked the patio. The door closest to our bench swung open and a red-bearded man stumbled out of his room with an ice bucket. He wore short shorts and had very hairy legs.

"You guys know where the ice machine is?" he asked.

"No," Richmond said. "We don't."

"Well, shit, I can't go without ice. I'm about to start a bender."

"Best part of drinking in a hotel room is the access to an ice machine," I said.

"Hell yeah," the man said. "And not having to clean up after yourself." He looked at Richmond. "Hey, I see you got a pack of cigarettes there, mind if I bum one?"

"Yeah, man, of course. You want to take my seat, too, want some french fries?"

"Oh no, man; no thanks, bro; just the cigarette. I have to continue my search."

Richmond stood up and gave the guy a cigarette. He lit it for him once he had it in his mouth.

"Thanks," the man said.

"Yeah, sure," Richmond said. He looked furiously at the guy's back as he walked away. I didn't understand what the big deal was. "But hey," Richmond said. "Do yourself a favor, man. They sell cigarettes inside. Go buy yourself a pack so you don't have to take people's shit all night. Someone with less manners than me might tell you to go fuck yourself."

The guy looked back with a confused expression and said, "Um, okay, man. Thanks."

He sped off quick. Richmond sat down and angrily chewed a french fry.

"Hey," I said. "What the hell was that about?"

"Nothing," he said. "Just giving the guy some friendly advice."

"With friendly advice like yours, who needs enemies," I said.

"Very funny," he said. "A guy with enemies needs a friend like me."

I'd known him long enough to know that the dude wasn't fine, he was feeling down about something. But maybe it was just nerves. It's crazy how your emotions build up when you have a show to play.

The venue was in the basement of the lounge and looked like a log cabin in outer space. Log beams in patterns along the middles of the space-gray walls. William stood alone onstage, tuning his guitar. Keith's bass and amp looked to be set up. Richmond and I walked from the back of the venue and stood at the foot of the stage. William stopped tuning his guitar and looked down at us.

"Where the hell were you guys?"

"Needed a quick snack after work," I said.

"Are you serious? We don't have a lot of time. I brought in some of your drums. The rest are in my car, you can get them yourself." He took out his keys and threw them at my face. Luckily, I caught them. But my palm stung from the impact.

"Dude," Richmond said. "What the fuck's your problem?"

"My problem is we have half an hour before sound check, and it takes you eight hours to tune your guitar."

"Fuck you, William," I said. "You could've taken an eye out."

"Yeah, man, you need to chill," Richmond said.

"No, I won't chill," William said. "You guys are being super unprofessional."

"You're the one being unprofessional," I said.

"Yeah, you're being a fucking bitch," Richmond said.

"Fuck the both of you guys," William said. "I don't care what you call me."

"Yeah? Well, fuck you," Richmond said.

He climbed onto the stage and got in William's face. The only thing between them was the guitar strapped to William's shoulder. I could see both of their faces. Richmond looked pissed. William looked unfazed. He was a few inches taller than Richmond, but at least ten pounds lighter. He smiled wide, showed his pristine white teeth. "I'm not scared of you, dude."

"No? Well, you should be," Richmond said.

"Go ahead," William said. "Go ahead and put me in one of your little wrestling holds, Mr. Macho Man. Show me how tough you are. But make it quick. We have half an hour before sound check, and you've got a lot to get done."

Richmond stopped his menacing glare. The two of them looked at each other and grinned, eyes sparkling dreamily. Lead singer and lead guitarist in cahoots. Richmond stood on his toes to kiss William's forehead.

"Okay, you win, you beautiful bastard. I'll go get my shit."

"Love you, dude," William said.

"Love you too," Richmond said. "We're going to kill it tonight."

I didn't love anybody. Richmond talked a good game, but he never seemed to have my back when it counted. I wanted to kick a hole in William's vintage Twin Reverb amplifier to get back at him for throwing his keys in my face. But who was I kidding? Only myself. William was untouchable tonight. I'd fight anyone who tried to touch him. Without our lead singer I wouldn't have a show to play, and if I didn't have a show I'd have nothing.

19

THE SOUND GUY WAS MORE confident than he was competent. A common sound person problem going back to my church days. He didn't listen to what we were telling him. My monitor mix was a mess. There was a lot of static. I couldn't hear the vocals. He kept saying he would fix it and it never got fixed. We ended up running through half our setlist before William was satisfied with the way things were sounding for *him*.

Once sound check was finally over, I took a nap on the green room couch. I woke up and the clock on the wall said ten past seven. Plaid Parenthood went on at nine. The green room walls were covered with posters and stickers and permanent marker. The room was quiet. Music bumped from somewhere far away. There was a stillness in the room that gave me the feeling I was the only living being on the basement level. No sound guy. No one preparing the bar. Just me. Floating alone in space in this spaceship log cabin. It was one of those times when I actually appreciated the feeling of isolation. In a couple hours the green room would be crowded, and I would be self-conscious.

I got off the couch, wiggled my arms and jumped up and down and moved my neck in circles. My body was intact, my mind fairly clear. I took off my shirt. Grabbed a bottle of beer from the refrigerator and pressed it against the back of my neck before using the bottle opener on the wall to pop off the cap, took a sip. I walked over to the clothing rack and took the dark green short-sleeve button-down off its hanger. I'd bought the shirt just for the show. It was expensive, but it made my arms look nice, was roomy enough to hide my tummy, and probably wouldn't look too bad once I started to sweat. It was expensive, but it reminded me of a shirt I'd worn in a family photo taken at a JCPenney portrait studio when I was a kid: in the photo, my father's hand is proudly placed on my shoulder, and my sister is somehow smiling after having endured hours of hair-care torture.

I looked in the mirror at my twenty-six-year-old self, hair still looking good from last week's cut, face only a little rounder than the image of myself that I had in my head. I adjusted my bolo tie and thought about pleasure and finances. In addition to the booze in the green room, I had three drink tickets and one meal ticket. Great, because money was tight. I'd been drinking pricier booze lately because it tasted better and gave me less of a hangover. *Champagne taste with a PBR pocketbook*, as my grandfather used to say. Premade healthy meals from the grocery store weren't cheap. Last week I bought a new ride cymbal. Then there was the hundred-dollar shirt on my back. It was nice that I'd gotten a two-dollar raise. But $80 more per week wasn't enough to support my lifestyle. As always, I wasn't going to be able to make rent and also pay the minimums on all my monthly bills. Something would have to go unpaid. But what? That was tomorrow's worry. Tonight was tonight. I gulped down my beer and tossed the bottle in the glass recycling bin before heading upstairs.

I ordered food and a drink in the lounge then headed to the patio. Keith was sitting on a bench close to the fire pit. I sat across from him with my back to the flames. The Spruce was filling up quick, and I was in a good position for people watching; I could see anyone who came onto the patio, and there were some cool-looking people. Keith informed me that William had left to meet Skyler at a vegan place and Richmond had left without saying where he was going.

"Think those guys have sex before the show?" he asked.

"Together?"

"With their ladies."

"Who cares," I said.

"I do."

"It's none of our business."

"Dude. Are you kidding? Of course it's our business. We need to be our best tonight. Just think about it. Have you ever been motivated for anything after sex? Sexual tension is one of the most powerful natural forces on earth. I read about it in an old *Playboy*. That's why I abstain for at least ten hours before big shows. Then I get onstage and put all that frustration into the music. I don't want our guys losing their edge. This is too big a night to play it half-cocked."

Keith always seemed to take everything back to sex. Which could be annoying, but at least he was consistent, never one guy one moment and another guy the next. The last time he got mad at me was for not wanting to play a song he thought would help him get laid. But he never yelled at people or threatened violence or threw shit at his bandmates. And I loved that about him, and I loved that once the music started, we'd come together as one and become the rhythm section.

I had just finished my steak frites and brussels sprouts when I saw Ida in a floral dress enter the patio holding a sweaty bottle of High Life and a small glass of whiskey. She looked great. Sadly, she wasn't alone. Her co-worker Jared was walking right behind her. I'd met him when he came in to help at the coffee shop dance party. I wasn't happy to see him.

"Don't turn around," I told Keith. "But the lady I'm into and one of her co-workers are headed our way."

I got up to greet them, Keith stood up too. I hadn't seen him properly since he put on his show clothes. He was fully dressed in vintage. Wore a fancy western shirt with pearl snap buttons, a bolo tie, a brown leather belt with a shiny bronze belt buckle, Levi's action slacks, and brown leather boots.

We went through introductions.

Ida sat next to me. Jared next to Keith.

"I like your bolo ties," Ida said. Her skin, her profile. Her voice.

"It was Keith's idea," I said.

"Just wait until you see us all wearing them onstage," Keith said.

"Very cool," Jared said. "You know there was a year when I decided to wear a suit and tie every day. But not because I had to. I was working at a grocery store as a greeter. And wouldn't you know it. My suit had powers. I felt better about myself and people respected me more. But then one day I decided to stop."

"What made you stop?" Keith asked.

"I'll tell you why I stopped . . ." Jared was a big talker. He was wearing cargo shorts. His pale legs were covered in tattoos, including one of Nelson Mandela. As soon as he got done talking about suits, he started talking about his wife and daughter. He said they were visiting relatives in Virginia. He didn't go with them because the flights were too expensive. "It was easier when the kid could fly for free. But man. I already regret not going, I just miss them so much." He took out his phone and started showing us pictures of his family. "We got married right after high school," he said of his wife. "She's my little dream," he said of his daughter. "I love them both so much." He sounded like he was about to cry. I wished he'd shut up. I was afraid I wouldn't get the chance to really talk to Ida before we had to go downstairs and start the show. But Keith was a natural wingman just like he was a natural bass player; he bailed me out.

"My twin nephews are around your daughter's age," Keith said to Jared.

"How old?"

"They're three."

"Nora just turned three last week!"

They got lost in baby talk. Ida and I turned around to face the fire. We split one of her spliffs. The sun was still winning, but the flames in the pit were acquiring depth. Ida scooted closer to me. Bumped my shoulder with hers.

"I'm excited to see you play. How are you feeling?"

"Like I'm about to make a fool of myself."

"Are you joking or being serious?"

"I'm serious," I said. "I'm terrified. And it happens every time. I have to trust that my body knows the songs, because right now I seriously can't remember how to play any of them."

"How long have you been a drummer?"

"Since I was eleven. I thought the drummer at my church was the coolest dude on earth. Marvin Randolph. Slick-as-fuck older Black dude who could play anything with ease and conviction. Phenomenal brushwork. Jesus couldn't help but come down from heaven with the way that guy finessed the cymbals. He gave me lessons."

"That's so cute. What was the best thing he taught you?"

"Music is a form of confession. If you hold back, God will know."

"So he taught you to play with conviction."

"I guess. He wasn't a patient teacher. When did you start painting?"

"My mother says I've been painting since before I could crawl. She's a painter too. She was my art teacher all through elementary school."

"My mom was my teacher too."

"Oh yeah? What subject?"

"Every single one; I was homeschooled until high school."

"I knew there was something funny about you."

"What's that supposed to mean?"

"You're genuinely kind."

I couldn't tell if being genuinely kind was a good thing or bad thing to her.

"The show is sold out," I said. "Did you get tickets?"

"We're all set. Richmond put me on the list."

Strange he hadn't mentioned that.

"Why didn't you ask me?"

"I thought it would be rude to ask you for something after I stood you up yesterday."

"Yeah, well, yesterday I cried in my poutine."

"Oh, I hope that's not true. I owe you an explanation. You want to hear it now or should we wait?"

"Does it end with you in someone else's arms?"

Ida slapped my thigh. "Shut up! No, why would I tell you if it did?"

"Okay," I said.

She told me on her way out of the door yesterday to meet me, she got a call from her ex. He'd bought Ida's truck as a birthday gift for her two years ago. It was still in his name. The registration was about to expire, and he was about to head out of town for a long trip. So instead of seeing me, she had to go over to his house so he could sign the title.

"Will it bother you if I talk about him a little? No? Okay. I met him three years ago when I was living in Seattle. Right after he moved back to the states from Peru. His name is Tyler, he's a little older than us. He paints these amazing portraits of South American peasants. All real people he's actually met during his travels. He has a personal story for every painting. But eventually I started to realize that he was just this privileged white guy from Utah taking advantage of other people's hardships, you know? He acted like he understood their suffering, but he didn't. If he did, he would never have painted their pictures and sold them for so much money without sending anything back to those people. I tried to explain that to him, but he couldn't process it. We drifted apart until our relationship was so obviously over. He's not an asshole or anything. He was the first boyfriend I'd ever lived with. I'll always love him in some way, but that door is closed now for good. Right now, I'm staying in a room in Jared's partially finished basement and sometimes sleeping in my studio. Anyway, I'm so sorry I had to leave you hanging. I felt horrible. I really wanted to see you."

"Thanks for telling me."

"You don't hate me for ditching you?"

"Of course not. I'm just happy you and Chuck are finally official."

"Good. Let's plan another time. I promise I'll be there."

"Let's do it," I said.

I'd tried to play it cool, but really, I didn't want to know a thing about Ida's ex-boyfriend and her undying love for him. It takes five seconds to sign over a title. Why couldn't she have seen me right after? Did they kiss? Make love? Spend the night together? I didn't want to know. Well, I did, but I didn't. Not that it would change the way I felt about her. I mean, those big brown eyes of hers and how they took in the world. Even sitting there listening to her talk about some other guy was the best time I'd had all week.

Keith tapped my shoulder.

"Eight-twenty," he said. "Time to roll."

"Break a leg," Ida said.

"Break hearts," Jared said. What a cheesy dude he was.

"Thanks," Keith said. "But we don't break hearts, we mend them."

20

THE STAGE WAS DIM. Venue half-full. I recognized other musicians, people I'd met at parties, Jackie the bartender from Klay's. I thought I saw my boss for a moment, but when the guy turned it wasn't him. Pre-show jitters had taken over. We flashed our wristbands to an employee sitting on a stool in front of the backstage entrance. They swished back the curtain. The green room was packed. Everyone white. This week our band had a write-up in the biggest Portland weekly, including a color photo of us standing in a thicket of trees at St. James Park. The other guys had been perfectly lit, but the tree-shadowed side of my face was just darkness. I hoped some of the people here recognized me from the half of my face that hadn't been shrouded, but either way, I was clearly the drummer for Plaid Parenthood, no one else in the room fit my general description.

Members of the headlining band were hanging out with friends and associates, including a comedian I'd seen on television. French Navy was from Seattle. They were blowing up. Pitchfork said their latest album was an 8.8/10. I agreed. Holly was their lead singer. Keith's dream girl. She sat in front of a lighted vanity mirror finishing her makeup and sipping white wine through a black plastic straw.

Our crew was sitting in the booth at the back of the room. We had to squeeze past a lot of butts to get there. William was chatting with Liesel and Skyler. Richmond was sitting at the edge of the booth, strumming his Telecaster. He was wearing his usual blue jeans, a black denim shirt, brown boots, and a bolo tie. Keith ran up and kissed his forehead.

"You look great! Absolutely great." He looked over at William. "Hey man, where's your tie?"

"It won't work with this shirt."

William was wearing a tight red sweater with tiny white hearts.

"Love the sweater," I said. "Where'd you get it?"

"It's mine from high school," Skyler said. "He looks great in it, doesn't he?" He did.

William's bolo tie was sitting on the table. Keith picked it up.

"Dude. The turquoise on the pendant goes perfect with your sweater."

"It makes me look like a joke," William said.

"If you don't wear it, we'll look like we're your lackies," I said. "Is that what you think is going on here?"

"No tie, no lead guitar," Richmond said.

"No bass, either," Keith said.

"And I won't sing any harmonies on those songs," Liesel said.

"Put the tie on, babe," Skyler said. "It'll be cute."

"Yeah?" William asked her.

"Yes," she said.

William put on the bolo tie. We took shots of bourbon to celebrate. Someone came into the green room and shouted we had five minutes until showtime. Liesel wished me good luck with a kiss on the cheek. The band huddled in the narrow corridor behind the stage. We put our arms around one another and rocked from side to side like the Chicago Bulls during the Jordan era. It was Richmond's turn to give the pep talk: "Gentlemen. We've worked way too hard for far too long in that stupid fucking basement not to go out there and kill it. I love you guys. Let's blow their damn minds."

"That's right. Baa-boom," Keith said.

We took the stage. I sat down, kicked my bass drum twice, turned on my snare, adjusted my throne, picked up my sticks, closed my eyes, took a few deep breaths, kicked one more time, nodded, looked up at the guys to make sure they were ready, then I counted off and we got rolling.

The first song went off without a hitch. It was our oldest and maybe best song; we could play it in our sleep. The trick was to keep up the energy and play everything like you meant it. I hit the snare slightly off-center, about the same spot every time, with intention and force, getting the tight marching band feel the song needed. In practice it was sometimes easy to lose steam, but being onstage in front of a crowd with lights shining in my face made me feel like I was boiling over.

During the second song, my hi-hat stand started to inch away from me. Every time I pressed on the pedal, it moved forward a little. Eventually I had to stretch out my left leg to get the right angle. My ankle got strained from pressing the pedal unnaturally. I started to cramp up. I almost fell off my drum stool trying to keep my foot on the pedal. But I fought my way to the bridge without missing a beat and used the four-bar break to pull the hi-hat stand back into position and pressed it down into the carpet. We finished the song just fine. The crowd cheered, but the feeling onstage was that our band could go even higher.

Our third song was our slowest and most dynamic. It was supposed to start out with just me and William. I was supposed to play the shaker, soft kicks on the downbeats. But I couldn't find the shaker anywhere. It wasn't in my stick bag. I didn't see it on the almost pitch-black floor. I started to panic. William turned around to look at me.

"What's wrong?" he asked.

"Can't find the egg shaker."

"Don't worry about it."

"Okay," I said. "Ready? One and two and three and."

He started strumming. Then he stopped. I got the feeling we were screwed.

Richmond walked over to us. "Keep playing. What are you guys doing?"

"Found it," William said. He bent down in front of my bass drum. He stood up and tossed me the shaker. He hit me with his surfer-boy smile. I shook my head and smiled back at him. We were brothers again. He went to the microphone and said, "My bad, folks."

I counted off again, *one and two and three and.* William and I synced up. A quarter way through the song, I put down the shaker to play the full kit, and the rest of the band joined in. My limbs moved on their own. My mind became clear. I looked out at the crowd. Full capacity. Over three hundred people. Outside of church, this was the biggest show of my life.

Ida was the only Black person I could see. She was standing next to Liesel who was standing next to Skyler who was standing next to Anne. Anne was standing next to her fiancé. It was the first time I'd seen him in person. He was a mediocre white guy in a crowd of mediocre white guys. He looked just like her. Same height, same oversized glasses, and wearing Patagonia like this was a nature adventure instead of a rock show. No wonder Anne didn't want me; I could never be her twin. She smiled when she saw me looking her way, and I pretended like she was mistaken, like I couldn't see her at all because of the spotlights, like she just happened to be where my eyes had randomly fixed themselves to. I didn't miss her anymore, but we once had something special. Now all we had were memories, and memories tended to disappear, suddenly and at random. I wondered what things about her I would never forget.

The vibration of Keith's bass interrupted my thoughts. I don't think he was joking when he told Jared that he was going onstage to mend people's hearts. He made me forget about the crowd, about Anne, Ida, about anything that wasn't music. I focused on what Keith was doing and what I could do to help him. It was a shame, there were people in the crowd who couldn't even tell you what the bass does or sounds like. Yet Keith was doing all he could to take away their pain, meter by meter. We were release valves for emotion. Ours and theirs, too. A connection to the spiritual world, a higher consciousness beyond language. When my faith was sliding and I was still going to church, I hated sermons because they never made me feel closer to God, only further apart. The only time I'd feel remotely close to a higher power in church was when I was behind the drums and people were singing and playing with all their hearts. I felt just as close to that power now, playing drums at the Spruce. I don't think it had anything to do with abstinence, but me and Keith could feel exactly where the other guy was going. One song he played right on top of me. The next song he sat back in the pocket and grooved. We weren't thinking anymore, the bullshit in our heads was only fuel for our limbs. I forgot all about my shitty monitor mix. The only thing that mattered now was vibration. How it could be harnessed and manipulated. I loved my new ride cymbal, the timbre. I loved my body and its power. The rest of the show I felt deeply rooted, yet lifted off the ground. Richmond ripped everything he played. Loud and distorted or quiet and pristine, everything full of heart. I couldn't hear William's voice very well, and for most of the show, all I could see was the back of his head, but when we practiced, he always faced me, so I knew he looked like a god when he sang his heart out. The way people in the crowd looked up at him, I knew they were in love. Liesel came onstage to sing harmonies on the last two songs, and the crowd was transfixed. When we got back to the green room, I could still hear people cheering. The comedian patted me on the back and offered me a hit of his joint.

21

STILL RIDING THE HIGH OF the post-show afterglow, I got a message from Ida saying she wished she could stick around but she had to go home. She said our band played great, and she'd call me tomorrow. She'd been up since five in the morning and was too exhausted to be any fun. I didn't get it. Tired or not, why couldn't she have at least stuck around long enough to say goodbye? Maybe she hated the music. Maybe I looked like a clown in my bolo tie.

Keith wandered into the crowd to schmooze. I didn't want to bump into Anne and her fiancé. I stayed backstage with William and Skyler and watched French Navy from the side of the stage. The band had a jangly indie-pop sound. Their music was the kind you played in headphones on a bus when you wanted to feel melancholy but ultimately resilient. There were people in the crowd who seemed to know the lyrics to every song. The place was at full capacity. Holly sang like singing was the easiest thing a person could do, she emanated energy and confidence. She crowd-surfed during French Navy's biggest hit and never missed a note. The last song was a new one.

She sang it on her knees, in tears. The crowd ate it up. Skyler told William to take note. After the show, the two of them left to hang out with Anne and her fiancé. Richmond and Liesel left without saying goodbye to me; I couldn't remember that ever happening before.

Keith and I stayed at the Spruce. We sat in the booth at the back of the green room with Holly and Jessica. We were the only people left. Jessica was French Navy's keyboard player. She had a little bit of cocaine in a tiny baggie. I'd only done coke twice before, both times I'd liked it. We finished the bottle of whiskey and did thin lines on a compact mirror. We walked upstairs to a busy lounge and patio. Jared was sitting on a bench by himself. I was cranky and didn't want him around. Keith gave him a bear hug and sat down next to him, which meant we all had to sit down with Jared, too.

"You guys were great tonight," he said. "Both bands, really great."

"Thanks so much," Jessica said. "How do you know Keith?"

"We just met today," Keith said. "His kid and my nephews are the same age."

Holly put her hand on my thigh under the table.

"Cool," she said.

"I came here with a friend from work," Jared said. "She had to leave before your set, but for the first time in years, I had no reason to go home early, so I decided to stay and see you. You ladies were fantastic. Ida get a chance to say goodbye to you, Julian?"

"Yeah," I said.

Hearing Ida's name made me feel guilty. Holly wouldn't stop touching me. We went to the bar to order more drinks. Fit our bodies between two occupied barstools. Holly carried herself like she knew she was the coolest person in the room. Her curly hair was dyed bleach blond and styled in way that would be considered a mess if she wasn't the rock star she clearly was. Multiple people came up to tell her how much they loved her.

The bar was busy. There were only two bartenders. The bartender who eventually served us was the woman who'd gotten annoyed with me and Richmond when we didn't know what we wanted. When she saw me and Holly smushed together between barstools, she smiled and came over right away. We handed her our drink tickets.

"How was the show?" she asked.

"Holly was great," I said.

"Julian is the hottest drummer ever," Holly said.

"All three of us are hot," I said.

"Why thank you," the bartender said.

We went down that path for a while, saying silly shit. The bartender didn't care that other people were waiting. We took shots of whiskey after the bartender proposed a toast to our hotness. Were any of us truly hot? Probably not. But that didn't matter. When we got back outside, Keith and Jessica were sitting alone on the bench. Keith had lipstick on his nose, cheek, and neck.

"Where's Jared?" I asked.

"He left," Keith said.

I had the feeling Jared probably saw me cozied up with Holly and decided not to say goodbye. That was no good. He seemed like the kind of guy who'd tell Ida everything he saw and suspected. Not that it should matter. Ida had no claim on me. She'd bailed on me two days in a row. Maybe her saying I was genuinely nice meant she thought I was going to sit around waiting for her.

My headache from the morning came back worse than it had been before. I wanted more cocaine.

"Oh, there he is," Keith said.

A dude wearing a Teenage Mutant Ninja Turtles bodysuit that went up to his neck, a sailor hat, and purple basketball sneakers drove up the walkway in a pink Vespa. He had a briefcase. A purple guitar strap was duct-taped to both sides of the briefcase and slung over his shoulders.

"You know this guy?" I asked.

"Oh yeah," Keith said. "But we're not on good terms. I had Jessica call him."

"If that guy doesn't have blow, no one has blow," Holly said.

"If I went around dressed like that, I'd get locked up," I said.

"So sad and true," Jessica said. "Fuck racism."

Yeah, I thought. *Fucking white people. Give me more cocaine.*

The guy hopped off his scooter and put down the kickstand. His bodysuit was tight like stuffed sausage casing. The balls on this guy. You couldn't miss them. People were staring. He thumbed through his phone like this was any other night. He made a call and Jessica's phone lit up. Keith turned his head so the guy couldn't see him.

"Hello? Oh, okay. Yeah. Where? Okay, yeah, okay, meet you there."

Jessica hung up the phone. "He says to meet him in the back hallway next to the ice machine. I can take one person, and it's okay if it's a guy, because he wants me to feel safe. Oh, he also wants whoever stays here to watch over his scooter."

Holly went with Jessica. Keith and I stayed and kept an eye on the scooter. He punched my arm.

"You ready for this, good sir?"

"Ready for what?"

"Jessica told me Holly's into people of color."

"Yeah? I hear Jessica's into tiny dicks."

"Great," Keith said. "Then she won't be disappointed. I told you these bolo ties would get us laid."

"Did she really say people of color?"

"Jessica? Yeah. She said Holly only seems to hook up with people of color. Men, women, whatever, just not white."

"You think it's intentional?"

"Who cares. The odds are in your favor."

"Yeah, but it's kind of weird, right?"

"Not at all, my good man. The dick wants what it wants, the pussy wants what it wants, whatever, it's just sex. Just listen to your loins."

"You're right," I said. "It doesn't matter."

"Seriously," he said. "You need to lighten up."

Keith didn't have to convince me of anything. The last thing I wanted to do was go back to the person I was before I got onstage and played the biggest show of my life. I didn't want to go back to my problems, to feel death creeping in with no sign of God. I wanted to forever be the person I was when I was onstage getting lost in the music.

Once we'd secured the drugs, we headed to the karaoke bar across the street. Before we walked in, we stood by the side of the building and did bumps off my house keys. We scooted into a tiny table next to a bachelorette party. Holly got her song request into the KJ right before the list was filled up for the night. I ate chicken fingers, drank beer, did bumps in the bathroom, and made out with Holly. Making out in public was something I'd never done before. It felt good. When it was Holly's turn to sing, our table got onstage and danced as she sang "Dancing on My Own" by Robyn. The bachelorette party got up and joined us.

Eventually Holly and I parted ways with Jessica and Keith and went to her hotel room back at the Spruce. The room came with a record player and a selection of records. Holly put on the Everly Brothers. Didn't fit the mood, but I went with it. We made out on her bed. She touched my erection pressed against my jeans. Traced it with her fingers. I took off my bolo tie. We took off our shirts. I got out of bed to take off my pants. Holly stayed in bed and slipped off her bra and white jeans. She had more tattoos than I'd imagined. Wolves. Spiderwebs. A naked woman. All kinds of symbols, including a cross.

"Do you have any protection?" she asked.

"No," I said.

"I'm sure the lobby does," she said.

The lobby. It seemed so far away. I put my clothes back on. I opened the door and walked along the second-floor balcony toward the stairs. I looked down at the fire pit where Ida and I had thrown a spliff in the flames about six hours ago. When I got back to the room, Holly was under the blankets.

"Any luck?"

"I didn't end up going."

Holly got out of bed. Wrapped the comforter around her body. She opened the minifridge and grabbed a bottle of water. Unscrewed the cap, took a few sips, then handed me the bottle. She put her head against my shoulder and yawned.

"Girlfriend? Wife? Boyfriend?"

"Not exactly," I said.

"Jesus?"

"Not exactly."

"What a fucking tease you are. No offense, I've had a lot of fun tonight, but if you don't want to fuck, you should leave so I can masturbate and crash."

She opened the door. I stepped out.

"I'm sorry," I said.

She leaned against the door to keep it from closing. I wanted to get my hands in that wild hair of hers. That's what my loins said.

"Stay the night," she said.

Bus lines wouldn't run again until the morning. Paying full cab fare was silly. Waiting around for someone to be in love with you just because you wanted them to be was even sillier. I suppose that was a thing about Anne I would never forget. Unrequited love was no fucking good. How did Holly know it was partly Jesus? All those sermons about sin, believing every word. Not wanting to disappoint the father above or the father sitting beside me in the pew. Well tonight I was choosing to forgive myself, forget the past shit, follow my desires, and be a man of the world. I stepped back inside. Holly moved away from the door and it slammed automatically. This side of the album was over. The record player spun only static and crackles and a rough, lopsided shuffle that always felt to me like the maddening anticipation of a spiritual release that was never going to come until someone flipped the damn record and put the needle to the edge.

PART THREE

22

GOOD THINGS HAD COME FROM our show at the Spruce. Important people had seen promise. Already my life was changing. The day after our show, we signed with a booking agent who, within a week of signing with him, had already booked us a tour. It was kind of a sad story how it all came together—but not too sad for me. Our new agent managed a band that had to drop out of their tour dates in Tacoma, Seattle, Spokane, Pendleton, San Francisco, Sacramento, and Los Angeles because their lead singer had a mental breakdown. Plaid Parenthood was taking their dates. We had two weeks from the day we found out about the tour to the day we were supposed to be in Tacoma. We'd been practicing and recording every day since we got the news. We were leaving for the tour in four days.

Everyone was doing all they could to devote more time to the band and be ready to go on the road. For William and his mysterious finances, finding that time was easy. Richmond surprised me though. He sold his prized 1972 Fender Telecaster. Which meant he was less flush with cash than I'd imagined. Keith quit his job at the doughnut shop but found a new gig as a bartender at the Sandy Hut, where he could start as soon as we got back. I didn't have that luxury.

Aside from being able to go on a date with Ida after the band voted to take that day off so William could go out with Skyler to celebrate her birthday, all that I could do to dedicate more time to the band was cancel all the time I spent reading books and daydreaming and worrying about God and death and romantic love. Trenton told me it was special that the boss was letting me use all five of my accumulated vacation days in a row, so I made sure not to mess it up. I got to work on time every day, no matter how hard it was to wake up, always tired as shit. I never called in sick. Going on tour and recording our first EP was worth every sacrifice.

I was waiting in line outside the sushi restaurant when Ida drove by in her truck. She took a left and disappeared. I shuffled up the line, feeling anxious. But nerves weren't all I felt. The rainy morning and afternoon, and the gray lid that had sat over Portland for the past week, had finally been lifted. The sun was out. The air was sweet, nature was flourishing, and I couldn't help but feel happy to be alive and living in this neighborhood.

Ida walked around the corner. Big sunglasses. Earrings that dangled. A quick hug.

"Hey, hey," she said.

"Hi," I said. "We finally did it."

"I know, right? A date. And I almost showed up on time."

"You're timing was perfect," I said. "If I'd had to go in there when it was finally our turn to be seated and tell them that my whole party wasn't present and experience their disdain and possible refusal to seat me, then you'd be late, but that didn't happen, so you're right on time."

Once seated we ordered beers, and when they arrived, we clanked glasses.

"So I'm dying to know," she said. "Is this your first-ever date with a Black girl?"

"C'mon," I said. "What makes you say that?"

"You live in this neighborhood and play in a rock band."

"Damn, alright."

"Well, is it true or not?"

"Okay, it's true."

"Ha! I knew it."

"Yeah? Well, you live in Portland too. What about you?"

"In high school, my mom said I was only allowed to date Black guys. Which was a ridiculous restriction in Bellingham, Washington, but I did it. Then my first week in Rhode Island I fell in love with this white guy in my spatial dynamics class who grew weed in the closet of his dorm room."

"Did he have dreadlocks?" I asked.

The server put our edamame and miso soup on the table. We thanked him. Ida waited until he left to reply: "I made him cut them off."

"But this is nice, right?" I said. "We're both Black. Our parents would be proud of us."

"Okay, goofball," she said. "Enough of the obvious."

We ordered way too much sushi but agreed that too much was better than not enough. Ichiro's was the only sushi restaurant in the neighborhood and was way better than the place off the Sunset Highway that John at work liked. Ichiro's had Texas-sized rolls. Fantastic and cheap.

We were seated across from each other at a small table in the middle of the narrow restaurant. Heaps of sushi to the point that we both found it hilarious. When I told Ida I got married at twenty-two and divorced at twenty-four, she dropped her chopsticks.

"I can't believe I'm on a date with a former child bride. This is a first."

"We were adults," I said. "Not children."

"What? Twenty-two? No, that's still a baby."

"How old do you have to be not to be a baby?"

"Older than me," she said. "I'm twenty-seven."

"I'm twenty-six."

"Do you still talk to your ex-wife?"

"Not since the divorce, no."

"Are you super religious? Do you still go to church? Sorry to ask so many questions. I'm just so curious."

"I don't mind. I grew up evangelical, but I'm trying to get over it. What about you?"

"Not much religion at all, but I sort of wish I'd had that background."

"You're lucky," I said.

"Am I? Because I feel like I'm missing out sometimes. So much art is based on the Bible. And then there's the Black church. So important."

"I guess those parts are interesting," I said. "But the guilt part is horrendous. You feel bad for just being yourself. It drives people to madness."

"Madness like early marriage?"

"Yes, exactly," I said.

She smiled. Her nose ring shimmered. "Oh. Before I forget. I told Jared I was seeing you today, and he wanted me to say hello. He also told me to ask you for Keith's number. He said they really hit it off."

I got a little scared. When I kissed Holly goodbye before walking out of her hotel room the morning after the show at the Spruce, I figured that was the end of things. But maybe Jared told Ida everything he'd seen and suspected. Was she testing me? Was I supposed to confess?

"Jared doesn't want *my* number?" I asked.

She reached over the table to pat my hand.

"Don't you worry," she said. "I already gave it to him."

My fear subsided. I told her more about my homeschooling. That every day was the same except for the music I chose to listen to that day and what happened in the books I read. Ida told me that while I was a child bride, she was backpacking in Europe with a Spanish guy she'd met at a hostel in Italy. We ate enthusiastically, messily, not holding back, made short replies to the other person's questions while our mouths were stuffed with rice and fish. The more we talked, the more I respected her. Halfway through the meal we abandoned chopsticks and ate with our hands. I began to understand that she was on her own life journey, and that right now her path was crossing mine, and that was how she saw life, like her foreign adventures with that Spanish dude from the hostel, that was just part of her path. And somehow along that same line of thinking, I no longer felt like I somehow wronged Ida by being with Holly; and even though I didn't want to know if she'd slept with her ex on the day she'd stood me up, it was okay with me if she did. Yesterday might as well have been a million years ago.

After dinner we went to the wine bar next door and sat on leather armchairs surrounded by tall potted plants. Ida leaned back in her chair after taking a sip of wine.

"Julian, I can't tell you how much I needed a night like this," she said.

"Same here," I said. "It's good not to be working."

"Ugh. Working and art. What else do we do?"

"Nothing," I said.

"But what about that kid across the street?"

I told her everything, including how when Claire had invited me over, I thought she was trying to seduce me. Ida thought that was funny, and she got me laughing about it too. I told her about the championship basketball game, how I blocked his shot and said *no, no, no, not today, nigga* and wagged my finger. I told her about Reggie storming off at the frozen yogurt place when I told him his parents were racist.

"Julian! Like, what the hell are you doing?"

"I know," I said. "And I want to fix it, but his parents won't give me a chance. They wrote me a fucking letter. They said I'm a bad influence and I need to stay away from their kid."

Ida put her hand on my shoulder to keep herself from falling over laughing.

"I'm sorry," she said.

Anytime she touched me, I never wanted her to stop.

"It's okay," I said. "I guess it's sort of humorous."

"A letter, though? What's wrong with these people?"

"They're lawyers," I said. "Any idea what I should do?"

"Not at all," Ida said.

I didn't feel bad about a lot of my sins. But messing up my relationship with Reggie was a mistake that would probably hurt forever if it didn't get fixed. I told Ida I didn't mind that she laughed, but I did.

"How's the painting life?" I asked. "When can I see what you're doing?"

"If you're lucky, you can see it when the project is complete. Hell, if *I'm* lucky and I get it finished without destroying myself or any of the canvases."

"Is it a series? What's the concept? What is it all supposed to look like in the end? Like the painting you last finished, how would you describe it?"

Ida took a sip of her wine, lowered her eyes, then stared at me unkindly. The first time I'd seen such a look. I'd touched a nerve.

"Words would be a reduction of what I'm trying to achieve, you know?"

"Totally," I said. "I'll be patient and wait for the master to finish her masterpieces."

She liked that. She put out her hand and I took it.

"Thank you, former child bride," she said.

We held hands while finishing our wine. It was the middle of May and beautiful and the sun was still up, but it was also Thursday night and we both had work in the morning. Once our wineglasses were empty, it was time to go. Ida insisted on paying for the drinks because

I paid for dinner. I was too poor to protest. We split a spliff as we walked to her truck.

"This was fun," she said.

"A blast," I said. "I'm happy we got to do this before I left."

"When do you leave again?"

"Monday."

"So soon. After tomorrow I'm taking time off work. I'm going to become an ogre who lives in her studio. Wow. Your first rock-and-roll tour. You must be so excited."

"I'm thrilled," I said. "But I'm already exhausted."

"Yeah, you look tired."

"Thanks."

"No, not in a bad way. You're dedicated. I like that."

"I like that about you too," I said.

Ida leaned against Chuck. We kissed. Our bodies pressed together, her breasts firm against the bottom of my chest. We kissed some more. No sushi breath detected, only possibilities of a mutual path. A group of people walked past us and stared. We were probably the only Black adults they'd seen all day, possibly all week, maybe for all of May; in this town that was possible. Ida got in her truck. She rolled down her window and yelled to me as she pulled away from the curb.

"Safe travels," she said. "Have fun. Strap up. Watch out for sketchy broads. I think I love you."

At least that's what I think I heard. It's possible after *safe travels*, she said something else entirely.

23

THE WHOLE BUNGALOW WAS WIRED for sound. From the second-floor control room down to the basement, cables ran up and down the stairs, along floorboards, through air vents, under area rugs, and across every entryway. Microphones everywhere, even in the bathroom—where William believed he got the best reverb when he craned his neck and sang into the mic that hung above the toilet.

I'd been tracking drums on the same song for the past two hours. Richmond couldn't be satisfied. One take, he told me to focus on the metronome and imitate a drum machine. The next take, to play like a confident drunk walking across a tightrope, teetering from side to side, so close to death but oblivious; he wanted me to swing with confidence. After that one, he told me I should play like I was back in church and invite the spirit of the Lord into the bungalow basement, so that's what I did. I thought that take was perfect, but still he wasn't happy.

His voice crackled into my headphones: "You almost got it, but the bridge should be four on the floor." He was in the control room.

I was in the basement. I wanted to grab the microphone hanging over my snare and bash it into the brick wall behind me.

"I've been playing it that way every time," I said.

Richmond's voice was in my head again: "I'm not hearing all the kicks. One more take. Same way you played it last time, but with a hard-hitting snare in the bridge and more fucking feeling all over everything."

"I'll show you hard-hitting feeling, asshole," I said.

"What was that, dude? I didn't catch that."

"Start the damn track," I said. "Hit record. This is the last time."

After I finished the take, I walked up the janky wooden basement stairs, grabbed a beer from the kitchen refrigerator, and went up to the second-floor alcove to listen to what we had. The rest of the band had already taken up the chairs. I sat to the side of them, back against the wall. Keith played the take I'd just recorded along with William's scratch vocals and Richmond's guitar. Olympia climbed into my lap. I scratched her neck, she purred with her head to the ceiling, eyeballs rolled back into her skull. I whispered to her that she was precious and the best cat around and my little baby. She started to scratch up my jean shorts. I tried to push her off gently, she held on tight, talons engaged. I pulled her off and tossed her onto the carpet. My shorts were now distressed. She hissed at me. After we finished listening to the take, Richmond said I was almost there.

"It's great," William said. "But if I'm honest, I don't see how it sounds much different than what he's been playing for the past hour."

"What are you talking about? Keith, play it back."

William reached toward Keith to stop him from pushing Play.

"No. Don't play it back. We got what we need. Time to move on."

Richmond turned his swivel chair to look at me.

"Whatcha think? You want to take another crack at it?"

William and Keith turned around to face me. And I thought, *How the hell did I end up with these three white dudes as my closest friends?* All three stared at me and waited for my response. The computer monitors, soundboard, and preamps glowed behind them.

"I've done all I can for this song," I said.

"You should play it one more time," Richmond said.

"We've got too much left to do," William said. "We need to move on."

"He's given us more than enough to work with," Keith said. "We can splice things together."

"Fuck that. Let's vote," Richmond said.

William was sipping herbal tea spiked with vodka, his favorite way to drink it, which is why it didn't make sense that he kept the bottle in the freezer. Keith had been sipping on the same warm beer for hours. He took his role as recording engineer very seriously. Usually, Richmond would smoke a little weed and drink a little beer, like me. Tonight he was drunk on bourbon.

Our band's biggest issue was that we didn't have a leader. William wrote most of the lyrics. Richmond wrote most of the music. Most of our recording equipment and the sound system we used for practices belonged to William, but Keith was the only one who really knew how to use them. If there was a disagreement, we talked it out and compromised. We only voted when it was something big. Like whether or not we should play at the Spruce or sign with a booking agent or go on tour or record a four-song EP to sell on the road. Voting on if I should play the same song again for the millionth time when we already had a bunch of great takes was an abuse of the system. I was done for the night, which meant I was done with my recording for our entire EP, my first album. I was proud of what I'd done.

"Are you sure about this?" I asked Richmond.

"Are you?" he said.

"This is a dumb vote," William said.

"Don't ever call something I do *dumb* again; if you do, I'll make you regret it."

"Give it up, Richmond," William said. "Give the tough guy act up. Go to therapy."

"Who do you think I should see?" Richmond asked. "You thinking maybe your girlfriend?"

"Go to hell," William said.

"Gentlemen," Keith said. "Play nice. We're about to spend a week on the road together."

"Let's have Julian decide," Richmond said. He leaned toward me. Bleary-eyed. "C'mon, Julian, one more time, you're *this* close to the perfect fucking take. I can feel it."

"I played my ass off every time," I said.

"No, c'mon. One more time. Forget everything I said before and just play."

"I can't stand your shit anymore," William said. "We're wasting time. Let's vote. Raise your hand if you think we're good here."

William and Keith both quickly raised their hands. I hesitated.

"Who thinks Julian should play it one more time?" Richmond said.

My hand shot up. I was shocked. My body must have known something my brain didn't. William shook his head at me as if my owing him rent meant I owed him my loyalty.

"Jesus. I can't believe this," he said.

"Never had a tie," Richmond said. "How do we square it?"

"Rock, paper, scissors," Keith said. "Best out of three. Can we all agree?" The four of us nodded in agreement. "Rock, paper, scissors has now been adopted into the Plaid Parenthood charter as the official means of breaking ties. We have Richmond, *the Jersey wrestler*, versus William, *the golden surfer boy*. Now, I want to see a fair fight, gentlemen. Good luck to you both."

William threw rock then scissors, Richmond threw paper then rock.

I headed to the basement. Richmond followed me. He tripped over the cable that went across the kitchen. I grabbed him before he fell. He looked at me with drunken gratitude. I didn't know what was going on with this guy, but I was sorry for him. Once we got to the basement, he put on a pair of earmuffs and lay on the area rug in front of the drums. He reached into a pocket of his forest-green zip-up hoodie to take out a pair of sunglasses and put them on. When the metronome started to click and the song began, I didn't think about being recorded or the other guys listening upstairs, I played for the man on the floor, my friend who believed I had more to give.

That take was my best playing ever. Richmond raised his arms in triumph. My work was done, I got hammered in celebration as the rest of the guys scrambled to record all four of Keith's bass lines. I woke up on the couch in the living room still feeling drunk from the night before. My bladder was beyond capacity. I got to the bathroom as quickly as I could, putting a hand against the wall behind the toilet as I peed to keep myself from falling over. William's bedroom had a door that connected to the bathroom; it was ajar. I looked in. He was sleeping in our house, alone, not with Skyler. Good for him. Funny thing was, last night before I passed out, all I thought about was how much I wanted to be next to Ida.

Keith had finished recording his bass lines around two in the morning. He did a shot every take, two songs he recorded twice; that was six shots in two hours. All of us caught up with Richmond and got wasted and joyous. Last night's drunk had been a happy one. The only kind of drunk I ever aspired to. We were almost finished with our first EP.

When I got out of the bathroom, I saw the clock on the microwave said it was almost noon. I walked into William's room and pulled his pillow from under his head.

"Why?" he asked.

"Liesel," I said.

I went upstairs. Keith was sitting behind the console, head against the high-backed office chair, waiting for Pro Tools to open. His sleeping bag was crumpled on the carpet behind him. The cat was napping on top of it.

"Coffee," Keith said. "Somebody needs to go out and get us coffee."

"We don't have time. I'll make some as soon as I wake up Richmond."

"How do you make it?"

"How do you mean?"

"How do you make your coffee?"

"In a coffeepot."

"An automatic drip?"

"Yeah."

"Yikes."

"What's wrong with that?"

"I usually do French press or pour over. What kind of beans? Do you grind them fresh?"

"Listen," I said. "You either take the coffee I make or go without."

"Does William make his coffee that way?"

"He only drinks tea."

"How un-American," Keith said. "We have access to such great coffee in this town."

I went to my bedroom. Richmond was the first person to crash last night and had determined that my mattress was the best place to sleep in the house. I hadn't known he was in there until I'd stumbled into bed in the late-night early morning and found myself lying next to him. I almost stayed, then thought better of it. Good to be next to a warm body for now, but it had the makings of an awkward morning, so I slept on the couch.

I shook him awake.

"The feng shui in this room is off," he said.

"C'mon. It's almost noon. Liesel will be here any second."

Aside from the mixing we were going to spend the rest of the day and night on, Liesel's background vocals and harmonies were the last things we needed to finish our EP.

When she walked into the bungalow, she was all business.

"Where do I record?" was the first thing she said. She was annoyed that we were hungover and slow-moving. "Did you guys forget the time you told me to be here?" Of course not, we told her. She said hello to me but didn't touch or say hello to Richmond. Keith set her up in the tiny room next to my bedroom, the windows covered with foam. The rest of us sat in the alcove and drank coffee and tea and ate buttered toast with jam.

Through the microphone in the makeshift vocal booth, Liesel told us that she didn't need to listen to the songs before she was ready to record because she'd already listened to the demos.

"Are you sure about that?" Richmond said into the talkback mic. "A lot of parts have changed. William's vocals are totally different."

"I don't think they're all that different," William said. Liesel couldn't hear him because he wasn't speaking into the talkback mic.

"I don't want to hear your voice again, Richmond. Start the song," she said.

"Okay, Liesel, here we go," Keith said.

She recorded all the vocals we needed in less than twenty minutes. When she was done, she opened the door to the recording booth and headed straight for the stairs. The front door slammed. The bungalow shook.

"Strange behavior," Keith said.

Most people loved Liesel, but those who didn't tended to despise her. Keith once told me in confidence he thought she was a stuck-up bitch.

"She was great," William said. "Lifted the album."

Richmond scratched the back of his neck.

"Yeah, so, I've been meaning to tell you guys," he said. "We broke up."

"When?" I asked.

"The night of our last show."

"That was weeks ago," I said.

"Why didn't you tell us sooner?" William asked.

"What a bummer," Keith said. "Who broke up with who?"

"Don't tell him," I said.

"*I* broke up with her."

"But why?" William asked.

Richmond laughed sharply.

"Looking for more song material? I think I give you enough of that."

"But Richmond," I said. "Don't you love her?"

"Of course I still love her. But this is best for the both of us. Believe me."

I couldn't believe it was over with them. Back when we'd go out, just the three of us, Richmond would ask me right in front of her: *Julian, isn't Liesel beautiful? Isn't she talented? Isn't she smart? She's such a badass. Don't you think she's a badass? Tell her, tell her she's a badass.* And I'd tell her to her reddening face that she was cool, smart, a phenomenal singer, beautiful, a badass. And she'd slap my arm or grab my hand and tell me to shut up, and the three of us would sit there just happy to be in one another's company, like a little chosen family. It didn't seem fair that Richmond got to decide that was over.

24

THE NEXT NIGHT, THE EVE of the tour, I was sitting on the couch in the living room copying cassette tapes on a boom box and watching *Antiques Roadshow* on the television when I thought I heard a noise, but I had headphones on, and when I wore headphones, I heard phantom sounds all the time, and if I stopped what I was doing every time I thought I heard something alarming, I'd never get anything done. I took a sip of bourbon. I flipped the cassette tape copy to listen to the EP from the beginning to check for quality. I'd wanted to put it on CD in addition to putting it online, but the rest of the guys thought cassette tapes were cooler.

Knock! knock! knock! I took off my headphones. The knocks sounded like government business. I stood up. Ready to be preached to or questioned or solicited or served or accused and roughed up and taken downtown. A dark face peered through the door window. It was Reggie. I undid the locks and opened the door.

"Can I borrow two eggs and a cup of sugar?" he asked.

"Sure," I said. "What for?"

"I'm baking a birthday cake for my mom."

I poked my head out the door and looked toward his house.

"Did they tell you to come here?"

"No," he said. "They just went out to dinner."

I left him standing on the porch and went to the kitchen to get the eggs and sugar. Put the container holding the sugar into a tote bag. The carton of eggs on top of the sugar. I went to the door and handed him the bag.

"Bring back what you don't use," I said.

"What are you doing now?" he asked. "You want to come over and help me?"

I studied him closely. Tried to figure out what his game was. He had the humble beginnings of a mustache, more pimples. It's remarkable what a month can do to a teenager.

"When are your parents coming home?"

"Not for a while. They just left. You can leave before they get back."

When we walked into the kitchen, I thought about the first time I came over as a guest of Claire's and we came up with a way for me to get close to her son. Reggie opened the refrigerator and told me there was lemonade, orange juice, soda water, and kombucha.

"I'll have a kombucha," I said.

"Kombucha tastes like butt sweat," Reggie said.

He handed me a bottle and pretended to gag when I took a big gulp.

"So good," I said. "Like butt sweat mixed with blueberries."

"Don't make me barf," he said.

On the island counter was of a jumble of dry ingredients in bags and containers.

"What recipe are we using?"

"The one on the back of the cocoa powder container. My mom's favorite."

We took measuring cups, bowls, and mixers out of the cabinets. Butter and milk out of the refrigerator. We read the instructions and made a plan of action. When Reggie went to the bathroom, I opened the liquor cabinet and poured some vodka into my kombucha. He came back and put music on the kitchen's built-in speakers.

"What the hell is this?" I asked.

"Justin Bieber. You don't know Justin?"

I went to a console next to the refrigerator and changed the station.

"Much better," I said.

"What's this?" he asked.

"The first track from Coltrane's *A Love Supreme*. The drummer is Elvin Jones. He's tied with Tony Williams for the best of all time. C'mon man, just listen to him."

"They're chanting."

"It's beautiful, isn't it?"

"It's weird."

"Fine, turn it back to the Biebs."

He put on the kettle before looking around the kitchen for the only thing we were missing: vanilla extract. I measured out the dry ingredients and poured them in a bowl. He found the extract. We started mixing.

"Middle school is almost over," I said. "How do you feel about it?"

"It started out rough, but I think I'm going to miss it. High school is going to be way better though."

"You plan to play basketball?"

"Of course. Catlin Gable is a smart people school. Their team isn't very good, so I might even play varsity as a freshman. You should come to my games."

"Totally," I said.

What a dream. Watching him in the layup line with his little mustache and his teammates and the high school band and the cheerleaders, knowing I'd had something to do with his footwork and his jump shot. Man, I'd be so proud, probably shed a tear. But that wasn't going to happen. Baking with him in his kitchen, it almost felt like the moratorium had been lifted or had never existed, like we were free to congregate. But that wasn't true. I still had the letter.

"Listen," I said. "I'm sorry I said that stuff about your parents."

"It's okay. I thought about it more and I know you didn't mean it how it sounded. And you were kind of right. There are things about me they'll never understand. But it's not because they're white, it's because they're old."

Once the two pans for the layer cake were in the oven, we started on the frosting. My heart jumped every time Reggie put down a bowl or tossed a spoon in the sink. I started to think every little sound was the sound of his parents coming through the door. They could be back any minute. But even if I left before they got back, I'd probably depleted too much vodka for it not to be noticed. Would they think Reggie drank it? I figured the worst that could happen to him was a stern talking-to and a possible reduction in allowance. He'd probably never caught a spanking for anything.

"I should get going," I said.

"That lady I played basketball with, is she your girlfriend?"

"Ida? Not yet."

"So, she might be someday?"

"I hope so. But I have to say, you were no help that day."

"Sorry about that. It's hard, because my parents think you're a bad influence."

"Yeah. I know."

"But I don't."

I patted him on the back.

"Ida thought you were cool."

Reggie smiled.

"She's cool too," he said. "I hope it works out."

"Thanks, man," I said.

The vodka was setting in, and what I wondered, although I'd never be drunk enough to ask him, was what his thoughts were on sex. Was he just going to have sex with whoever he was dating, whenever he thought he was ready? Without guilt? Without any thoughts of marriage? People raised without belief. Where did their guilt even come from? How could anything haunt him if he didn't think God was watching and judging and knowing the depths of his soul? Life without fear of God's wrath was even more unimaginable than a life without debt.

The timer dinged. We checked the cakes with a toothpick. We took them out of the oven to cool.

"These cakes are perfect," he said

"We're a real fucking team," I said.

Reggie shook his head.

"My dad says swearing is lazy."

"Sorry," I said.

"We are a great team though," he said.

The job was done. If no one checked the vodka levels, you wouldn't even know I was there. Reggie could frost the cakes on his own.

"I should get going," I said. "Where should I put this kombucha bottle?"

"You should take it with you," he said. "They know I don't drink it."

"Alright, then," I said. "Bring it in my guy. This was great."

As I was hugging Reggie, Claire and Peter walked into the kitchen laughing and stumbling. They were dressed about as formal as anyone could expect for going out to dinner in our neighborhood. Blue jeans and a turquoise blouse. A black polo, a blazer, the latest high-tech running shoes. Peter had his hand firmly placed on Claire's butt. Their faces were red and flush. It took them a while to register what was going on in their messy kitchen. Claire didn't say anything.

Neither did Peter. He took his hand off his wife's butt, but he didn't say a word. I edged away from their son. Afraid to make any quick movements.

Reggie spoke first: "Hi, guys."

"Hello, Son," Peter said. He looked at me and blinked a few times. "Hello, Julian."

"Hey," I said.

"What's going on here?" Claire asked.

"Julian helped me bake a cake for your birthday," Reggie said.

"He came by the house for eggs and sugar and asked if I could help," I said.

"He wanted to help," Reggie said.

Claire looked confused. "But Reggie, we have eggs and—" Peter touched her arm.

"Smells great in here," Peter said.

"Happy birthday," I said. "I should get going."

I was halfway down their driveway when Peter shouted my name. When I turned around, he was right in my face like he'd taken a single leap from the front door to where I stood. I was prepared to use the empty bottle of kombucha I was holding as a weapon. He smelled like a bottle of red wine. He was holding my bag with the sugar and the eggs.

"You know, I was thinking," he said. "You like to sail?"

"Never tried it."

"Never? I grew up sailing. A lot of weekend regattas, that sort of thing. Sailed the Caribbean for two months right before Reggie came along. There's nothing better than open water. I have a boat at the club across the river. A twenty-four-footer. Sails like a dream. But I'm so busy these days, I rarely get to take it out. Since you've never had the experience though, I'd be more than happy to make the time."

"Wish I could, but I'm going on tour tomorrow."

"Awesome. Then let's do it when you get back. Be good to have a talk, don't you think?"

"Maybe so," I said.

He gave me the bag. We shook hands and said goodnight. Turning my back to him felt dangerous. I kept listening for his footsteps behind me. Once I was safely inside the bungalow, I locked the door, shut the blinds, sat on the couch, and put on my headphones. I turned up the television volume but still read the captions. The cat jumped on my lap, and I just about died. I didn't know she was in the room. I scratched her back until we both calmed down to our usual anxiety levels. High alert, but no blaring alarm in our heads.

PART FOUR

25

IT WAS A TWELVE-HOUR DRIVE from Pendleton, Oregon, to San Francisco, California, and in the beginning, Keith drove and I sat shotgun, pushing down the highway in a blue twelve-passenger van from the early 1990s that we'd borrowed from a jam band in exchange for use of our bungalow recording studio while we were away. KOREAN UNITED PRESBYTERIAN CHURCH was stencil-painted on both sides of the van in English and Korean. There was a radio and a tape deck. The glove box stuffed with cassettes. Most of them terrible, a lot of hair metal from the 1980s. Skyler was with us. I had no idea she'd be coming along until I walked outside the bungalow on the morning of departure and she was standing by the van holding a large canvas duffel bag. Now she was sitting on the third-row bench, cuddling William and reading a book.

Richmond was sitting by himself on the bench behind us. Fifth day of tour and still he wouldn't tell me what happened between him and Liesel. So far, he'd messed around with a different woman every night since we'd been on the road.

I popped in a Bob Dylan album I'd never heard. I never knew he'd gone through a gospel phase. Keith didn't know either. I turned around to look at Richmond. He was typing something on his phone. When he realized I was watching him, he took off his headphones and glared at me.

"What do you want?" he asked.

"Listen to that guitar," I said.

Keith looked at him in the rearview mirror. "Bob Dylan's got me wanting to go to church. Who would have thought?"

"Sounds like Dire Straits," I said.

"Good for you guys," Richmond said. "Mind if I put my headphones back on?"

He didn't wait for a response. He loosened his seat belt to the point that it no longer provided safety and turned his body sideways to lay on his back. I could see his phone screen for a moment as he turned, and it looked like he'd just received a message from someone with a very short name. I thought it said Ida. But that couldn't be. I hadn't heard from her in days.

We switched drivers in Weed, California. First time I'd ever set foot in the state. Keith got the middle bench to himself because he was the last person to drive. William got behind the wheel. Skyler sat shotgun. Richmond and I sat in the back bench and ate Taco Bell. We talked about tour stuff but not about women. Skyler scanned the radio until she found the local NPR affiliate. According to the radio, technology was probably driving people further apart instead of closer together—and that was my current experience. Ida's last message before the three days and counting of silence was sent right before the band hit the stage in Seattle: *miss you. break a leg! diving into this project so I can maybe be free when you get back.*

Jittery from the trucker pills I'd taken to stay awake, I took one of Keith's muscle relaxers to get some rest. I woke up in a traffic jam on the Golden Gate Bridge. Drool on my face from sleeping upright, but no pain in my neck. On a busy street, the van pulled up to our venue for the night, a place called the Rickshaw Stop. We parked the car in an emergency zone to unload our gear. After that, we ended up having to park the van at least a quarter mile away from the venue. We walked up what felt like an endless hill to a falafel place that William said he went to every time he was in town. He was a California boy back in his home state. He'd played in bands that had played at the Rickshaw Stop before. Our lives had been so different up to now.

Rickshaw was the only big venue on this tour where we were the headliners. A local band named Wild Eagle opened for us. I watched them from the balcony. The lead singer presented himself as a guy who fled the family farm in the middle of the night after a great tragedy—I didn't buy it. He played guitar and banjo. The music was clean and polished, a lot of pretty harmonies, big vowel sounds stretched out to build emotional resonance. The crowd ate it up, which wasn't a good sign for us. Our first two songs were our newest ones, and they were great, but they were also pretty loud and out of left field. I couldn't see these ladies with their nice handbags and the men with their polished boots loving those tracks. This was a folky, mainstream crowd. Richmond made the setlist, so in the green room before we went on, I told him we should change the order and start with something softer.

"No way," he said. "If they don't like the tracks, then fuck 'em."

Two hundred people shrank to one hundred by the time we started our second song. Instead of watching them leave, I kept my eyes on the actual rickshaw sitting stage left. People walking out seemed to inspire Richmond. The rest of the night I listened to him in wonderment. He'd been great all tour, but tonight he played licks I'd never heard before—menacing, soulful, and downright nasty stuff.

We found out after the show that we'd been given the last slot of the night because the venue's manager knew that a lot of White Eagle's dedicated fans would also be interested in the even bigger show just down the road, so having them play early gave their fans time to make it to both shows. There was nothing we could have done to stop them from walking out.

William had family friends who owned a bed-and-breakfast in the Mission District who were letting us stay there for free. He and Skyler decided to turn in early. The rest of us followed White Eagle to a raucous warehouse party. Keith busted out every move he had. His impersonation of Mick Jagger doing his best impersonation of James Brown was his best stuff. Every time he did it you couldn't help but love him. Richmond spent most of the party bumping and grinding with one of the women who'd come to our show and stayed, a thirtysomething blonde with a long, lean butt that looked great in her high-waisted denim. I stuck to the perimeter until I got drunk and someone gave me a bump. A Barry White song came on and when he said, "one ticket please," the dance floor became the only place for me. I moved my shoulders and bent my knees like Ida had taught me.

I met a woman named Rose. She'd said the DJ at the warehouse party looked like Heath Ledger in witness protection. I couldn't stop laughing because that's exactly what he looked like. She was a dark-haired Jewish comedian who lived in Oakland. We had fun, but it didn't go further than getting close on the dance floor and a kiss goodnight, because I couldn't get Ida out of my mind. Pretty wasted, I cut out of the party before Richmond and Keith, took a cab to the B&B, and somehow got into my room.

I woke up alone in a wedding suite. Got up and drew a bath. I went back under the covers until it sounded like the tub was almost full. As I slipped into the big marble tub, it felt romantic to be hungover and forsaken. I'd been sleeping on couches and living room floors since the tour began. The van was a gas guzzler, and we were making peanuts, so the only way to make the tour work was finding free places to stay. And none of those places had been this comfortable. None of them had big marble tubs and great-smelling bubble bath. I never wanted to leave this place. I felt like Charlie Chaplin in the movie *City Lights*, a vagabond in the lap of luxury.

I heard the door to my suite unlock and creak open.

"Hello? Anybody in here?"

"Yeah. In the tub," I said.

Richmond walked into the bathroom wearing the same clothes he'd worn the night before. He didn't look like shit though, he looked like a road-worn guitar player, more scruff on his face than I'd ever seen him with. He sat on the edge of the tub.

"Look at you, taking advantage of the situation. If I had known our accommodations were this plush, I might have invited her here instead of going to her place. Where's Keith?"

"Water's getting cold," I said. "Do you mind?"

He turned on the faucet, put his hand under the water and adjusted the temperature.

"There you go. You'll be warm again in no time. You know, you look great in this tub." He turned to look behind him. "There's a shower in here too? Baller shit." He stood up, grabbed a clean towel, and went into the bedroom. When he came back a minute later, he was naked except for the towel around his waist. He was holding something in his hand. He sat back down on the edge of the tub again. I asked him to turn off the water.

"Anything for my drummer," he said. He had his small glass pipe. He lit it with a lighter and took a hit. "Want any?"

I held up my hands.

"Too slippery."

"Okay. Here. I'll hold it for you."

He reached out his arms. I put my wet hands on the side of the tub and leaned forward until I could get my mouth on the tip of the pipe to smoke it. I leaned back in the tub, holding in the smoke. When I exhaled, the weed brightened everything.

"Thanks," I said.

"My pleasure." He got up and paced around the bathroom. Aside from a little paunch, he still looked like a wrestler, had visible veins on his biceps. He didn't go to the gym, but he did a lot of push-ups, and despite all his drinking and drugging and smoking, he jogged a few times a week. "I've been a dick to you recently, haven't I?"

"You have," I said.

"I know, man, and I'm sorry. I love you. Liesel just has me fucked up."

He sat down again at the edge of the tub and took another hit.

"If she has you so fucked up, then why are fucking around like this?"

He exhaled a cloud of smoke and shrugged.

"Hard to explain," he said.

Richmond's guitar playing last night was powerful and yearning, infinitely deep, mostly indescribable; you had to hear it to believe it. He was some kind of genius, but words are still important, and when it came to expressing his feelings through language, Richmond could be shitty, and the most frustrating part about it was that it didn't seem to have anything to do with his capacity for speech—so did he really not know why he was fucking around with all these women if he was still in love with Liesel, or did he think that if I didn't already understand, I never would? Because I understand a man's desire for freedom. I just didn't understand why he'd want to be free of Liesel.

There was a knock on the door and a shout. William walked into the bathroom looking refreshed and clean-shaven, not a hair out of place. "Sorry to interrupt, but have either of you guys heard from Keith? He left me a really weird voice mail last night, said he was lost and needed me to find him. Called him back this morning and his phone went straight to voice mail."

"Last time I saw him was at the party," I said.

"Was it a good party? Sorry I missed it."

"Shit," Richmond said. "This is the only place we've stayed where turning in early would have made any sense."

"When did *you* last see Keith?" William asked.

"Same as Julian," Richmond said.

"What should we do?" I asked.

"Nothing," William said. He looked at us for a while. I guess his drummer in a tub with his guitar player sitting on the edge in a bath towel probably was an amusing sight to etch into memory. "Once you two lovebirds are finished bathing each other, come down and have brunch. We don't need to leave town for another two hours. We'll stay here and see if Keith finds us."

Once William left the bathroom, Richmond stood up and put his glass pipe and lighter next to the sink. He took off his towel and hung it on the rack next the shower. He got in the stall and turned on the water. Hopped around from the shock of the cold. His naked body visible through the glass until the steam from the shower made him disappear. He hummed a cheerful tune. I wished he wouldn't. I was starting to despise him.

26

KEITH CALLED WHILE WE WERE eating brunch. We jumped in the van to pick him up on our way out of town. Skyler drove. William sat shotgun. It was Saturday, our sixth day of tour. When we rolled up to last night's venue, Keith had his thumb out like he was hitchhiking.

"Can't we just leave him here?" Skyler asked.

"Babe, no," William said. "He's our bass player."

Keith got into the van. "Hey guys, thanks," he said. "Let's go to Sacramento."

Luigi's Fun Garden was a matchbox-shaped pizza parlor and venue in downtown Sacramento. After sound check was over, I stepped outside to call Ida. It rang and rang without an answer. She hadn't answered when I'd called her in Pendleton or San Francisco, either. Those times I'd hung up. This time I left a voice message: "Hey. It's Julian. Just calling to say hello. Haven't heard from you in a while. You alright? Did you drop your phone in a body of water? Happens. One time I was floating down Sandy River with Richmond and Liesel. Did you know they broke up? Have you talked to either of them since? Anyway, we tied our tubes together so we could all stay close. It was one of those days where the world feels like it was made just for you. Wildflowers everywhere, even on the rocks. Sunlight flashing behind the trees. Everything was great until we approached these two big rocks. After the rocks there's a rapid, so you aren't supposed to be tied together because it makes it harder to navigate, but we were tied together, and the dangerous rocks were rapidly approaching. I tried to untie my tube from the one I was connected to, but the rope was wet and knotted up tight, so I couldn't untie it. Things were looking bleak. Then, out of nowhere, this high school kid who was supposedly a lifeguard came at me with a large knife. He cut the rope. My tube flipped over, and I was stuck underwater. I went down the rapid that way: upside down, fighting for my life. Scratching my arms and hands against the rocks while trying to protect my head and the rest of my body. For a moment I thought I was going to die. Wouldn't that have been sad? To be a Black man who drowned in a river surrounded by white people? Man. If I ever die like that, please let the media know I was a decent swimmer and the only reason I had THC and alcohol and whatever else in my system was because I was trying to live my life as a child of privilege like all of my friends. When we got back to Richmond's car, I realized I had my cell phone in my swimming trunks. I went home and did the rice thing but it didn't work. Did something like that happen to you? Did your phone take a bath and now it's dead? I hope not. I miss talking to you. Did I already say that? Because I really do miss you a lot, Ida. Tour is cool. I mean, it's mostly just being in the van and waiting for the venue to let you in to set up your shit, and then playing and doing everything you just did before you played in reverse while drunk. But I'm so happy to be doing it. And if you ever want to go floating down Sandy River, I'm totally down. Hope to hear from you soon."

As soon as I hung up, I regretted leaving the message. Clearly her phone wasn't dead if it rang that many times before going to voice mail. And we'd only been on one date. Just one! Kissed a couple of times. That was all. My message may have hurt my chances. I'd sounded so desperate.

Luigi's Fun Garden served only wine and beer. That wouldn't do. I liked to start my nights with whiskey and end them with whiskey. I headed to the van for the handle of Seagram's under the back seat. When I slid the van door open, William and Skyler were sitting in the back seat necking like Christian teenagers. Sitting up instead of lying down. Tongues so far down each other's throat they couldn't hear the van door sliding open on its busted tracks. Eyes shut too tight to register the intensified sunlight and the backlit Black man only two feet away from them. Skyler's hands were folded in her lap. William had a hand on her chest—over her clothes, not under them. I cleared my throat. Banged a fist on the side of the van. Skyler opened an eyelid, the eye fluttering until it landed on me. She moved away from William. She used her hand as a visor and leaned forward. William turned his head to look at me, squinting from the sun.

"What do you want?"

"Whiskey," I said.

He reached under the bench seat and handed me a tote bag. I slammed the van door, because a gentle push would have left it ajar. I went back inside the pizza parlor and asked the kid behind the counter for a Diet Coke, then took the pebbled red plastic cup into the tiny bathroom in the back of the employee break room and locked the door. I wanted to forget about that message to Ida. I drank down some of the Coke, added a little Seagram's, drank some Coke and Seagram's, and topped off the cup with more Seagram's.

The band liked to stash the whiskey inside the venue for easy access. There was a wooden shelf above the toilet, topped with rolls of toilet paper, paper towels, and various cleaning supplies. I tried to move back the bottle of bleach to make room for the handle of whiskey. Window cleaner fell off the shelf, the spray handle hit the rim of the toilet and broke from the bottle, the bottle fell into the toilet bowl. Blue water splashed onto my blue jeans and sneakers. I no longer smelled like fancy San Francisco bubble bath. I was filthy again.

I stepped back into the break room. Took a sip of my drink. It didn't seem to be contaminated. I put the whiskey tote inside an empty locker. The break room was no place to relax, just a big closet with lockers and padded chairs with yellow stuffing bursting out. The sight of the chairs was nauseating; ever since the night I did Molly at the Woods, seeing the insides of something out in the open caused serious cosmic horror. We'd passed by a lot of roadkill recently, and every time I'd made sure to avert my eyes.

I got out of the break room. Skyler and William were sitting in a booth and eating pizza. For their sake I hoped I'd caught them in a chaste role-play earlier and that wasn't how they normally operated. But when I thought about it, they were sexier than they were sexual. I'd never caught William looking at a butt, not ever.

I headed back to the van. Keith and Richmond were standing beside it, smoking cigarettes and drinking wine from red pebble cups.

"Stashed the whiskey bottle in locker number four," I said.

"We were just talking about Skyler," Keith said. "Can you believe she called me a woman chaser? That's bullshit. I'm a progressive."

"She wasn't serious," Richmond said. His scruff was gone; he'd shaved at the bed-and-breakfast. "She was just annoyed that we had to go out of our way to pick you up."

"I wasn't that much out of the way," Keith said. "And I think it's bogus she gives me shit and not you. Especially because she's friends with Liesel."

"That's a fucked-up thing to say, Keith," Richmond said. "Why the fuck do you have to bring up Liesel in all this?"

Keith looked at me. He stroked his big bushy beard thoughtfully. "Before we got to talking about Skyler being rude, Richmond told me the woman he went home with last night was a district attorney. Isn't that strange? Not only did she look a lot like Liesel, she also happened to share his father's profession."

"Did you tell her your old man was a judge?" I asked.

"Never came up," Richmond said. "But let's get this straight, guys. Everyone grieves in their own way, and I don't like to be alone when I'm grieving, so really, all this messing around is because I'm still in love with Liesel and I'm trying to get over her."

"Makes sense to me," Keith said.

"Thank you, doctor," Richmond said.

"No," I said. "That doesn't make sense at all."

Richmond smiled at me.

"Why not? Word on the street is you hooked up with Holly from French Navy the night we played at the Spruce. Too bad she wasn't in Seattle when we were there for our show, huh? And then last night I saw you kissing that Cuban girl."

"She wasn't Cuban," I said.

"Julian's becoming one of us," Keith said.

"No I'm not," I said.

"I'm not trying to give you shit," Richmond said. "All I'm saying is you had a nice date with Ida before we left for the tour, and still you've been fooling around, and that's okay, you're not dating her, so that's just the way it is. All I'm asking for is the same understanding."

I replayed the moment from yesterday in the van when he'd turned over so I wouldn't see his phone.

"Have you talked to her recently?" I asked.

"Who?"

"Ida."

"Don't worry about that," Richmond said. "Our band is a brotherhood. I would never tell her about the Cuban girl. She thinks you're a choir boy."

I wanted to grill Richmond further but I knew that would get me nowhere. Maybe his great shiftiness came from his wrestling days and his father being a judge. Funny, my father was a detective, yet I was no good at reading people's motives. But that was okay. I could gather evidence. I could steal Richmond's phone the next chance I got.

Our performance at Luigi's was the best of the tour so far. The crowd was small because the pizza parlor was tiny, but the place was packed, and the people there really seemed to like us. It felt great to get lost in the music and to feel understood by strangers. But as soon as the show was over and I saw I had no new messages, missed calls, or voice mails, I was back to feeling dejected. After our show, I went over to where Elijah and his wife were standing. We kept getting billed with bands that sounded nothing like us. A husband-and-wife duo, "Elijah and Pam," had opened for us tonight at Luigi's. Pam played acoustic guitar and the mandolin. Elijah played the violin and the harmonica. They sang country-tinged folk. Mostly love songs. They wore flip-flops and torn-up jeans. Onstage they'd told a cute story about first meeting as tennis instructors. Pam was white. Elijah was Black. I told them I enjoyed their set. They nodded their heads and said thanks very quietly. Elijah acted awkward, like us being the only Black people in the room was the reason why we shouldn't speak instead of the reason why we should, like he was afraid I'd say something to blow his cover. But he became jovial when Skyler and William walked over.

"You've got some pipes, man," Elijah said. "Me and Pam were just saying."

"Really great," Pam said.

"Thanks a lot," William said.

"Your music is so intimate," Skyler said. "I just loved it. Can I buy a CD?"

"You can have one," Pam said.

"We'll give you our cassette," Skyler said.

The four of them formed a tight circle with no space for me. I went to the break room for the handle of whiskey.

During my shift at the merch booth, Skyler and I sat on the same side of a table with our backs against the wall. Our wares displayed in front us. Copies of our EP cassette tape and a newsletter sign-up list, all we had to offer. The place was clearing out quick.

"How's the search going?" Skyler asked.

"Not good," I said.

Every other city there had been a connection for a place to stay, but no one knew a soul in Sacramento. During the drive to Luigi's, we had made up a loose plan for how we were going to convince strangers to let us crash at their place. We decided first we would talk to the band we'd be playing with; next, people who worked at the venue; and if that didn't work, we would broaden our net and let Skyler take the lead. We figured having the lady in the crew asking for a place to stay instead of a dude would be key in assuaging the understandable fears of our preferred host: a lonely woman with a spacious home. That's when Skyler told Keith she didn't want him making any moves on these women. Pretty much calling him a woman chaser.

"I think we're going to stay with Elijah and Pam," Skyler told me at the booth.

"Are all of us staying at their place?" I asked.

Skyler turned to me and shook her head sadly.

"Unfortunately, they don't have room. William and I are going to sleep on the pull-out couch in their living room. They have kids."

"What about the rest of us?"

"I'm sorry, Julian. I tried."

She sounded so sorry about the whole thing, it made me think she wasn't sorry at all. Like she was happy to put us out on the streets. William came over to relieve me of my duties. When I got up, I fought the urge to shove him.

"You cool with this?" I asked.

"Cool with what?"

"Putting us out on the streets."

"No one's putting anyone on the streets. They just don't have the room."

"That's what I told him," Skyler said.

"It's not right," I said. "A band is a brotherhood."

"No it isn't," Skyler said.

Maybe she was right.

"You'll find a place," William said. "If not, I'll pay for a hotel myself."

"No you won't, William," Skyler said. "Doesn't he already owe you six hundred dollars?"

"Babe . . ."

"He doesn't even do his share of the chores."

"It's five hundred and fifty dollars," I said.

Skyler scoffed. "What makes you act so entitled? William could easily charge you three hundred more a month than he does, and maybe, I don't know, ask you to pay your half of the utilities, but he doesn't." She seemed a little drunk. "You won't even drive the van. Everyone drives the van except for you."

I didn't drive the van because I didn't trust myself not to hit a fire hydrant, another vehicle, or a person; I was afraid that if I got behind the wheel I might kill Plaid Parenthood.

"If you're going to be with us on the road, you might as well do something useful," I said. "So, thank you for driving."

"You're a fucking asshole," Skyler said.

She got up from the table. William stood between us. His surfer hair flew as he moved his head back and forth from her to me in rapid motion. "Julian, she's part of the band too. Babe, no need to swear at him. You guys both need to chill. We're going to figure this out."

"Either we're brothers or we're not," I said.

"Dude. Are you serious? Of course we're brothers."

"You men," Skyler said. "I can't wait to get back to Portland and start a cleanse."

"Stop lying, William," I said.

"I love you man," William said. "Let's be reasonable,"

He reached out for a hug. I brushed past him and headed toward the counter. I wanted to say a lot more to him, but not around Skyler, he didn't hear me the same when she was around. Maybe I was being unreasonable like he said, but I just didn't care. I was hurting. "He's such a baby," I heard Skyler grumble as I walked away.

I used my last drink ticket on a glass of red wine and scooted into a booth where Keith and Richmond were sitting with Miranda. She'd introduced herself to us after the show. She had dark eyes and large lips painted bloodred. She had come to Luigi's all alone. Had a confident nature. I grabbed the last slice of pizza on the pan on the table. It was lifeless and cold, a horrible chew. Richmond could see something was wrong.

"What's going on?" he asked.

"Skyler and William are staying with Elijah and Pam."

"Are we staying with them too?" Keith asked.

"No, that's what I'm trying to say, they're staying there without us."

"Well fuck those guys," Richmond said. "They'll be asleep in an hour anyway."

"Sleep sounds pretty good," Keith said.

"You guys can stay with me if you want," Miranda said.

"The three of us?" Richmond asked.

"Yeah, it'll be fun. I never have people over."

"Are you sure?" I asked.

"I wouldn't offer if I didn't mean it," she said.

After everyone in the band was way past wanting to leave, we started to pack our gear. Each man carried what he could and put it next to the van, then he waited for someone else to arrive before going inside to get more. We didn't talk, just worked. Once we had all our stuff piled up, William went back inside the venue, Keith hopped into the back of van because he was short enough to almost stand up in there, I handed him the gear. Richmond stood by smoking until I was about to pick up his guitars, then he stepped in front of me and put them in the van himself.

Miranda came outside as we were finishing up. She fished around her large backpack and produced a joint. The four of us walked to the other side of the van to smoke it. Faced a clean concrete wall without a hint of graffiti or mischief. We passed the joint and looked over the wall toward the lit-up overpass. Quality weed. Everyone was silent. Ida on my mind, Richmond's phone on my mind, I decided I would steal it as soon as he was asleep.

The van door quaked open and shook us out of our collective haze. We looked at one another with wide-eyed, weed-fueled panic. We crept to the other side of the van. William and Skyler were grabbing their bags.

"You were great tonight," Miranda said to William.

"Why thank you."

Skyler slammed the van door and stepped between them.

"Hi, I'm Skyler."

"Miranda, nice to meet you."

"Hey, Miranda, I'm William."

"It's a pleasure to meet you."

"Miranda offered to let us stay at her place," Keith said.

"That's so nice of you," Skyler said. "Sure you want to put up with these ruffians?"

"I'm rough too, so it should work out just fine," Miranda said. "I'd offer to put you guys up as well, but I don't have the room. Not unless you two want to share a bed with me and Julian."

She was messing with Skyler on my behalf. I appreciated that.

"You're so funny," Skyler said. "Thanks for the offer but we're all set."

A forest green minivan pulled up next to us. Pam was driving. Elijah was in the passenger seat.

"We should leave town by noon tomorrow," William said.

"Los Angeles or bust," Keith said.

They waved goodbye as they drove off. I didn't wave back.

Richmond gestured toward our vehicle.

"Hop in the van," he said.

"No thanks," Miranda said. "I got my skates." She sat on the curb behind Luigi's Fun Garden and took a pair of neon-green roller skates and a white helmet out of her backpack. She took off her checkered slip-on canvas shoes and put on her skates and helmet. She wore a short purple dress and black fishnet tights. "Skating home tipsy and stoned is easily my favorite part of any night out."

She started rolling down the sidewalk. Richmond drove the van and kept it close to her, driving slowly. I found a metal album in the glove box and put it in the tape deck. We rolled down the windows and cranked the music. We passed around the handle of bourbon and finished it off, only two pulls each. At first she was easy to follow because of her neon skates and her white helmet, but as we rolled along, the outside of the sidewalk began to be lined with palm trees, and sometimes we'd lose sight of her behind the trees or under the dark shadows made by the fronds. She'd disappear only to appear again later, further down the road.

27

MIRANDA STOPPED IN FRONT OF a two-story brick apartment building and told us to park right in front. We grabbed our bags, covered the gear in the back of the van with blankets, hoping any would-be crook would see dirty blankets in an old church van and move right along. We entered a small lobby lined with mailboxes. Walked up the stairs to the second floor. Went down a long hallway. Her apartment was the last one on the right. It was a small studio. She offered us chocolate stout, the only booze she had. She put an empty coffee mug on the carpet and handed Richmond a joint. Keith and I sat on the love seat. Richmond and Miranda sat cross-legged on the floor. The living room window was open and there was a warm, dry breeze coming in.

Miranda told us she didn't smoke cigarettes, but everyone else in her building seemed to smoke like chimneys, so it was okay if we did. Keith lit my cigarette before he lit his own. Richmond stuck to weed, only taking small hits. He and Miranda sat very close. They got to having a one-on-one conversation about relationships and astrology.

"I'm a Gemini! No wonder I always get bored. Doomed from birth."

"Sagittarius," Richmond said. "My sign has never been the problem."

They kept talking like they were the only two people in the room. Keith was staring out the window at the brick church across the street with such intensity that I had to know what it was. I put my head close to his to catch his line of vision and saw a church bell.

I wondered what was going on at Pam and Elijah's house. I wondered if he felt any remorse for shunning me. How many times did one have to turn their back against their people until they became numb to it? Clarence Thomas knew. But I didn't want to know. I thought about the time I went to a weeklong Christian summer camp in Lake Geneva, Wisconsin. I'd run to the basketball court as soon as my parents drove away because playing sports was the only way I knew how to make friends. There was this mountain of a kid who really stunk it up. He had to look down at the ball when he dribbled so he didn't lose it. The whole time he dribbled, he huffed and puffed. He couldn't walk and dribble at the same time. He shot the ball with both his hands and never made a basket. Once everyone determined this house of a kid had no skill whatsoever, he was relegated to the sidelines in every aspect of the camp. He had no friends. No one picked him for anything. Trouble was, he was my bunkmate. A few days into camp, right before lights out, we heard him laughing in the shower room. Everyone in the cabin ran in to see what was happening. My duffel bag was drenched. I ran into the stall to turn off the water. He laughed so hard he had to put his hands on his knees to catch his breath. The other boys started laughing too. I ran up to him and pushed him. When he tried to grab me, he slipped on the wet floor and fell onto his side. Screamed like a baby. We laughed at him, we howled. For the rest of camp, his arm was in sling. He was the only other Black boy at the camp, just the two us. I hadn't known better then, but I knew better now. God, did I miss Reggie.

I took sips from my glass of water, looked around the living room for a bookshelf and didn't see one. A poster of Van Gogh's *Almond Blossoms* was stapled to a wall. The edges of the poster were torn and pockmarked as if it had been stapled and unstapled many times, from one place to another. I figured Miranda must have done a lot of moving.

Keith finished his stout, asked me if he could finish mine. I picked it off the carpet and handed it to him. He lit a cigarette, rested his head against the couch's upholstery, and fell asleep. On the way to San Francisco, we'd talked about our fathers. How they'd both expected more out of their only sons than working dead-end jobs and chasing childish dreams. Keith's father was a paramedic. I shook his shoulder. He jolted awake and put the mostly unsmoked cigarette into the bottle of chocolate stout I'd given him. There was a singe. He scratched his beard.

"Where do you think I should sleep?" he asked loudly.

Miranda and Richmond looked up from their conversation. They were planning to sleep together. That was obvious.

"You should probably take the couch," Richmond said to Keith. "You're the only one who would fit."

"Fine," Keith said.

Miranda put her hand on Richmond's knee.

"You can sleep with me," she said to him.

Their vibes made me uncomfortable. Miranda was cool. She also seemed lost, like me, spiritually lost, forsaken by many, I didn't know how I could tell, but I could. Richmond was a waste of her time. But it was none of my business.

"I'll take the floor," I said.

We took turns in the bathroom getting ready for bed. I got into my sleeping bag, but I wasn't trying to sleep. Richmond's phone was charging in the kitchen, and I planned to wait for a bit and then grab it.

It couldn't have been more than a few minutes from when I'd gotten into bed that I started to hear Miranda moaning. Softly at first, then louder and louder. There was no door between us, only a sheet on a rod that covered the bedroom doorframe, and it did nothing to muffle her moans of pleasure. Then Richmond started moaning too. The bed started creaking.

"Motherfucker!" Keith whispered. He rolled onto his side and within seconds started snoring. Everyone in the tiny apartment was doing some kind of sleeping except for me. I unzipped my sleeping bag. I stepped quietly into the kitchen and unplugged Richmond's phone from the charger. I closed the door to Miranda's apartment and stood in the hallway.

I knew Richmond's phone code because he'd had me send a message to Liesel for him a few times while he was driving. I'd never forgotten it: 3323. Larry Bird's jersey number, then Michael Jordan's number. Once the phone was unlocked, I scrolled through his messages. I knew I was betraying his trust, but I just didn't care, I had to have answers. I scrolled down and down. No messages from Ida; no messages from Liesel, either. Impossible. He must have deleted them. I went through his call log, plenty of calls with Liesel, but none since we'd left for the tour. Then I scrolled past Ida's name. She'd called him the day after we'd gone on a date, the same day he had me record on the same song over and over; the call had lasted fifteen minutes. No way they spoke without sending messages beforehand. If they did, then it had to have been serious. And why had he deleted his messages with Liesel? Something sinister was going down. If I were actually a detective, I'd get subpoenas for phone records and start a formal investigation.

I was running out of time. Sex didn't take forever, so I had to get back before Richmond noticed his phone wasn't there and neither was Julian. I turned Miranda's door handle to get back inside. It was locked. Nothing was going right. I put my ear on the door and didn't hear a thing. Richmond's phone felt hot in my hands. I couldn't let him catch me with it. I bent down and slid his phone through the gap under the front door in a moment of pure panic. But that didn't fix a thing. Now his phone was on the ground in Miranda's living room, and I was still stuck outside.

Two older women came out of an apartment down the hall. I took my own cell phone out of my pocket so it wouldn't look like I was just standing there up to no good. I had no new messages or missed calls. Ida was dead, kidnapped, or wanted nothing to do with me.

The women in the hallway exchanged urgent whispers and quick glances in my direction before they hugged and kissed goodbye. One woman went inside her apartment. The other one headed for the stairway. I didn't want to scare the lady who was leaving by making her think a big Black man was following her at one o'clock in the morning, so I waited a few beats. My best bet for a place to sleep was the van. The passenger door didn't lock unless you had the handle turned upward when you slammed it closed. I was pretty sure I hadn't done that when I shut it earlier. If I jiggled the handle, I might get lucky for the first time that day.

After what felt like half a minute, I started for the stairs. The woman who had just gone inside her apartment opened the door and poked her head out. She had a big white curious face and sharp, kind eyes.

"Everything okay?" she asked.

"I'm okay. Going to sleep in my van."

"Geez Louise, get kicked out by one of my crazy neighbors? Let me guess . . . it was that roller derby girl, right? Women are nuts, I tell ya. You saw. I just finally got my old lady out of my hair. I mean, the woman has never heard of a quickie. As a matter of fact, I'm not sure she's done anything quick her entire life. I'm going to drink some scotch to celebrate my endurance. Would you like to join me? I hate drinking alone."

I had no better options. I followed her inside. She said her name was Susan. Her apartment was twice the size of Miranda's. Plants everywhere. The walls covered with tapestries and paintings. She was proud of the place, I could tell. She gave a little tour, told me most of the paintings were done by her grandfather. Paintings of valleys and prairies and farms. The tapestries were old, but not as old as the time periods they depicted, white men in robes riding horses in forests with women in profile and dogs and wild animals. On the wall above the bar cart was a picture of an old man standing beside a very young Susan in an open field. No longer young, Susan poured scotch into two crystal tumbler glasses. She raised her glass to the picture. I raised mine as well. We toasted the man in the picture, her grandfather. The scotch tasted like a raging bonfire underneath the ocean.

"My grandfather was a pioneer. The first Communist mayor in America," Susan said. "Hard to believe, right? It was a long time ago in a struggling town in South Dakota. Gramps helped the farmers and factory workers fight the bosses and creditors. Would you like to sit down?"

I sat on an old and well-kept leather couch. Susan sat across from me on a matching armchair. A large coffee table between us. She offered me a cigarette. I took it. She said she was a history teacher at an alternative high school. I told her I was a drummer in a band from Portland and we'd just played a show at Luigi's Fun Garden.

"I've never been to a show there. But I love their marinara sauce. A couple of my students work there. Outside of school, I avoid those fuckers like the plague. Was it a good show?"

"It was."

"That's great. Some people like to shit on Sacramento, but people here have taste." Susan took a sip of her scotch then settled back into her chair.

"This is the best scotch I've ever had," I said. "Thank you."

She smiled. "This is kind of peculiar, isn't it?"

"What do you mean?"

"This. Us. Two strangers. A strapping young man with a middle-aged lady sitting in an apartment drinking expensive scotch at one o'clock in the morning. Now don't get me wrong, I've got no intentions. Proud lesbian. Very proud. I was just thinking about what it might look like to somebody else."

"No stranger than the rest of my life," I said.

"Ha, I like that, well said. I'm sure a traveling musician sees a lot of things. You know, I'd be happy to put you up for the night if you'd like."

"You sure? But you don't know anything about me," I said.

Susan pointed at her head.

"I've been a teacher a long time, my friend. I've got a sixth sense. You're one of the good guys."

"I'm not so great."

She pointed at me with enthusiasm.

"Now you see. You've just proved it by denying it. Besides, I've got nothing worth taking except for what you're already drinking."

I wondered what her sixth sense would have to say about Richmond and Ida.

"Are you sure?"

"Save sleeping in your van for another night." Susan got up and lumbered toward the kitchen. She was wearing a red sweatshirt and thin baggy blue jeans. "I'll go get us some water. Take off your shoes. Put your feet on the table."

I took off my shoes. I picked up the thin hardcover book that was sitting on the coffee table and rested my feet in its place. Susan came back from the kitchen and put a glass of water on the side table next to me. She sat in her chair and lit another cigarette.

"So where are you off to next?"

"Los Angeles."

"Yuck."

"Not a fan?"

"The world would be a better place without it."

"*The Death of Ivan Ilyich*," I said. I held up the book that had been on the coffee table.

"That's right. Never take a small bump lightly."

"Of cocaine?"

"I take it you haven't read it?"

"I tried to read *Anna Karenina* but didn't get very far."

"*Ilyich* is Tolstoy's best work, and I'll fight anyone who disagrees." Susan put out her hand. "Here, I'll show you. I'll read it to you."

"Now?"

"Sure," Susan said. "It won't take much time at all. It's a novella,"

"Can I borrow it and mail it back?"

"That's my only copy and it can't leave this house. It was my grandfather's. And like I said, I got a sense, I think you need this story, and I think if you leave without me reading it to you, you may never pick it up again."

I didn't want her to read me the damn book, but she kept her hand out, waiting for me to give it to her. I gave her the book and tried to pretend like I wasn't annoyed. No one ever seemed to do a kind thing without expecting something in return. It seemed like letting her read to me was the price for crashing on her couch and drinking her scotch.

She switched on the Tiffany lamp on the table beside her. Wiggled in her seat until she was comfortable, cleared her throat, and began to read. Her voice was strong and soothing. A judge had died and now there was an open position, that's all I was catching. I was lost, so many Russian names and I couldn't tell them apart. When she stopped to light another cigarette, I told her about my confusion. She gave me a summary of what she'd read so far and told me not to worry about the names. I imagined she was a great teacher. She told me to have another cigarette. She started reading again and I was rapt. She smoked Marlboro after Marlboro, taking drags during pregnant pauses, lighting new smokes with the butts of her old ones between pages. The only times she stopped reading was when she poured us more scotch and when she threw a pillow at me to make sure I was awake, but I was awake, I was just listening with my eyes closed.

When Ivan Ilyich finally stretched out and died, I felt a deep sadness. I was beginning to believe I had no good friends, that only my parents and sister loved me, and even with them, they only loved who I used to be, the child in me, not who I was or was becoming, and I feared that the emptiness I felt now was an emptiness that would eventually lead to my death, and when death finally came, I'd have nothing and no one to hold on to and no hope of heaven, my soul would be finished. Susan got up and sat next to me on the couch.

"It's rough stuff, isn't it? Here. Have another cigarette."

"No thanks," I said. "But not because of cancer. As the story finely states, I could die at any moment."

"Yes, of course that's true. But that's not the point."

"The dude died because he bumped his leg while putting up some stupid curtains."

"Yes, don't you see? He died from doing something meaningless because he led a meaningless and unexamined life. He was dead before he ever bumped his leg."

"What about the God stuff?"

"I don't believe in God. But it's okay if you do. It's like that poem about angels. If they exist for you and they dance, then I'm happy for you. I'm no philosopher, but my grandfather the Communist was a very deep man. I used to spend my summers with him. Nature was his church. Cigarettes are my church, so I've never cared much for walking around aimlessly, but hiking with him was the best thing in the world, his love for every living thing was infectious. And when we hiked, he'd let me talk his ear off about anything I wanted, so I did, and I was a wacky girl, and then an angry young woman, but nothing

I said ever pushed him away. And you know, our best moments were the ones where I ran out of things to say and we were silent, I see that now. He's the one who taught me what love was, real love. Toward the end of his life we snuck outside the grounds of his retirement home so he could sneak one of my cigarettes. He told me he would have died thirty years sooner if I hadn't been in his life, I told him I'd have died too, and I meant it. That man saved my life. And he did it with love. Love is the only thing I believe in."

"You're a hippie," I said.

"Maybe I am. Love for yourself and love for others. That's all you can hope to achieve. And that's why I teach. I complain about those kids, but I believe in their future. I love them. I love to drink scotch and I love to make love to my girlfriend and obviously I love cigarettes way too much. I know I'm not saying anything profound here, but if you actually lived a life of love to any degree of success, I think you'd find that all the other shit wouldn't seem like such a big deal. Death is coming for all of us, my friend. Worry about the things you can control. She's moving in next week, by the way."

"Who?" I asked. I was ready to pass out. I couldn't believe I was still awake.

"My girlfriend," Susan said. "She's moving in with me."

"Congrats," I said.

"Meh, I go back and forth about it, to tell you the truth. I've lived alone in this apartment for twenty years. Loved every minute of it. You see, there's that word again, *love*. But I guess in the end I love her more than my freedom, and this is what she wants. The only condition is that I get to keep the place decorated how I like. You love playing your music?"

"That's why I'm here," I said.

I was half-asleep.

"Good. Don't just do things out of fear or pressure from the outside world, that's how they kill your spirit, that's how you become

Ivan Ilyich. Same with women, or men, but I get straight vibes from you. If you love her, keep her; if you don't love her, let her go."

"I love her, but I don't have her."

"Then fight like hell for her. And fight like hell to find your own meaning. But then again, what do I know? Like I said, my grandfather was the philosopher. I'm just a bullshitter up way past her bedtime."

28

A HEADACHE THE SIZE OF my debt. The ringing of church bells. Lungs so fire damaged I vowed to never smoke again. It was morning. Susan's bedroom door was closed. I found a piece of paper and a pen and wrote her a thank-you note, included my email address and phone number.

In the hallway I looked over at Miranda's door and considered knocking but thought better of it. It was still pretty early. Eerily quiet. The whole building seemed to be asleep except for me. My phone said it was nine in the morning. No missed calls or messages. I tiptoed down the stairwell.

The van was locked tight; thank goodness for Susan's hospitality. I looked over at the church across the street. Maybe life's meaning for Susan didn't include God, but for me, I wasn't sure. Without God, everything was supposedly vanity and vexation of spirit. So says King Solomon, the Preacher, in the book of Ecclesiastes: "For in much wisdom is much grief." That part checked out; the more I knew, the harder life seemed to get.

The church bells were no longer ringing. An organ was playing. I crossed the street. The side door to the church was cracked open. The congregation was singing in Spanish. I peeked inside. There was an old woman standing at the end of the pew closest to door. She saw me looking in, took a step out of her pew, and beckoned for me to join her.

When the song was over, I started to take my seat, but everyone else in the congregation stayed standing, I shot back up. The minister wore a white robe with gold buttons, gold embellishments, and gold piping. He said something and the congregation responded in unison. Everyone closed their eyes as he began to pray. When I saw the Virgin Mary on a stained-glass window to my left, I knew for certain I was in a Catholic church. A life-sized ceramic Jesus hung on a cross high above the altar. He was white. Head tilted to the side. Shoulder-length hair with a medium-length beard, wearing a crown of thorns, arms outstretched, legs crossed, nails in hands and feet. Those were features of crucified Jesus that I was used to. What struck me was how emaciated he looked; I could count every rib. If the loincloth had been real, it would have fallen off his bony hips. Even in death I was used to seeing depictions of a strong and healthy-looking Jesus. For this one on the wall, all hope of resurrection seemed lost. His lance wound looked fatal. I kept my head down but snuck looks at him, hoping he would give me some kind of sign. A slight turn of the head, a wink, a chorus of angels coming down from on high, an unexplainable breeze—I'd take anything.

When the priest finished praying, everyone crossed themselves and opened their eyes. I did what everyone else did. We sat down and the priest began his sermon. I've heard a thousand sermons, so it was nice to be in church without having to suffer through another one. My two years of Spanish in high school had taught me next to nothing. I had no idea what the priest was saying, except for when he said Jesus or Mary, but when he said something moving, people in the congregation nodded, especially the old lady next to me. Every time she started nodding, she'd have a coughing fit and reach into her purse full of napkins.

When the music started up again, everyone got up and shook hands. I knew just enough Spanish to say "hello" and "good morning" and to say that I was feeling good. I got a lot of curious glances. The only white person in the church was super dead ceramic Jesus. Everyone else in the church was brown. But I was the only Black one. There was a family of three in the pew in front of us: a mother, father, and son. The boy had a mohawk, looked to be around ten. He shook my hand loosely, without making eye contact, but with a little smirk on his face, like, *Holy shit I'm shaking hands with a Black guy, this never happens.*

Altar boys approached the priest from the back of the church, walking down the aisle with measured steps. One carried a large chalice filled with wine, the other a curved metal plate filled with wafers. I knew the Catholics believed that once the priest blessed the sacrament, the wine became Jesus's real blood and the wafers become bite-sized pieces of his flesh. The literal body of Christ.

The old lady pushed down the kneeler on the back of the pew in front of us. I kneeled alongside her and closed my eyes. I tried to pray but couldn't. Praying felt as absurd as shouting at the top of my lungs right there in the church. When I closed my eyes, all I could feel was an increase in darkness. Once prayer time was over, we got off our knees to line up for communion.

Last night's cigarettes had deadened my senses. I must have smelled horrible. I was probably the source of the old lady's cough. I was wearing the clothes I'd slept in, the clothes I'd worn yesterday. My jeans stained with window cleaner. I didn't want to go up there and have a taste of Christ. Even if I did, I figured the priest would take one look at me and deny me sacrament.

It was time for our row to shuffle into the aisle and join the line that led to communion. The old lady kept shoving her body into mine to move me along. I wanted to stay back. We kept getting closer and closer to the end of the pew, to the point of no return. I tried to stop moving but she wouldn't let me. I looked down into the determined eyes of this forceful old woman. I tried to find something to say. But I didn't even know how to explain myself in English. She grinned at me before she hip-bumped me hard. I was off the edge of the cliff, into the aisle. *Fuck it*, I thought. I filed behind the kid with the mohawk.

We pressed on toward the altar until it was time for the mohawk kid to receive the wafer from the priest. The priest said something and handed the kid the wafer, the kid said, "Amen."

Then it was my turn. *Here I am, God*, I thought. *Here I am, Jesus. Remember, I came to you. You wouldn't come to me, so I came to your house, and if you kill me now for taking communion as an unrepentant sinner, at least I'll know you're up there and that this old lady behind me is going to go to heaven when she dies, and that my grandfather is already up there, and when my parents die they will join him, their faith rewarded. All the slaves, God, all my ancestors, even Emmett Till wouldn't have died in vain, because all of history will have been part of your grand plan. This isn't me testing you, I know better than that. I'm a sinner and I feel bad for almost everything I've ever done that has brought me pleasure. If I get to keep living, just please stop hiding.*

I opened my mouth. The priest took a wafer out of the golden chalice and placed it on my tongue. He mentioned Christ, I said, "Amen." I took a sip of wine and headed back to my pew. Spiritually, I felt rejuvenated, my thoughts had turned into prayer, I'd taken communion and wasn't dead, God was with me, or he wasn't with anyone. Physically, I could easily eat a million wafers.

Service ended. I shook the old lady's hand and headed for the exit. I walked out of the main entrance of the church. Went down the steps and onto the sidewalk. An IHOP sign two blocks down was the clearest sign I'd seen in years. I slid into a booth by the big front windows and ordered from the menu like I didn't owe my roommate money. I ordered a Denver omelet, hash browns, pancakes, orange juice, and coffee.

At a table to my left, a little girl in pigtails sat in a booster seat with her family. A server set a funny-face pancake down on the table in front of the girl. The pancake had maraschino cherry eyes, a chocolate chip mouth, and a whipped cream nose. I thought it was cute, but the little girl hated the sight of it. She bashed the pancake with her fists until her father grabbed her hands to stop the carnage. She shrieked in protest. Her father let her go.

When I was married and miserable, I'd spend nights next to Lauren on the living room couch, drinking whiskey, listening to music on headphones, and writing poetry in a notebook as she watched trashy television. If I thought a poem was decent, I'd type it up and do some revision before sending it off to journals. All but one had been rejected. I hadn't written anything since Lauren got pregnant. At first it was because I was too overjoyed. Both of us were. Forget about me wanting to kill myself, our brief separation, the horrible fights, our incompatibility, that didn't matter anymore, our marriage had been saved. We were going to be parents. I was going to be a father. Have purpose. What a gift. Who needs poetry when you have all that hope? My heart began to expand. It broke a month later. Poetry and prayer died along with everything else.

But it was time to try again. I could feel it. I could write about this girl and her funny-face pancake. I could write about a friend whistling happily in a hot shower while my bathwater turned cold. Roller skates. Cold pizza. Emaciated Jesus. The mohawk kid. The old lady at the church. Communion. Marlboro cigarettes. Ivan Ilyich. Death. Desire. God. The soul. All the big questions. I could write a poem titled "Sacramento: To Susan, with love." At least for now. I could always change the title, I could always change everything, but I could never make up for the time I was wasting.

The little girl's plate was a gruesome scene. She picked up a large chunk of pancake and started to chew on it slowly, taking little nibbles as it dangled from her mouth. She looked upset; she looked like Saturn gloomily eating his newborn. I wanted to write that down, but there wasn't a pen or a pencil on the table and my waitress was standing by the kitchen talking to a cook. There was a box of crayons on the messy table next to me that hadn't been cleared from previous patrons. I got up to grab the crayons and quickly sat back down. The box was sticky with syrup. I took out a stubby purple crayon and started writing on syrupy napkins. Not thinking. Only feeling. Drinking coffee. Getting lost. Until the waitress set down two heavy plates on the table with a bang. I looked out of the window to see the little girl driving away in a car with her family. The table they'd been sitting at got cleared, and it was almost as if she had never been there at all. But I'd written her down. So she'd never be gone completely.

PART FIVE

29

MY PHONE DIED AND I didn't notice. The band found me drinking coffee and writing poetry in the IHOP thirty minutes after we were supposed to have left town. William and Skyler were pissed at me. No surprise there. But Richmond, perhaps feeling guilty for subjecting me to his sex sounds the night before, defended me and said I had a shitty sleeping situation, so he understood why I'd left Miranda's in the middle of the night. He said the band was lucky to have a drummer as dependable as I was, especially given the long history of drummers who'd go missing for days. "But here he is," Richmond said. "Plaid Parenthood's secret weapon." It was a pretty good speech.

But I still didn't trust him or anybody else. And he didn't ask me how his phone ended up on Miranda's living room floor, but if he had, I would have lied to him.

We didn't need to worry about finding a place in Los Angeles, because William had plenty of connections. He'd gone to a college called Pomona, which was located very close to Los Angeles and seemed pretty impressive when I looked it up online. He was the only other English major in my group of friends. I think his being an English major is part of why his lyrics were so good. I'd never told him I liked his lyrics, and I wasn't about to start now, but to ease the tension from last night's fight at Luigi's and the morning's IHOP snafu, we talked about books we'd recently read as he drove and I sat shotgun on our way to Los Angeles. I told him I'd just finished reading *The Fire Next Time* by James Baldwin. He said "Letter from a Region in My Mind" changed his life. I asked him how, he told me he couldn't remember, it had been so long since he'd read it. "I just remember being floored," he said. I wondered if he really believed in his heart that I was equal to him. I wondered if it was even possible for someone like to him to believe that.

After our show at the Troubadour in Los Angeles, the band had one agenda: to celebrate a great show and the end of a mostly successful tour, all beefs put aside. We partied as hard as we dared with some of William's college friends and his down-for-anything, pay-for-everything, party-animal uncle. Turns out his uncle was a producer for one of the big network television shows my ex-wife loved so much. I was impressed. I didn't share Susan's opinion of Los Angeles. I'd never seen so many beautiful faces in one place. We stayed at the uncle's mansion in the Hollywood Hills. My last lines of coke were with Skyler and an actress. Lines on a mirror on the kitchen counter. It was evident that Skyler had no idea that the woman she was speaking to was well known, and it never came up because they discovered pretty quickly that they both grew up doing 4-H. After that, it was mostly just animal talk. But at some point we were alone, and Skyler got serious and told me she was sorry for being rude in Sacramento. I told her I was sorry that I made them drive around looking for me. We hugged. And somehow, possibly related to the drugs and my willingness to listen to her and the actress talk about pigs and summer 4-H conferences with serious interest, it seemed that she liked and respected me more than she had before we'd left for the tour. I was never going to forgive her for calling me entitled, but I was cool with her otherwise. I passed out on a plush and lengthy window seat with an awesome view of a sprawling Los Angeles below.

Los Angeles to Portland was a fifteen-hour drive, and I was ready to do my part. I drove the van from Fresno to Redding. I waved to Susan and Sacramento as we drove by. I knew she'd be proud of me for overcoming a fear. I didn't feel freaked about driving anymore. Even when the van rocked from heavy winds, I stayed steady. Roadkill was nothing but roadkill, not an existential crisis. Afterwards I sat in the beloved middle bench, my perk for having driven.

Outside of Salem, Oregon, desperate to be home, I got a call from Claire. She said the bungalow was on fire, at least that was what it sounded like. I put my phone against my chest and shouted at Keith and Richmond to turn down the music. I put the phone back to my ear.

"Claire, can you repeat that?"

"I can see flames in the second-floor window," she said.

"Flames? So, it's a serious fire?"

"It doesn't look good. The firefighters might be getting it under control. There's a lot of smoke now. Where are you? Are you still on tour?"

"We'll be home in an hour."

"Reggie thought you were in there. I had to stop him from . . . Hold on . . . What was that? I have to let you go, Julian. I need to speak with this firefighter. I'll keep you updated. Be safe."

I filled everyone in. Keith pulled the van into the left lane and gunned it. Skyler yelled at him to slow down before he killed us. Richmond turned around to look at me. He asked me to repeat again what Claire had said about only seeing flames in my bedroom window.

"Then it's not downstairs, right? She said the basement seemed cool, right?"

"Shut up, Richmond," Skyler said. "Julian and William might not have a place to live anymore."

"Yeah, c'mon, Richmond," William said. There were tears in his eyes. "Olympia is dead. I just know it. And all you care about is your stupid gear in the basement. I've lived in that place for four years. My whole life is in that house. My studio. Jesus. Thousands and thousands and thousands of dollars. I can't even do the math."

"You got home insurance?" Keith asked.

"Yeah," William said.

"Then everything can be replaced," Keith said.

"Not everything," Richmond said. "I've got a Strat in that basement that's one of a kind."

Richmond was being so insensitive, he couldn't even pretend his guitar wasn't all he cared about. I felt bad for not thinking about the cat until William brought her up. The first thing I thought about when I heard about the fire was rent—if the house burned down, I wouldn't have to pay it. Anything I owned worth anything was in the van. Laptop. Drums. The clothes I wore most often.

Then I thought about the cardboard box in my bedroom that I used as a nightstand. It had probably been destroyed. Old love letters and pictures, yearbooks, wedding photos. Gone up in flames. That was fine by me. Fuck the past. But that meant my old writing notebooks, my birth certificate, my ancient immunization records, my social security card, and a copy of the issue of the obscure and now defunct literary journal that had my one published poem was gone now too. And shit, maybe a place to live. When I thought about it that way, the fire was a really bad thing.

I sent up a quick prayer, but what could God do now, unless he was going to change the weather and bring a rainstorm. I checked the forecast on my phone to see if there was going to be a miracle: Portland was dry and only going to get dryer. There was a three-day national wildfire warning in a city known for rain. This was a job for the firefighters.

The only person I knew who'd been through a fire was my ex-wife, Lauren. Her childhood home burned down on a hot summer day in Texas. And maybe that's part of the reason she loved the winter. The first romantic moment we shared was in the snow. We'd both gone to the winter celebration service the December of our freshman year of college. Both sat in the chapel balcony. We knew each other but not too well, not yet. My future wife sat with some of her softball teammates. I was by myself. When the service began, the captain of the rowing team, Ingrid, a beautiful Swede, walked into the dimly lit chapel wearing a long white robe, and atop her cascading blond hair: a crown of burning candles. She led a procession of fellow Swedes from the back of the chapel to the stage. The women wore garlands. The men white cone hats with stars on the top. Everyone was holding candles and wearing white robes as they marched toward the cross and sang in Swedish. Their faces shadowed and glowing. It was the scariest shit I'd ever witnessed in a place of worship.

And I knew my feelings weren't their fault, this was a school full of Scandinavians, and this was a tradition. They were liberal as far as Evangelicals go, most of them kind toward me, and so for them this had absolutely nothing to do with the Klan, but still it made my skin crawl. Lauren had Swedish roots too, but she was from the South. She came over and sat in the empty seat next to me and asked if I wanted to go walk in the snow that had just started to fall.

At my college, if you were a guy, it was the trend to wear as little as possible in the winter months to show your mental and physical toughness, so I wasn't wearing proper shoes or a warm-enough jacket or gloves for the heavy snowfall. Big cottony flakes, Chicago in a snow globe. I got cold and wet but didn't care at all because Lauren was in rapture, she just couldn't stop grinning and opening her mouth to catch snow on her tongue. She thought blizzards were the most heavenly thing. She was the only one I knew personally who had lost her home in a fire.

In the carboard box I'd kept a copy of Grandfather Strickland's funeral program. At his funeral, after looking at him in his open casket and seeing his soulful smirk, I could barely breathe, I needed fresh air. Lauren and I snuck out of the church and went to the gravel parking lot across the street. We hid behind a van and lit cigarettes. Her father was a pastor. She considered herself a Christian rebel. Her mild rebelliousness was part of the reason I fell in love with her. I thought I was rebellious too. I was editor in chief of the college newspaper, I fought for the right to publish photos in color, and sometimes I climbed up the student services building late at night to drink whiskey and write poems in a little notebook while feeling sad about my lack of faith and my sinful mind. I thought I was deep. For most of college, Lauren and I only smoked cigarettes when we were drinking or sometimes with our friends after dinner. Smoking tobacco in designated areas was about the only debauched behavior our Christian college condoned. They didn't even provide condoms. We didn't start buying cigs regularly until after we ran out of the free packs the tobacco companies handed out like Halloween candy outside Churchill Downs on Derby Day our senior year of college. In the cardboard box there was a photo of our old crew sitting in a Waffle House in Louisville, Kentucky. Seven of us. Me in the middle, the only Black guy like always. Lauren on my right. My soon-to-be best man, Brett, on my left. We thought we were the Evangelical Christian avant-garde. As if that could ever exist. We were there to celebrate our graduation and Lauren's and my engagement. We drank coffee, smoked cigarettes, and devoured heaping plates of food, smothered, covered, and fried; hoping and praying all the calories and saturated fat would prevent us from losing our guts and minds in the derby infield later that day. My only memory of the actual running of the downs was rolling in the mud and vomiting up mint juleps as the hooves and spindly legs of thoroughbred racehorses shot past my blurred line of vision on the other side of the fence.

My mother had caught us smoking in the gravel parking lot during the funeral and was furious. I told her Grandpa Strickland was a lifelong smoker and smoking wasn't why he had a heart attack. My mother slapped me in front of my wife. What happens to the losing horses anyway? Are their hooves in the Jell-O shots at Klay's Cosmopolitan?

William was on his phone talking to someone quietly. I felt a hand on my shoulder. I turned and it was Skyler. Our faces were almost touching.

"Hey, how you are holding up?"

"Worried," I said.

"I know, so am I. This really sucks. But what's most important is that everyone is safe."

"What about Olympia?" I asked.

"I bet she's drinking water from the toilet as we speak."

"Anne check on her this morning?"

"I think so. She left to visit Ryan in Colorado this afternoon."

"You know, maybe it was Anne who set the fire, some sort of jilted-lover thing."

"But aren't you the jilted lover?"

"Shit," I said.

"Don't worry. Whatever happens, we'll make sure you're okay."

She smiled and patted my shoulder, then leaned back in her seat.

I thought about calling my parents, but I didn't want to hear half of what they'd say. My father would tell me to put my faith in the Lord, that God would never give me a challenge I couldn't handle. My mother would say that maybe this was a sign I should move back to Illinois. I loved them but no thank you. Often when I was in distress, talking to them hurt my spirit more than it helped me, and I'd feel lower than I did before we spoke.

I thought about my sister. We used to spend almost every waking hour together. For most of my childhood she was the only friend I had. I'd always thought that part of the reason she chose to go to Spelman was so I couldn't follow her. But we never talked about it. We were the kind of family that kept our deepest feelings so deep we had trouble accessing them ourselves. I'd only spoken to her once since Christmas. She'd called to ask if I wanted to chip in for an anniversary gift she was buying for our parents. I said sure, but I never got around to sending the money. I couldn't even remember what the gift was. Did I feel guilty about that? Very.

I wanted to tell Ida about the fire, but that didn't seem like a good idea either. She'd never been inside my home. She wouldn't understand what I was afraid of losing. And I wasn't going to risk leaving another rambling voice message.

I looked at my phone. I had a message from Claire.

"I just got word the fire's out," I announced to the van.

"I said it was out ten minutes ago," William said. "Weren't you listening?"

The van went silent except for the engine. There was nothing to say. All we could do was wait. We got off the highway and pulled onto Macadam Avenue toward the St. James Bridge. Less than fifteen minutes until we reached the bungalow. Everyone was distressed and beyond tired. The air in the van smelled acrid. Body odor and the contents of food wrappers rotting under the seats. I wanted so badly to be away from these people.

We rolled up to the bungalow. Broken glass and blackened wood around my bedroom window. The firefighters were packing up to leave. I waved to Reggie, Claire, and Peter, who were standing in their driveway. There had been plenty of spectators, apparently, but now there were none. It was three o'clock in the morning. A fireman said the fire started at the power outlet connected to the soundboard on the second floor. Most of the damage on the first floor was contained to the ceiling. Olympia was nowhere to be found. The basement had gone unscathed.

Keith took the possibility of the cat's death harder than I thought he would. He was pissed. He blamed the fire on the jam band. William reminded him they only used the recording studio the first two days we were gone, and Anne had been checking in once a day.

"Well, maybe they didn't turn the soundboard and amps off," Keith said.

"Whatever happened here was an accident," Richmond assured him. I felt like he was trying to hide his elation about his gear being safe.

"Sorry this happened to you guys," the fireman said.

"Thanks for everything," Skyler said.

"Our poor cat," William said. "Our poor, poor Olympia."

Poor cat and poor fucking me. It was the wrong view to take—heretical, I guess—but wouldn't a father who doesn't protect you, neglects you, actively works against you, be considered an abusive father? Was I just supposed to keep on taking it? Was that what the Christian faith was all about? Suffering? Really? Was that love? Let it all burn if it be God's will? Be crushed by the weight of it all to glorify him? To get to heaven? Complete surrender until there is nothing left? Or was this the price for my sins? Why did I seem to be paying a higher price than everyone else? No wonder so many people only believed in prosperity.

30

NINE O'CLOCK IN THE MORNING. First day back, and everyone in the office had their hands all over me. Arms, back, shoulders, and neck. The boss closed his eyes and began to pray, "Dear Lord. We pray for our brother Julian. We thank you for watching over him and protecting him when his house caught fire, God." The boss's palm rested on the middle of my chest. He kept tapping where my heart was.

"Yes, God. Thank you, Jesus," John said, as he pressed a knot by the base of my neck. I couldn't believe the guy, I wanted him to get off me. The only person whose hand I didn't mind was Trenton's. He was patting my back in a manner where I could tell he was trying to keep me calm because he knew how much I hated every moment of this.

"We know this has been a trying time for our brother, Lord God. But we also know that if he puts his faith in your son, Jesus Christ, you will never give him a burden that he can't handle. We know that your wisdom goes beyond all our understanding. And that Julian will come out of this trial and tribulation stronger than ever through the power of your love."

"Yes, God. Thank you for your love, Lord," John said.

"Holy Father, may you continue to bless Julian and give him the strength and peace of mind he needs in this trying time of uncertainty. May he continue to put his faith in you. We pray these things in Jesus's holy name. Amen." We opened our eyes. Everyone took their hands off me. I let out a deep breath. The boss smiled at me like he'd taken my sigh as a sign of God's immediate work in the repairing of my soul. My coworkers left the conference room and then it was just me and the boss standing by the doorway.

"You going to be okay to work today?" the boss asked.

"I've got no other place to be," I said. "And I could definitely use the money."

I had about five hundred dollars in the bank, and the student loan people were demanding three hundred dollars and were threatening to garnish my wages if they didn't get their money soon, so forbearance was no longer an option. On tour I'd somehow managed to spend more money than I did when I was at home. I bought a locally handcrafted pair of selvedge jeans in LA to replace the jeans that were stained in Sacramento. And now I had no place to live.

"I get it," the boss said. "Diving into work is how I cope with trouble as well. But don't feel like you've got to jump into it at regular speed. Ease into it."

"Thanks," I said.

"My daughter did a good job when you were gone," he said. "I'm thinking of having her coming in and working the phones all summer."

"So am I being replaced?" I asked.

"Replaced? No way." The boss put his hands on my shoulders in a way that made me think of Richmond for a moment, his face flashing in my head as the boss spoke. "I want you to learn how to sell then join the sales team."

"Me?" I asked. "In sales?"

"That's where the money is, my man, and I think you've got the chops. Pray on it. We'll circle back around next week."

Back at my desk, I couldn't focus on the screen. I could make out the letters if I squinted, but I had trouble putting them into words and sentences that made any sense.

All the days and recent events were a blur. When we'd pulled up to the fire-damaged bungalow last night, the firefighters told us we couldn't go inside, and I'd ended up sleeping in Anne's room because she was in Colorado. Being in her room had sparked memories. I'd masturbated. Afterwards I thought about Olympia. That sleek black body. That cute little nose. Those all-knowing eyes. I didn't think she was dead. That cat had too many lives left to live. I would have prayed for her if I thought it would help. But prayer had gotten me nowhere but homeless.

I should have laughed in the boss's face. Get fired and go on unemployment. I was no salesman. As a matter of fact, I had no natural abilities aside from the drums. At everything else, I sucked. If the cat was still living, a prayer from me would probably kill her.

31

ANNE'S HOUSE WAS ONLY A place to sleep, it wasn't a home, and I didn't like being there. William and Skyler were always hanging around, and we were sick of one another. For three days in a row, right after work, I would take the bus downtown to Powell's City of Books. It was easy to enjoy a whole evening there without spending much money except for buying a cheap dinner like pizza or a cheeseburger or last night's splurge of fish and chips and a martini. I finally read *Hamlet* and *Leaves of Grass*. I read poems by Charles Simic, Audre Lorde, Mary Ruefle, Derek Walcott, Louise Glück, and Stephen Dunn. I worked on the Sacramento poem.

Friday after work, I was on the bus headed to Powell's when Ida called. She apologized for not getting back to me sooner. She'd heard about the fire and was so very sorry. We made plans to meet the next day for coffee.

When I walked into the Ugly Mug, Ida was already sitting at a table. I'd purposely come five minutes earlier than our agreed-upon time so I could be the first to arrive. Being the second person to get there, yet still arriving early, felt like defeat.

She smiled and waved, didn't get up to greet me. I returned her wave before I went to the counter and looked up at the big chalkboard menu on the wall like I was trying to decide what to order even though I knew I wanted an Americano. I needed time to recover. Seeing her hit me with the same force as the first time I saw her. Life would be good if she wanted me, no good if she didn't.

I changed my mind and asked for drip coffee. An Americano, I'd have to stand around awkwardly while the barista pulled espresso shots. Drip coffee was ready to go, and I was ready to sit down. My mug was overflowing. I spilled coffee every step I took. When I sat down, Ida had napkins ready for me.

"Thanks," I said. "It's great to see you."

"It's great to see you too," she said. "This is a cute little coffee shop on a cute little street." She reached out like she was going to touch me for a second, then pulled back like she'd forgotten I was contagious.

"The fire," she said. "So horrible. How are you doing?"

"Not well."

"I heard you lost everything you didn't have with you on the road."

"Who'd you hear it from?" I asked. "Liesel?"

"No, Richmond."

"You and Richmond. You guys seem to talk all the time."

The brightness in her eyes dimmed. She took a sip of her coffee before she replied.

"Not all the time, but sometimes."

"But you messaged him a few times while we were gone, right?"

"A few times, I guess. Why?"

"No reason," I said. "It's just that, and I know this sounds petty, I think it's bogus you had time to message him and not me."

"Julian." That's all she said. My name. She picked up her mug and had another sip of her coffee. I wished we could have started the conversation over again. I wanted to talk about us. I wanted her to remember how much we liked being with each other and end this coffee date with a kiss and a promise of more to come. But instead, I brought up Richmond and sounded like a jealous man-child, and maybe I was, but I didn't want her to think that about me.

"Well, how are you doing?" I asked. "How's the series coming along?"

She looked at me and smiled faintly.

"Good," she said. She shifted her gaze to the coffee mug she was gripping firmly with both hands. "I have three of four done." She looked out the window again. I wanted to ask her what was going on outside that was so damned interesting—was it the promise of freedom after we said goodbye? "But the last painting is giving me a lot of trouble. I can't find the proper contrast."

"I'm sure you'll figure it out," I said. "I believe in you."

"Thanks," she said.

"Of course."

There was nothing left to say. Not until she said whatever it was she was clearly holding back. Our wobbly wooden table and the bulletin boards on the wall nearby covered with colorful flyers of wholesome neighborhood events and the sounds of other people happily chattering over the pleasant music and the gentle light coming in from the windows and the sound of a newspaper ruffling and nice warm air coming in through the propped open door and the rich aroma of fresh coffee and the memories of those kisses we once shared made the silence between us feel like a momentous, ever-increasing, and potentially irresolvable distance. I sipped my coffee and kept my eyes down until I couldn't take it anymore.

"So," I said.

I stared at her until her eyes met mine. Her face was plain. The last time I saw her she wore makeup. I liked her more this way. She had nothing worth hiding. I could never truly describe what she did to me. I smiled at her. She looked at me nervously.

"So," Ida said. "Yeah. Sorry for the lack of communication while you were away. I was working a lot and doing a lot of thinking about myself and where I am right now, and you know, with my recent breakup, and the project I'm trying to get done . . . I think it would be better for me if I didn't try to get into a relationship right now."

It was like the house fire all over again.

"Are you sure?" I asked.

She bit her lip. "Yeah," she said. "I'm sorry, I am."

"Was it something I did or didn't do?" I asked.

She'd reached in her purse. I was afraid she'd get up and leave any second, and that made me want to give up on life.

"Not at all. You're a great guy. Really, it's not you at all. I'm just not in the space."

"But I'll give you all the space you need," I said. "We can just be friends."

I knew I sounded desperate, but hell, I was desperate.

"Julian," she said.

"Is it Richmond?"

She sat up straight, further away from me and the table.

"I don't know how to answer that," she said.

"Just lay it all out," I said. "Lay it on me."

"It's not what you're thinking."

"Then what is it?"

"I just need space," she said. "At least for now."

"Fine," I said.

I pushed back my chair to get up.

"Let's not leave it like this," she said.

She looked upset. But why? She was the one who was being unreasonable. Not me. I was ready to be brave. We had a chance, a serious attraction, like nothing I'd ever felt, and I knew in my heart she felt the pull just like I did, and yet she didn't have the guts to find out if we could truly love each other.

“See you around,” I said.

Somehow, despite my anguish, I was able to stand, and I was proud of myself for that. I figured the best thing I could do for my dignity was walk out and leave her all alone in this charming little coffee shop I used to love but was now forever ruined.

32

THE LAURELHURST SALOON WAS THE only honky-tonk hippie joint in town. A place for people who loved everything about the South except for its history. The closest anyone would get to supporting the Confederacy was singing a heartfelt rendition of "The Night They Drove Old Dixie Down." The place had live music six nights a week and sometimes it got rowdy in a pleasant kind of way. But it was Sunday afternoon, so we pretty much had the place to ourselves. Onstage a white guy with long white hair and a long white mustache sat on a chair and fingerpicked a worn guitar. "This one's called 'Walk on Boy,'" he said. Every song he played like he'd been playing it for the past forty years because he still believed in its power. What a nice way to be.

I was with Liesel. We had coffee with our food. Then we moved on to champagne cocktails. I took the first sip of my drink, and for a moment I didn't feel bad about anything at all. Then Liesel brought up her ex.

"So how many women did Richmond sleep with on tour?"

"Are you serious?"

"Yes."

"Seventy-five."

"Be serious."

"Let's not talk about him, okay?"

"Did he make you swear to never tell me? He can be very persuasive."

"He didn't make me swear to do anything," I said.

"Don't bullshit me, Julian."

"As far as I know, he didn't sleep with anyone."

"As far as you know?"

"As far as I know, okay? Can we just not talk about him? Not Ida anymore either? Let's just talk about ourselves."

We ordered a second round of champagne cocktails from a lanky middle-aged bartender who wore a straw hat and overalls. No undershirt. And he really pulled it off, he could wear that to the bank, no problem. Before he walked away to make our drinks, he gave Liesel one of those, *hey girl, what's up?* looks, and she smiled in return like she appreciated his attention. I didn't like that he assumed we weren't together. But then again, if he'd heard any of the conversation I'd had with her while we were eating our meal, he'd know that I was hurting over a woman named Ida who told me yesterday she wanted nothing to do with me.

"What is William going to do about the house?" Liesel asked.

"He isn't sure yet," I said.

"Would you want to live there again?"

"With him? I don't know."

"Well, what do you know?"

"Nothing, except that I've been feeling mixed up, homeless, and unlovable."

The bartender came back with our second cocktails of the day. He gave Liesel a flirty little nod again. She smiled and thanked him before he walked away. What a guy. The last person I'd seen rock overalls so well was Ida, but I was trying not to think about her. I had planned to take a break from drinking after I got back from the tour, but there kept being good reasons to hold off. Like not having a place to live, that was a good reason to drink, so was heartache, so was going to brunch with Liesel. The reasons went on and on.

Day drinking can be fantastic and whimsical. The trick is to keep it classy. If it's only noon and you're drinking well liquor and cheap beer, then you're demonstrating alcoholic tendencies. But if you get tight on good booze, you're simply exercising your God-given American right to have a good time whenever and wherever you please.

Liesel asked me how work was.

"Still horrible," I said. "And on top of its usual horribleness, the boss wants me to become a salesman."

She laughed. "You, a salesman? Like calling people and getting them to buy something?"

"Yeah," I said. "Can you imagine me doing something like that?"

"No. I really can't," she said. "What are you going to do about it?"

"I don't know," I said. "I wish I could afford to never go back there."

"How is staying at Anne's house?"

"I hate it," I said. "But I don't have much longer there anyway. Anne's coming back from Colorado this Wednesday. Then I'll be sleeping on Keith and his roommate's couch."

Liesel reached over the table and took my hand.

"You're going through so much." she said. "How can I help you?"

"I don't know," I said.

This was the first time I'd seen Liesel since she stormed out of the bungalow after recording vocals for Plaid Parenthood's EP. When her call woke me up that morning and she asked if I wanted to go out to brunch, I'd said yes, got dressed, and caught a bus without any hesitation.

She was still holding my hand. She told me she was thinking about getting out of town because she didn't want to be around when Richmond started dating someone new. "It'll happen any day now," she said. "If it hasn't happened already. He doesn't know how to be single."

"Where will you go?"

"Brooklyn. My best friend from college lives in Williamsburg and wants me to be her roommate. She says she can get me a job. I have money saved up and my Portland rent is so cheap I'm just going to keep paying it until I know if I'm going to stay in New York."

She let go of my hand and waved down the bartender before grabbing it back again.

"Don't go," I said. "This town is no good without you."

"I know," she said. "And I'll miss Portland dearly, but I need an adventure. You left Illinois right after your divorce, right?"

"Yeah," I said.

"And did it work?"

"Did what work?"

The bartender came over and we ordered another round. This time he didn't give Liesel a flirty look.

"Does your ex-wife still have power over you?" she asked.

We were still holding hands.

"Not at all," I said. "But she never really did. I don't think we had that kind of love. When it was done it was done."

"But do you ache for her?"

"No, nothing like that."

"Good. That's what I want," she said.

The bartender came back with fresh champagne cocktails. We clanked glasses and took sips. We were getting good and toasted.

"Why don't you try dating someone new?" I asked.

"No thanks," she said. "I'm not dating for at least a year."

"That sounds impossible," I said.

She pulled my hand until our heads got closer.

"Not celibacy, silly. Casual sex. All you have to do is be up front and honest with the other person. And even more importantly, honest with yourself."

"But what if I honestly just want Ida?"

"Oh, Julian. I think you need to stop giving her so much of your energy. As her friend, I love Ida. She's cool and amazing. But she can also be a cruel bitch sometimes, you know?"

I couldn't believe it. The two times I'd seen them together, Liesel clamored over Ida, and now that she wasn't here to defend herself, Liesel was calling her a bitch. I was disappointed in her, but she was holding my hand and that was comforting. She sipped her cocktail and looked into my eyes. She made up her mind about something and tightened her grip.

"I don't think race makes any difference, do you?"

"You think I only like Ida because she's Black?"

"Of course not, but c'mon, isn't that part of it?"

"What do you know about it? Richmond's white and so are you."

"Jesus, Julian, it's not like Richmond's the only lover I've ever had."

"Do you call all the people you've slept with lovers?"

"What do you call them?"

"One I call my ex-wife, the other I call Anne."

"Geez, that's all? You never slept with Ida? No wonder you're obsessed. You're practically a virgin. You need to sleep around. Oh God. Forget it. Don't listen to me. I didn't mean to offend you. I'm drunk."

"It's alright," I said. "I'm pretty drunk myself, and maybe you're right."

"I just want what's best for you," she said.

The man onstage finished his last song. We let go of each other's hands and applauded. Liesel finished her champagne cocktail and put a finger inside the glass to scoop up the mixture of sugar and bitters at the bottom. The finger went into her mouth, she pulled it out slowly, sort of absentmindedly. She was looking up to the ceiling, she was scheming, or so it looked.

"What are you thinking about?" I asked.

"Let's go see a movie," she said.

"What's playing?"

"Who cares. We'll sober up and then I'll give you a ride to wherever you want to go."

In high school I could walk the mile faster than I could run it. Most people walked too slow for my taste. But Liesel and I kept the same pace naturally. We walked on Northeast Thirtieth Avenue, then took a right onto Couch. It was a sunny day, where any shaded spot felt ten degrees cooler. We slid down the sidewalk gracefully until my foot hit a chunk of concrete raised by the root of an overgrown tree. I almost grabbed Liesel's hand for support, but even inebriated, I knew taking her hand now would mean something different than it did when we held hands while discussing our relationship woes at the bar.

We bought sandwiches at a deli. We put them in my backpack and snuck them into the theater. We drank mega-sized cups of ice water and Diet Coke while watching a bro movie about drunken high jinks in Las Vegas. After finishing her sandwich, she put her head on my shoulder and promptly fell asleep. It was nice to be with her, to not feel so alone. We seemed to have an unshakeable faith in each other, that strange, inexplicable thing. I woke her up during the credits. The lights came on in the theater and she said it felt like waking up to a brand-new day, and it was true, my drunken past was nothing more than a lingering headache.

We left the theater and went in the direction of her car. She stopped to admire a dress in the window of a secondhand clothing store on Twenty-Eighth Avenue.

"Think I should try it on?" she asked.

"I bet you'd look great in it," I said.

She grabbed my arm and led me inside. She asked the lady behind the counter to take the dress off the mannequin. I sat with my head against the back of a salmon-colored wing chair. I closed my eyes until I heard a creak and saw Liesel come out of her dressing room. There was a full-length mirror next to the chair I was sitting in. I got up to give her more room, stood about three feet behind her. The dress was short-sleeved and periwinkle blue. She took her curly brown hair out of its ponytail and shook it until it was touching her shoulders. We met eyes in the mirror. We'd always been good friends, never crossed the line into anything else.

"How do I look?"

"Fantastic."

"My boobs don't look nonexistent?"

"Can you turn slightly? No, not at all. They look great."

"Yeah?"

"Totally."

"And it's only fifteen bucks," she said. "Fuck it. I'm buying it."

She went back to change. I perused the tiny men's section and found a tweed jacket with a suede patch on the right shoulder. The sleeves were short, but other than that it fit perfectly. I decided to buy it. I handed it to the woman behind the counter.

"Great jacket," she said.

"Why is there only one shoulder patch?" I asked.

"It's a shooting jacket," she said. "The patch on the shoulder is where you rest the butt of the gun." She fixed her arms like she was holding a rifle, closed one eye, put the other on the sight, then turned until she had me in her crosshairs. "Ka-Powww."

We paid for our clothes and continued the long walk toward Liesel's car. It was parked all the way on Belmont, in front of Stumptown Coffee. She'd been hanging there before our brunch and had decided to walk to the Laurelhurst Saloon instead of driving.

"Are you in a rush?" Liesel asked.

"Not at all," I said.

"Then let's walk through the park."

It was Memorial Day weekend. The park was jumping. There were people dressed like warriors, knights, and peasants, striking each other with fake swords and axes, protecting themselves with spells, footwork, contortions, and homemade shields. Pet owners were huddled in conversation while their unleashed dogs roamed designated areas. People were on tightropes tied between trees. People jogged around the outside path. Groups of teenagers threw frisbees or sat around on blankets having serious teenage conversations. There were ducks in the pond. The water was shallow and brown. On the other side of the pond, men with shopping carts and backpacks drank beer and smoked cigarettes. Even the down-and-out people seemed to be having a decent time. It was just one of those days. And I hadn't had one like this, so bright and full of hope and so effortlessly casual, since the days I used to spend with Anne, walking around our neighborhood. Maybe Anne had been right, maybe I never loved her at all, maybe I'd just loved her company. But what about love? For the past two months I'd been in love with Ida.

Liesel bumped me with her shoulder.

"Do you have any plans for the rest of the day?"

"Nothing set in stone," I said. "Not even anything tentative."

"Want to go to see the Oregon Symphony at the Schnitzer?"

"My only suit got lost in the fire."

"I'm sorry to hear that, but you don't need a suit. This is Portland. Practically no one wears a suit to the symphony. Wear your new jacket. I'll wear my new dress."

"Did you already buy tickets?"

"Kind of. I traded for them. Do you know Diane? The violinist? No? She always comes to my shows, and she's been to some of yours. She plays in the symphony, second chair. We're both part of an online exchange group. I offered up a Crock-Pot my mother bought me that I never use, and Diane offered symphony tickets."

"Cool, well, I'd love to go," I said.

"I'm jazzed," Liesel said. "I'll make us dinner. Show starts in about three hours."

We stopped at Stumptown and downed double espressos. Then got in her car. On the way to her place, we stopped at Plaid Pantry. I ran inside and splurged on a fifteen-dollar bottle of red wine.

Liesel lived off Killingsworth. Only four blocks away from where Richmond lived. She said they hadn't bumped into each other since they'd broken up. "But it's hard," she said. "I think about the places he likes to go and the times he likes to go there, and then I go someplace else."

"What about New Seasons?"

"That's my turf," she said. "If he needs groceries, he can go to Fred Meyer or QFC."

We parked in her driveway. She punched numbers in a keypad. The garage door shook and began to rise. We scooted past a pool table topped with boxes and a bicycle hanging from the ceiling and walked inside her house. She started cooking right away. I offered to help, but she said there wasn't room for two cooks. I sat on a stool at the bar counter and drank wine. I watched her move gracefully in her tiny kitchen, wearing a yellow apron over black jeans and a gray T-shirt, sipping wine, laughing, cutting up vegetables, telling a funny story over the sound of the sausage sizzling in a cast-iron skillet, stirring a small pan, getting sauce on the stove, and wiping away the perspiration on her brow with her forearm. Richmond was my friend and my bandmate, but he had to be biggest idiot in the world.

Liesel asked me to set the table and told me where everything was. I set it for two. Just as we sat down to eat, her roommate, Becky, came in through the front door in a huff and took the seat between us. She banged her elbows on the table, rattling the silverware. She took a sip of Liesel's wine before she started complaining about how emotionally unstable her younger brother was.

"I love him, I do, but he's either so sad or he's so angry and I just don't have the capacity to carry one more ounce of his burden. I mean, let's be real. I can barely hold it together myself."

"That's how I feel when someone on the street asks me for money," I said. "Maybe they can't see it, but I'm just about bankrupt."

"Exactly!" Becky said. "I had a tarot card reading last week that pretty much said the same thing."

"Has he tried therapy?" Liesel asked.

Becky took a slice of baguette from Liesel's plate and tore it in half. Her fingers dripped with garlic butter.

"Everyone in my family goes to therapy." She spoke with her mouth full. "Our family demands madness and then they demand therapy, if you aren't born crazy, they'll drive you to it, and then they'll drive you to the shrink. Oh my God, I'm starving."

"There's more in the kitchen," Liesel said. "Make yourself a plate."

Becky ate our food and drank our wine, but she made up for it by rolling a fat joint and putting on a solid playlist of Ethiopian jazz. We ate dinner, got stoned, and talked about family. Liesel said when she visited her parents in Eugene last week, she concluded that they didn't have a sexual relationship and probably never had, they seemed to be asexuals deeply in love. I said I believed my parents had been in love at some point but now all I knew for certain was that they couldn't live without each other. Becky thought that was sweet, she said her aristocrat parents were divorced and now married to other people and didn't know what love was at all. She said she'd take parents like mine or Liesel's any day. I could understand that, I said, but would she give up her inheritance for it? She laughed and said no. I respected her honesty.

After dinner, Becky left for a dance party at the Goodfoot. I helped Liesel clear the table and load the dishwasher, then followed her into her bedroom. It felt like the natural thing to do, waiting for her in her bedroom as opposed to sitting in the living room. Liesel picked up the pile of clothes on her bed and threw them onto an armchair. She apologized for her room being a mess. She said when she got depressed the first thing to go was her cleanliness. I told her the room seemed pretty clean to me. And it did, compared to my own standard of living. Liesel told me the bed was more comfortable than the chair. She closed the blinds before leaving the room to take a shower.

I put my wineglass on the nightstand and my backpack on the floor. Took off my sneakers and sat on the bed. An ancient iPod connected to a small speaker system sat on the nightstand. I wheeled through the albums, clicked on *Songs from a Room*. Alone at night, the album was tragic; I'd cried many times to "Bird on a Wire." But on a bright day like this one—with a full stomach, stoned and sitting on Liesel's bed while she was in the shower on the other side of the wall—the songs were valiant accounts of those who had struggled to live an honorable life against the forces of darkness that saturated everything. On a day like this, the music made the shit of the past, the haunted memories, and those awful sleepless nights feel like the inevitable journey I'd been required to take to be here now.

I didn't smell so good. I reached over the side of the bed to grab my backpack, the closest thing I had to a home. Inside were the essentials: a toothbrush, a pair of 5A sticks, my writing journal with the sticky IHOP poem napkins pressed inside the front flap, band cassettes, a phone charger, an old winter issue of *Tin House*, a change of clothes, deodorant, and the condoms I'd purchased at Plaid Pantry just in case. I put on deodorant.

I was leafing through Liesel's copy of *The National Audubon Society Field Guide to New England* when she came back into her bedroom wearing only a bath towel. Her hair wrapped in a T-shirt. I kept my eyes on the book until she turned around to face her dresser. There was a circular mirror attached to the wall above it. But I couldn't see her reflection like I'd hoped. Her back blocked the mirror. She opened the top drawer of her dresser and pulled out underwear. She slid them on and let her towel fall to the floor.

"What are you reading about?"

She had a birthmark on her left shoulder. Her acoustic guitar leaned against the wall next to her door.

"Blue jays store their chestnuts in the ground," I said.

She looked at me over the shoulder with the birthmark.

"Why?" she asked.

I didn't know, I'd been too busy staring at her back.

"Probably to keep them safe," I said.

"What does the book say?"

"That's all it says. It doesn't say why."

"I doubt that," she said.

She rifled through her dresser, started at the top and worked her way down. The bottom drawer wouldn't open. She pulled it, kicked it, pulled at it again, it wouldn't budge. She stood up and looked through the top drawer again, then turned around to face me, her left arm pressed against her breasts to hide her nipples. I'd seen her in a bikini before, but I'd never seen her naked. She was slim, strong hips, the shoulders of a swimmer. I was almost twice her size, but I had the feeling she could crush me.

"The bra I need is in the bottom drawer and I can't get it open. Can you help?"

"Sure," I said.

I hopped off the bed. Got on my knees and started working on the drawer. Pulling it and pushing it as I shifted it from side to side and up and down. Liesel stood close by. The scent of her freshly showered body was in every breath I took, and it gave me the strength to wrench the drawer halfway open. I looked up at her. Her hands were on her hips and her nipples were soft. I was hard. I wanted to grab her and to bring her to bed without saying a word, but how could I ask for permission without speaking? She took a deep breath, then pushed the air out slowly, her abdomen tightening.

"Okay, that's enough, thank you," she said.

"You sure?" I asked.

"Yes. I can take it from here, thank you."

"I can do more if you'd like."

I looked in her eyes, they were glossy and red, she was stoned. So was I.

"That won't be necessary."

"Okay," I said

I got off my knees and returned to the bed, stayed hunched over to hide my erection. Once I was back in bed, I took out my sticks and hit them on my thighs to work on paradiddles and forget about her body. Back to flaccid, I went to the bathroom to freshen up the best I could. When I got back into the room she was rummaging through the pile of clothes on the chair for her bra.

"Shit," she said. "We're running late now. Can you look under the bed?"

I got on my knees and looked under the bed. I grabbed what looked like a bra. It was a gray men's sock; most likely Richmond's. If he knew where I was and especially what I was thinking about, he'd kill me. I threw the sock aside, found the bra.

"Here it is."

"Oh, great."

I tossed it to her. She slapped it against the dresser. Dust floated in the rays of light that came through the slats of the blinds.

• • •

We sat quietly in the back of a Radio Cab. White cab drivers didn't exist in Chicago, but in Portland, every job was a white person's job. The driver spoke emphatically to someone on his headset about a board game.

"Dude," the driver said, "fuck the friendly robber. Always take resources."

As the cab climbed the Burnside Bridge, the big neon-lit PORTLAND OREGON sign came into view. I first saw the sign three years ago, crossing the bridge in a cab just like this one with my ex-wife on our way to her college roommate's wedding in the Pearl District. We were recently married ourselves. It was winter then, the white stag at the top of the sign had been sgiven a red nose like Rudolph, and my ex had said it was a sign of good fortune, onward and upward to a prosperous, God-fearing marriage. But now it was almost summer, three years later, two years divorced, my gold wedding band lost way before the fire could have burned it, and the white stag's nose was naked.

Liesel told the driver to let us out in front of the liquor store on Tenth Avenue. We bought a pint of whiskey and started to walk toward the Schnitzer. As the concert hall got closer, I realized I wasn't in the mood for classical music.

"Mind if I stay at your place after the show?" I asked.

"Sure," Liesel said.

"Great."

"We can cuddle, but that's it, Julian, we can't play around."

"Of course," I said.

She grabbed my arm and put her head against the left shoulder of my shooting jacket. "Good," she said. "I'm happy we're on the same page."

The pleasant day was cooling down fast as it shifted into evening.

Right before we'd left her house to jump in the waiting cab, Liesel had decided to wear a black motorcycle jacket over her blue dress. And I just loved it. There was something about her today. All I could come up with was that she was the height of American realism. I didn't know what that meant exactly, but that's how I felt, like I was living the American dream. The sky was blue and orange. The sun was hiding behind a skyscraper. And I just wanted to love her, that was all, I wanted to make love to her as a friend. Tonight. No care about tomorrow. Like that Bob Segar song. Casual sex if that's what she wanted to call it. I made up my mind to be frank . . . *to hell with the concert* . . . I wanted to say . . . *to hell with Richmond . . . we both know what's going on here, right?* but before I could work up the nerve, a group of white guys started to yell at us from across the street.

"Jungle love!"

"Jungle fever!"

"Voodoo magic!"

"Hey, lady, has he hypnotized you?"

"Do you need us to save you?"

There were three of them. Liesel tightened her grip on my arm.

"Don't engage," she said. "Ignore them. Keep walking."

We walked faster, keeping our eyes straight ahead. They stayed three steps behind so the only way to see them was to turn in their direction. They made kissing sounds. They pretended to moan with pleasure. I couldn't believe it was happening. They were going to ruin everything.

We were almost to the concert hall when one of them made monkey sounds and the other two busted in laughter. I looked over and one of them was waving his arms and pretending to scratch himself like a monkey, hopping from side to side. I yanked my arm from Liesel's grasp and ran toward him. If I could punch the monkey imitator in the face once or twice it would be worth the damages.

For a second, they all froze as if they hadn't expected confrontation. But when the monkey man started running away, the other guys followed him. They turned right, heading down a dark street. I mustered all my rage and went into an all-out sprint. I was on their heels. I reached for the flailing jacket of the guy I was closest to. I touched the hem of his garment but couldn't get hold. Then my left hamstring seized up and it got harder to breathe. I lost the ability to run about halfway down the block. They reached the end and veered left.

Liesel ran toward me. I was next to a dumpster with my hands pressed against a brick wall. I turned and slid down the wall until my butt found concrete.

"Are you okay?" she asked.

"Out of breath," I said.

"Then you should get up. The ground is full of rat poison."

I got up and wiped my hands on my jeans. I put them up for her to see.

"No dirt." I said, still struggling for air.

Liesel crossed her arms.

"What were you thinking, Julian?"

"I was thinking I wanted to beat the shit out of those guys."

Her bottom lip quivered.

"Well maybe that's what they wanted. You ever think of that?"

"To get their asses kicked?"

"For you to get angry."

"I almost got hold of the chubby one."

"You're lucky you didn't. They were minors, Julian."

"Kids?"

"They were wearing fucking letterman jackets."

"Didn't you hear them? What else could I do?"

"Ignore them. All they wanted was attention, and you gave it to them."

"You don't understand."

"Why? Because I'm not a hotheaded man? You don't think I get catcalled?"

I stepped forward, she stepped back.

"This sucks. I hate this world sometimes," I said.

"Me too," she said.

Blatant racism. What a cockblocker. The magic between us had died. For me it was when those guys started heckling us. For Liesel, maybe it died when I chased them. We walked in silence, shaky and uneasy. The Schnitzer was only a block away.

We stopped at will-call just as it was about to close. We rushed into the empty atrium. Someone who worked there told us the concert would begin in five minutes. Liesel insisted I hurry into the bathroom to wash my rat-poisoned hands. We found our entrance. An usher took our tickets. He squinted at the tiny numbers and letters on the bottom and nodded once he'd seen enough.

"Row J, seats three and four. Follow me," he said.

As we followed the usher to our seats, I looked around at the audience. Almost every person I set eyes on could have been the parent or grandparent of a white teen in a letterman jacket. Our seats were in the middle of the aisle. The usher shined his light. Liesel went in first. And as I followed her, I bumped into a few old knees, apologizing every time.

I felt an abundance of eyes on me. People wanted to know who I was and why I was here and what I was about. I didn't blame them. If I'd seen another Black person in attendance, I would have wondered the same thing. I couldn't find a comfortable way to sit. It got so bad I thought about getting up and leaving. The lights in the hall dimmed and the orchestra began to play, and I started to feel invisible to everyone but Liesel. We snuck the whiskey bottle back and forth and got lost in Rachmaninoff. We became warm again. I grabbed her hand. We smiled at each other. She rested her head where the lady at the store counter earlier that day had said you're supposed to put the butt of a rifle.

At the end of the night, we stripped down to our underwear and fell asleep in each other's arms. It was easier not to fool around than I thought it would be. Just being close to her was almost enough. When we awoke, I was achy and sore in the joints. Liesel said she felt more rested than she had in a long time. We decided to get breakfast at a place we both knew Richmond hated, but when we walked into the diner, there he was, with Ida, in a booth, holding hands.

33

WHEN THEY SAW US STANDING at the entrance to the diner, they let go of each other. But that didn't make any difference. Liesel walked right up to Richmond and slapped him in the face.

"Holy fuck," he said. He put his hand to his cheek.

"You fucker!" Liesel yelled. "I can't believe you."

"Liesel, oh my God," Ida said.

Ida had me messed up. I wanted to yell at her and ask her what the hell was going on. Or better than that, sit down calmly and ask her what the hell was going on, but things were happening fast, and I was afraid she'd be the next victim, and despite anything potentially going on with her and Richmond, I wasn't going to let Liesel put a hand on her. I pulled Liesel away from the table, but not before she knocked over Ida's mug and coffee went everywhere. We had the attention of the entire restaurant. A waitress rushed over.

"Ma'am, this unacceptable," she said. "You need to leave the premises immediately."

Richmond scooted toward the end of the booth as if he were thinking of getting out of it. "Wait. Guys, let's talk."

Ida looked at us pleadingly. The both of them looked pathetic. Sitting there with their frightened faces and their clothes doused in coffee. I hoped it ruined everything.

"We're going," I said.

Liesel and I hurried out of the diner. We got in her car and drove off.

"Maybe they're just chilling like we are."

"Richmond isn't like you, Julian."

"What's that supposed to mean?"

"If they spent the night together, they fucked."

"Why did you guys break up?"

"Huh?"

"You and Richmond."

"He didn't tell you?"

"No. I tried to get him to, but he wouldn't."

"Of course not, that bastard."

Liesel had a grip on the wheel like she was trying to crush it. I put my face in my hands. Ida and Richmond were the center of their own universes, that was something I'd respected about them, but how could they do this to me? Especially Richmond. He fucked all those women on the road and then got back home and fucked the woman he knew I was in love with. Our friendship was over.

We went to Grand Central Bakery and ordered coffee and breakfast sandwiches to go. It was crowded. Not enough room to talk about betrayal. We stood against a wall, buried in our thoughts until someone called our names. Once we had our food, we got back in the car. Liesel started the engine. She put her right hand on my headrest and looked out the rear window as she reversed out of the parking space.

We drove down the road. It was a beautiful day, but it made no difference.

"Why won't you tell me what happened between you guys?" I asked her.

"Because I don't want to give him the satisfaction."

We pulled up to her house. She told me her garage code, where I could find her hiking boots, weed, and rolling papers. I wasn't in the house for long, but I hated every second I was alone. I purposely left my backpack next to the bed so I'd have a reason to come back.

We drove to Forest Park and sat in the parking lot with the windows slightly down. We didn't talk about Richmond and Ida. We didn't talk about anything. We listened to the latest Sharon Van Etten album, ate our sandwiches, drank coffee, and smoked half a joint. Every breath I took was slow and deliberate, bites quietly and thoroughly chewed. I coughed into my shoulder, terrified it would destroy the stillness in the car that I never wanted to end, this break from reality. People parked next to us. They made noise getting out of their car and talked loudly as they walked away, but they didn't exist in our universe. After a while we both put a hand on the armrest between us and interlocked our fingers, lightly, still not saying a thing. Then Liesel opened her door, and there was the ugly, no-good world again to greet us.

Parts of the world were beautiful, though. And Forest Park was serene. So, like in the car, it was easy not to speak. We were close to the top of the hill when Liesel tossed her Nalgene bottle onto the ground, leaned against a tree, and started to cry. She buried her face in my chest, I wasn't ready for it, got knocked back a few steps, close to the edge of the hill. She put her arms around me in a bear hug. I put my arms around her and pushed against her to move us away from the edge so we didn't fall to our deaths. I looked at Pittock Mansion towering above us at the top of the hill. A historic mansion built from the profits of paper mills. The trouble I felt right now, though, money couldn't help. Not prayer, either. I thought about that Psalm—*Where does my help come from?*

"Fuck those guys," she said.

"Yeah," I said. "Fuck 'em."

She moved out of my arms. Her face puffy and wet. She looked at me.

"Julian, I thought Ida wanted *you*. I thought you guys were going to be a thing."

"So did I."

"Do you think I should call him?"

"What are you going to say?"

"I don't know. How about you call Ida?"

"That's the thing. We were never together."

"Is that really how you see it? You're just going to let it go? Because I'm not."

"No, of course not," I said. "But Ida doesn't want anything to do with me, she's been clear about that. And Richmond, I don't know how I'll ever face him again."

"When's the last time you saw him before today?"

"Not since the night of the fire. I've been trying to avoid him, to tell you the truth."

"Why?"

"Because he was an asshole on tour."

"God, I can't believe I slapped him. I shouldn't have."

"I thought you were a pacifist."

"I am. It was the first time I've ever really hit someone. Where's the rest of your stuff?"

"At Anne's."

"Come stay with me?"

"That'd be great."

She drove me over to Skyler and Anne's house. The front door was unlocked. I grabbed my duffel bag from Anne's room and rushed out. No sign of William and Skyler, and that was for the best. I don't know what I would have told them if they asked where I was going.

34

LIESEL CAME WHILE SHE WAS on her side and I was on my knees behind her. I watched her walk out of the room as she headed for the bathroom. How wonderful. I looked up at the ceiling. Sex always changed everything, at least for a while. She got back into bed, turned onto her stomach, and propped herself up on her elbows. I turned onto my side and moved my left hand across her back until it rested on her right butt cheek. Goose bumps. She bit her bottom lip.

"This is nice," she said. "We should do more of this before I go."

"Yes, please," I said. "But where are you going?"

"Brooklyn, remember? My flight's in three days."

"I didn't know you already booked the ticket."

"Yes you did. I told you yesterday."

"I don't think you did. Not about leaving so soon, anyway."

"Stay with me until I go? I have to clean up and pack, but other than that I'm all yours."

"And after that?"

"Then I leave and we're just friends again. Anything more would mess things up."

I kissed her so she knew I understood. She grabbed my penis and looked in my eyes. I was hard again. She laughed. I pushed her onto her back. There was a knock on the door.

"Umm, Liesel, are you in there?"

It was Becky. She sounded concerned.

"One moment," Liesel said. We sat up in bed and held the bedsheet up to our necks. "Come in."

Becky opened the door, rushed inside the room, and shut the door behind her. She walked to the front of the bed.

"Umm, guys, so I'm all for what's happening here, but umm, Richmond's here."

"Richmond?" I whispered.

"He's in our living room."

"Why the hell did you let him in the house, Becky?"

"It was reflex. I mean, how many times has he knocked on our front door? I let him in and told him I'd tell you he was here."

"Jesus, Becky, Jesus."

"Geez, I'm sorry, okay?"

"Does he know *I'm* here?" I asked.

"No. And I didn't even know you were in here until just now, but I heard some music, so I knew Liesel was here. Not that I don't want you here by the way, I think you're a nice guy, but yeah, clearly there'd be a problem if he knew you were here, right?"

Becky had her eyes on the opened condom wrapper sitting on the nightstand. Liesel got up from the bed, fully naked. She put on a red zip-up hoodie and a pair of yoga pants and stormed out of the room. Becky and I gave each other a look, like, *oh shit, some shit is about to go down.* I threw off the bedsheet unconcerned about what Becky might see and quickly put on my clothes.

From the living room we heard Liesel yelling: "Get the hell out of here! How dare you come into my house. How long has it been going on, Richmond? Is she the real reason you broke up with me? You stupid asshole, get the hell out of my fucking house."

Becky and I were standing at Liesel's bedroom door. The front door slammed, then there was silence. Becky poked her head out to look down the hallway to the living room and front door.

"They must have gone outside," she said.

"I can't risk Richmond seeing me," I said. "Can you go out there and look around?"

Becky walked into the hallway. I poked my head into the hall to watch her. She walked out of sight into the living room, reappeared in the hallway, went out of sight into the kitchen, came back into the hall, then turned to me and whispered: "Come. Come quick."

I followed her into the kitchen. We stepped into the garage. Becky motioned her head toward the closed garage door, where we could hear them talking on the other side in the driveway.

"Can you stop calling me names? You slapped me today, remember?"

"And you deserved it, you deserve a lot more."

"I'm telling you the truth, there's nothing going on with me and Ida."

"Bullshit. You lie too much, and the worst part about it is that you've never been a good liar. But I put up with it because I loved you more than anything ever. But then you break up with me and do all this and still you lie. You've wasted three years of my life. I think I kind of hate you now."

"Liesel, Leese, c'mon."

"Goodbye, Richie."

"I swear, babe—hey, you can ask me anything and I'll tell you the truth."

"Okay, how many women have you slept with since you left me?"

"What? Are you serious? None."

"Well, I don't believe you. I want you to leave."

He left and we had sex again.

Still naked in bed, we talked about what I was going to do about not having a place to live. Liesel texted her uncle who was going out of the country for two months, to see if anyone was watching his house while he was away. We were drinking wine and eating big salads for dinner when her uncle texted back and said the person he had lined up to house-sit had just backed out. He was leaving in a week. Liesel got me the gig.

I called in sick for two days in a row. Tuesday and Wednesday. Ignored all calls and messages. Liesel and I spent most of that time in her bedroom. Then came Thursday, the morning of her flight. At the airport, I was hungover, drained, and in disbelief about everything that had happened. I took Liesel's suitcases out of the trunk of her car and put them on the curb. She grabbed her guitar out of the back seat and put it next to the suitcases. We hugged, then looked around before a quick kiss goodbye.

"I'll miss you," she said.

"Do you really need to go?" I asked.

"We can't spend the rest of our lives hiding from our problems."

"But we made a great attempt."

"Epic," she said. "No regrets."

"I'll miss you dearly."

"Are you going to tell anyone about us?"

"No," I said. "Are you?"

"No. It'll be our own little thing. A juicy secret."

"That's right," I said.

We shared one more hug before she picked up her things and headed for the entrance. There was plenty of luggage being carted around outside the terminal—car engines rumbled, people yelled, but I could still hear the wheels of Liesel's luggage rattling on the concrete, getting fainter, moving faster, until the only friend I could depend on disappeared through the rotating doors.

I stood there at the airport without a course of action. What was I supposed to do? Where was I supposed to go? A traffic cop must have seen my confusion. He blew his whistle to get my attention. I put my hands up, like, *What do you want from me?* He pointed at me. He pointed at Liesel's Jetta. I got into the driver's seat. The traffic cop was right, the car was mine until she got back. He pointed down the road. I put on my seat belt and drove to work.

35

FEELING SHITTY ON A BUS surrounded by other down-and-out people was a bummer. Driving was nice, but it would have been even nicer if Liesel's car had an automatic transmission. Stick shift always gave me trouble. I sat at a stoplight, waiting to get on the highway, the car in neutral. When the light turned green, I tried to let out the clutch to put the car in first. The engine went through the human experience: rattles, grumbles, and death. The guy behind me laid on his horn. I turned around and gave him the bird. He drove around me. We both had our windows down. As he passed me, he said, "What the hell, man?"

I gave him the bird again and screamed: "Go fuck yourself, motherfucker!" I managed to get the car in first without stalling and started down the highway. I felt like an animal. Like the only capabilities I had left were the means of survival. Which is why I had to go to work. Survival required money.

Back when I'd first gotten my driver's license, I was driving around town one night in the family minivan, nervous as hell, a sheltered Black evangelical teenager with no idea about the world except for that it was full of evil. I followed every traffic rule, every road sign. Made sure to keep a three-second distance between the minivan and the car ahead of me, but then some cars going in the opposite direction started to flash their high beams and honk their horns at me. I started to panic, I started to cry, I even started to yell, Why, oh why? What is it about me that you hate? Is it my skin? Is it me in particular? Am I some kind of joke? Can you see my sinful heart? Do you know I'm no good?

Turns out my headlights were off.

I arrived to work an hour late. The boss had his blinds open. He saw me walk into the building and waved me into his office. He was behind his desk, looking angrier than I'd ever seen him.

"Close the door," he said. "Sit down. Where the heck have you been the past two days?"

I squirmed in my chair. I decided to cut to the chase.

"I've been sad," I said.

"Sad?"

"Yeah," I said. "Sad. I'm sorry, but I've been too sad to work."

The boss didn't look so angry anymore. I don't think an employee had ever taken this angle with him.

"I'm sorry to hear that, Julian," he said. "I know you've been through a lot. But you can't do what you did and get away with it. You only called and left messages when you knew I wouldn't be in the office to answer the phone. And you never returned my calls. Not to mention you being an hour late today."

"It will never happen again," I said.

"I hope you're right because it can't happen again. Miss work again, you're fired."

"Sounds fair to me," I said. "Thanks for understanding."

We stood up and shook hands. He looked me in the eye and said, "Julian, you're my brother in Christ, man. And I really want you to work here. I pray for you all the time. But you have to want it too, bro. I need you all in. I don't associate with half-steppers."

"Okay," I said.

"Good."

I went back to my desk. Trenton stopped by and whispered, "Just tell me it was about sex."

"Sure it was," I said.

"Don't get fired. The boss wants me to start teaching you how to sell."

"But I don't want to learn how to sell."

"You won't be saying that once you start making commission," Trenton said.

After work I ate a big Korean meal in Beaverton. Far away from where any of my friends or associates lived. I didn't see anyone I knew, which was perfect. The house-sitting gig started in four days. I thought about getting a hotel, but the forty bucks I'd spent on dinner had put me dangerously low on funds. I had about two hundred in the bank, and I was waiting for my paycheck to deposit at midnight like it usually did, but I wasn't confident the check would properly include my vacation time and the holiday. I couldn't spend another dime until I knew for sure, I just couldn't do it. And I didn't want to stay with anyone I knew. But my neighborhood, St. James, was calling me.

I drove to St. James Park. A block from my former home. A place where cops rarely patrolled. I parked in the park's parking lot and passed out pretty easily in the front seat. The sun woke me up at six in the morning. I checked my bank account on my phone and saw that my paycheck was bigger than I'd expected. The two-dollar raise was a blessing, the boss was right.

I went to the gym, the person at the counter told me last month's membership payment had been declined. I told her I'd fix it next time I came in. I went to the locker room and put on my swim trunks. I sat in the sauna, trying not to feel homeless.

I figured it was only a matter of time before Richmond came looking for me, and I needed to stay a step ahead of him. It was already suspicious enough that he'd seen me with Liesel at the diner and I hadn't answered his phone calls or messages since. And he'd been sending some pretty earnest messages—saying he was sorry and he could explain everything and he just wanted to meet up and talk—and I'd ignored every one of them. I'm sure that had pissed him off. I wouldn't be surprised if he had put some facts together by now and was looking to beat me up for sleeping with his ex.

After a long shower, I put on the last pair of fresh underwear I had in my duffel bag and the least dirty and wrinkly work slacks and button-down shirt. I had forty-five minutes until I had to be at work, so I went to the grocery store, filled out an order form for a bagel breakfast sandwich, and headed for where they kept the bottled water. Someone put their hand on my shoulder. It had to be Richmond. My body told me to attack. My brain overruled. I turned around slowly, it was Anne.

"Hey there, stranger," she said.

"Oh, hey," I said.

She didn't look like a stranger at all; as a matter of fact, she looked the same as she'd always had, and when I thought about it, so did the grocery store, the workers, and the shoppers. Spring was just about over. Signs promoted summer produce: peaches, plums, figs, snap peas, beets, cucumbers, and berries. But other than that, it could have been March instead of early June. Nothing much had changed.

"How are you?" she asked. She reached for my elbow. Nothing much had changed except for me. For the first time ever, I didn't want her to touch me. I jerked my arm away and took a step back.

"Why are you shopping so early in the morning?" I asked.

"I'm still on mountain time from traveling," Anne said. "But I'm also an early bird, remember? But not you. You're never up and out this early."

"That's not true," I said. "And my being here now is proof."

"Well, how are you? Did you get the messages I sent after the fire?"

"I did."

"Then why didn't you respond?"

"Because I didn't feel like talking then, and I don't feel like talking right now either, okay?"

"Geez. Excuse me for caring."

"You don't care," I said. "Stop playing."

"You two doing okay over there?" the lady behind the deli counter asked. She was talking to Anne, not me.

"Yes, thanks," Anne said. She moved to the medicine aisle. I followed her out of habit. "Seriously," she said. "How are you? I haven't seen you since before the fire. What have you been up to?"

"If I tell you I'm fine, will you leave me alone?"

"I've missed seeing you."

"I haven't missed you at all," I said.

"Now you're just being a jerk."

She was right. But I couldn't get myself to act any different. I didn't mean to be rude, but I had no energy for her or the past pains she brought to the surface. Seeing her made me want to give up on life. Get in the fetal position in the middle of the grocery store and not get up until I was dragged away.

"You're right," I said. "I'm not being very nice, and I don't think I can be today. I should keep moving. I have to get to work."

"No, Julian—" Anne tried to reach for my arm. I didn't want her touching me. I jerked my arm away from her, hitting the handbasket she'd been holding hard enough to knock it out her grasp. The basket and its contents flew across the floor. She touched her cheek as if I'd slapped her instead of the basket. I almost reached out to touch her but stopped myself.

"I'm sorry," I said. "I didn't mean to do that."

Anne moved away from me and glared.

"Fuck you, Julian," she said. "You've lost your mind."

She pushed past me and walked out of the store.

Despite my not wanting to talk, I hadn't been trying to make another enemy. I had too many of those already. Her handbasket was toppled over in the middle of the aisle. Blood seeped out of butcher paper and spread across the floor to the bruised bananas and the French baguette. I stepped over the mess and searched for bottled water, beef jerky, and trail mix. Feeling low.

When we were kids, my sister and I would pretend that half of a store's floor was molten lava, and we would hop and jump for safety. And now here I was, an adult walking through the grocery store parking lot with a paper bag clutched to my chest as if it had the power to make me invisible.

After work I went to the downtown Powell's. I walked through the fiction aisles and picked out books from authors I'd told William I'd read even though I never had. I read a few sentences from Dickens and Dostoyevsky. I had no idea what they were talking about. Morrison was a winner. As was Joyce. I turned a corner and there was Skyler, wearing a light denim dress and a green baseball cap.

"Hey, Julian. Oh my gosh. *Beloved.* '124 was spiteful.' Toni Morrison is a saint. She's magic. My absolute favorite. Where have you been?"

"Just kicking around," I said.

"No one's heard from you. Why aren't you returning people's calls?"

"I've just been needing some space, you know?"

"Where have you been staying?"

"Around. I've got a house-sitting gig coming up."

"Great. Where?"

"On Seventeenth Street, but I'd rather you not spread that around."

"Well, good. I'm happy you'll be in the neighborhood. William doesn't understand why you won't talk to him, he's worried, we both are. Richmond's worried too."

"Have you talked to Anne today?"

"No, I haven't."

"I saw her this morning at New Seasons. And when I saw her, I accidently knocked over her handbasket, but I think she thinks I did it on purpose."

"Shit. Did you?"

"No, it was an accident."

"Did you apologize?"

"I did, but I don't think she accepted it."

Skyler rolled her eyes.

"Her partner is the nicest guy on the planet and all you do is rile each other up. I don't know why you two ever picked up in the first place."

Her and William in the van being chaste popped into my head.

"Yeah, you're right," I said. "Being riled up is just about the worst thing ever."

"Well, if you're looking for a place to relax," Skyler said, "I recommend reading by the waterfront. I did that yesterday for hours. A delight. I'd say you have about two hours of sunlight remaining."

I was happier to see Skyler than I thought I'd be. She was who she was, as someone once said. I knew where I stood with her. If she had a problem with me, she'd tell me. "That's a fine idea," I said.

"Take care of yourself," she said. "I want to see you again soon. Call William."

I drove to St. James waterfront park, sat on a bench that overlooked the river, tried to read but couldn't concentrate, there were too many people to watch on the stretch of beach below me. Sunset was coming soon. A woman partially covered with a shawl slipped a shoulder out of her one-piece purple bathing suit and freed a breast to feed her baby. On the other end of the beach, the other end of the age spectrum, an old man in a loose red speedo was walking barefoot in the sand. He struggled with every step, like a tin man in need of oil. He was smiling, his teeth white and gleaming. Between the distance of the baby and the tin man, a platform packed with teenagers floated in the river. Boys in board shorts that hit below the knees. Girls in bikinis that left nothing to the imagination. All of them trying very hard to look effortlessly cool and sexy. Standing tall with hands on hips, flexing, flirting, laughing. A group of rowdy boys pushed girls into the cold river. The girls pretended to be surprised.

A riverboat tour went by. It blew its horn. People on the boat waved to the people on the beach. The old man and the teenagers waved back. The mother turned her head. The baby kept nursing. I envied everyone I saw for having a place in this world carved out for them, at least for today, right there on the beach. But me on that beach? I would have changed the whole dynamic.

36

MY FIRST NIGHT SLEEPING IN the car had been easy because I'd been too exhausted to do anything but pass out. Tonight was tougher. I took a weed gummy and tried to relax. There were plenty of bars to go to and I thought about calling Keith, but I didn't feel like seeing my friends and I didn't want to see any strangers, either. I felt like I was forever stuck on tour and all I wanted to do was be home.

I reclined the driver's seat and tried to doze off. The car was parked behind the park's restroom building so it couldn't be seen from the street. I thought about Liesel. Not just the sex, the conversations, the quiet moments in bed. But I did think a lot about the sex. And those pleasant thoughts got me to thinking about Ida and all the bullshit. I still believed we could have had something special.

In my weed-clouded dream, someone or something was pounding on my head. I woke up to metal taps on the car windows. I opened my eyes to rays of light shining in my face. I leaned forward, keeping both hands visible within the crossbeam of the flashlights so they could see I was unarmed. "Roll down the windows, sir," a cop yelled. I didn't know what to do. The key was in the ignition. But I was afraid to move my hands. The cop on my left took his gun out of the holster and pointed it at me, the other cop put a hand on his gun and moved toward the front of the car to beam his flashlight through the front window. I put my hands up next to my head. "Roll down the windows now!"

Here comes death, I thought. A flashlight followed my right hand as it slowly moved to turn the key forward a click. The radio came on. A Russian-sounding violin concerto, a good song for homicide. Why had I taken that second weed gummy? The flashlight followed my right hand as I slowly pushed the knob to turn off the radio. I put my right hand into the air, then slowly moved my left hand to press the two buttons that rolled down the front windows.

The officer at the driver's-side window hunched down to get a better look at me, but I couldn't see much of him, his flashlight was shining in my face. "Evening, sir," he said. "License and registration please." His name tag sparkled from the beam of his partner's flashlight. It read, *D. Darlington.*

"Evening, Officers," I said. "May I ask what the trouble is?"

"Park is closed after dusk," said the cop at the passenger side.

"My wallet is in the center console. I'll have to open it."

"Okay, sir. Go ahead," Darlington said.

Making every move slow and deliberate, I opened the middle console, took out my wallet, and handed him my license.

"Registration too, please."

"It's probably in the glove box," I said. The other officer moved his flashlight to the glove box. I tried opening it. "It's locked," I said. I took the key from the ignition to unlock it. The glove box was stuffed with paper and loose compact discs. The flashlights hurt my eyes. I had to squint. I pulled out all the papers that looked promising. Put the pile on my lap and searched for the registration. I thought I might faint. A twenty-dollar bill fell out of a Christmas card.

"Is this your car, sir?" asked Darlington.

"A friend of mine's," I said.

Wrong answer. Darlington took a step back from the car and put a hand back on his gun. I dropped the papers I was going through and put my hands in the air. If he pointed that thing at me again, I didn't know what I'd do.

"So this isn't your vehicle?"

"No," I said.

"Anything in the car you want to tell us about, Mr. Strickland? Any weapons? Drugs? Paraphernalia? Anything illegal?"

My eyes must have looked okay or else he wouldn't have asked.

"No, sir," I said.

"Okay, Mr. Strickland, we're going to have to ask you to exit the vehicle."

"But why?" My eyes were watering.

"Probable cause. We need to determine if this vehicle has been reported as stolen or if there's a warrant for your arrest. Do you understand? Now go ahead and exit the vehicle slowly with your hands up."

"Do you want me to keep my hands up? Or should I do what I need to do to exit the vehicle?"

"I couldn't have been clearer. Exit the vehicle on your own before we have to force you out and put you in custody."

I managed to comply without being shot or tased. I sat on the curb next to the park's restroom building in handcuffs. The other officer's name tag said *Smith*. He had taken my backpack out of the car and was looking inside it, touching all my shit with his dirty cop hands, probably messing up my poem napkins. He stood about five feet away from me. He threw my backpack on the ground. There wasn't anything in that bag to find. The weed gummies were under the driver's seat. He held his heavy-duty flashlight next to his crotch like a mechanical dick with a spotlight on the tip and pointed it at my chest.

"Hey man, if you live in Portland, why are you sleeping in your friend's car?"

I wanted to tell him to go fuck himself, but I didn't want to get shot.

"I was taking a nap," I said.

"Shit," he said. "I get it. The sun and the beer just sucks it right out of ya."

"I haven't been drinking," I said.

"Not at all? Not a little nip or two before the nap? A little marijuana maybe? It's not a big deal, you can tell me."

"Nothing at all, Officer," I said.

While Smith tried to get me to admit any wrongdoing, Darlington sat in the squad car trying to determine how unlucky he could make me with technicalities of the law, I thought about my father. I used to play with his handcuffs all the time. How many people had he put them on and terrified like this? I'd rather not know. Here I was a homeless, God forsaken drummer with dreams of being a poet, stoned on weed gummies, sitting in handcuffs in a parking lot late at night. When my father was my age, he'd already had two kids and was doing exactly what these guys were doing. I'd grown up around guys like this; I was the one Black kid at their kids' birthday parties.

"My dad is a detective in Chicago," I said to Smith.

"Is that right? Hey, Darlington, this guy says his dad's a cop."

"I have his police union card in my wallet if you want to see it," I said.

The union card saved me. They uncuffed me. All thanks to my earthly father. Darlington gave me three citations: one for being in the park past dusk, one for parking in the park past dusk, and one for living in Oregon for over forty-five days with an out-of-state driver's license. The fines added up to about half of what I had in my freshly paid bank account. When I got back my driver's license, it had been cut in half. "That way you remember to get a new one," Darlington said. I didn't tell him to go to hell like I wanted to. I thanked him and said goodnight. They were letting me get in the car and drive away. And for that I was grateful. I had more living to do. Too much shit to figure out. I drove around a little until I was sure I wasn't being followed. I parked the Jetta in the driveway of the burned-out bungalow and cried myself to sleep.

37

REGGIE WAS KNOCKING ON MY window. Claire was there with him. I opened the door and stepped out.

"Did you sleep in there last night?" Reggie asked.

I pointed at the house that used to be home. Yellow tape saying CAUTION DO NOT ENTER went across the front door. The siding on the second story was blackened with fire damage, my bedroom window was boarded up.

"I've got a house-sitting gig that starts on Monday," I said. "But for now, all I have is this car."

"You should go camping," Reggie said.

"I don't have the gear."

"Come over to the house," Claire said. "We just made breakfast."

Peter had gone on a run. I sat down at their kitchen table. Waffles, bacon, eggs, and coffee. Claire sat across from me. Reggie to my left. The food was fantastic. Coffee exquisite. The kitchen table was made out of wood fit for the coffin of a king. The white marble countertops, the fine dinnerware, the soft linen napkins put me at ease.

After eating a bit of her waffle in the cleanest and most proper manner I'd ever seen someone eat a waffle, Claire said that when the bungalow was burning, Reggie thought he saw me trapped inside my bedroom.

"He ran toward your house," Claire said. "He kept shouting your name. Peter had to tackle him on your lawn and pin him to the grass until he calmed down."

"I thought I saw you in your window," Reggie said.

"You were going to risk your life for me?"

"You should have seen the look in his eyes," Claire said.

"I just wanted to see if there was anything I could do to help you."

"I really appreciate you trying to save me."

"Of course. You're my friend," he said.

"Maybe you saw the cat."

"Oh, how horrible," Claire said. "That little black cat that used to sleep on your porch?"

"Olympia," Reggie said.

"Right," I said. "No one knows what happened to her."

"I know it sounds crazy, guys," Reggie said, "but it wasn't Olympia. Maybe a shadow is the wrong way to describe it. It was like a human face being pressed against the glass."

"*My* face?"

"Somebody's face. I really saw something."

"Alright, M. Night Shyamalan," Claire said. "Too many scary films for you."

"C'mon, Mom, I know the difference between movies and real life, and this was a real face."

"I'm not a fan of scary movies," I said.

"Why?" Reggie asked. "Do you really think that stuff is real?"

"No, but it's how I was raised," I said. "Anything with possessions, or ghosts, or demons, I can't handle. It gives me nightmares."

"But you're a grown-up," he said.

Claire laughed, then she said in a deep voice, "REG-GIE. REG-GIE." She threw her linen napkin at her son's chest. Then she shook her head like she'd come out of a trance and said, "Wait, what just happened?"

We all cracked up laughing. Claire was such a different mother than my own; making fun of demonic possession would never fly in the Strickland household.

"My birthday's tomorrow," Reggie said.

"Awesome," I said. "Fourteen, right?"

"Yep. Will you come to the party?" he asked.

I looked at Claire and she nodded her head.

"Sure," I said.

"Great," Claire said. "It's tomorrow in our backyard. We would have sent an invitation in the mail, but we didn't know where to send it."

I wasn't sure why, but something had changed. Claire was being kind. Nothing like that nasty letter. Maybe it was the fear of losing me in the fire; or maybe something had clicked and she'd realized she should have never agreed with her husband to put that damn letter in my mailbox in the first place.

Whatever caused the change, I was grateful. I took the last bite of my delicious waffle and washed it down with a gulp of coffee. My stomach was full. The water was sparkling. Blood and oxygen were flowing. The sun was on my back. *Weekend Edition* played softly on the kitchen radio. Reggie got up to load the dishwasher. Claire got up to refresh our coffee cups with the rest of what was left in their Chemex. She sat back across from me, closed her eyes, and massaged the right side of her neck, her forearm pressed against her breasts. What a sight.

All was calm until Peter walked into the kitchen, glistening with sweat. Claire's eyes were still closed, but she could sense him. She put a hand on her shoulder. "Hey, babe," she said. Peter squeezed her hand and bent down to kiss the top of her head. Probably his typical

Saturday morning after a run: the kitchen silent except for the radio, his son cleaning up, his beautiful wife in a moment of meditation. The perfect life as far as I could tell. Then he looked up and saw me sitting across from his wife, drinking coffee out of his Stanford Alumni mug, and he started to look angry, but only for a second before his face quickly shifted to a smile. He came around the table and reached out to shake my hand. Pulled me out of my seat and hugged me hard with his clammy body.

"I probably don't smell too good, but it's so great to see you, man. How you holding up?"

He released me from his grasp.

"I'm doing okay."

"Yeah? I mean the fire. My God. We're heartbroken for you. I can't even imagine."

"Julian's coming to my birthday party," Reggie said.

"That's great," Peter said. "Did they tell you about the clown?" He opened the refrigerator, pulled out a clear plastic bottle layered with separated liquids, and shook the contents vigorously to mix it. He looked at Reggie and smiled. "You didn't tell him, did you? Because you know it's bizarre."

"What clown?" I asked.

"I'm having a clown at my birthday."

"But why?"

"Because I've always really wanted one."

"Always? A clown?"

"I'm serious. Mom and Dad know."

"For Reggie's first birthday he really wanted a clown," Peter said. "So we booked one."

"But the person canceled last minute," Claire said. "Reggie was so sad, we thought he might never forgive us."

"Next birthday he didn't want a clown, he wanted a laser tag party."

"Then the next year we went to Egypt to see the pyramids," Claire said.

"That was an awesome trip," Reggie said.

"Totally awesome," Peter said. "The clown thing never happened because we kept doing better and better things. Then two weeks ago, out of the blue, Reggie wants a clown."

"It's going to be hilarious. None of my friends believed me when I told them I was getting one. One of my friends bet me it wasn't going to happen."

"I hate clowns," I said.

"All clowns?" Claire asked.

"Yes," I said. "When I was a kid, I somehow saw a TV special about a serial killer named John Wayne Gacy who dressed up as a clown and went to children's hospitals. He lived in Illinois just like me. He killed young boys and buried them in his floorboards. Also, Bozo the Clown used to be popular in Chicago, and my dad would make us watch reruns of the show because it reminded him of his own childhood, but Bozo was scary and his show was weird. I could go on with examples. I could tell you about the recurring clown nightmares I used to have."

"Okay, we get it," Claire said. "You've had some terrible clown experiences. But the clown I booked has a million good reviews."

"A million, honey? More like three," Peter said. "But hey, if this guy actually shows up, he'll already be doing better than the last one."

Was this always how they acted as a family? Sort of jokey and carefree. Or were they putting on a show?

"Hey, Dad," Reggie said. "We found Julian sleeping in a car this morning."

"Christ, Julian, the car parked in your driveway? What's going on, man?"

"I told him he should have gone camping," Reggie said.

"It's a temporary thing," I said. "I got a house-sitting gig coming up."

"When?" Peter asked.

"Monday."

"Well, we can't have you sleeping in a car until then," Claire said.

She looked at Peter. A look I couldn't decipher: marital code. Peter walked over and stood beside her. She put an arm around his waist. She looked up at him and he looked down, and they smiled at each other. Then they turned their heads to look at me.

"You can stay in our guest room," Peter said. "As long as you need. Door's open. Only condition is you have to go sailing with us after I freshen up. It's beautiful outside. Great wind. We have to get out there."

38

CLAIRE SAID SHE HAD TO stay home to get the place ready for tomorrow's party. The rest of us piled into Peter's Range Rover. We crossed the St. James Bridge. Turned onto a small road that led to the sailing club parking lot. We walked down a long landing to get to the dock. The boat was sleek. Hull painted dark blue. The rest of it white and brown. Peter told me to hop in first. He handed me a cooler and a grocery bag, told me to take a seat. He untied the front of the boat, hopped on, and stood behind the wheel.

Reggie untied the back. He didn't get in. He stood there with the rope in his hand, letting the boat drift further and further away from the dock.

"I thought Reggie was coming with us," I said.

Peter smiled. He turned around and looked back at Reggie.

"You coming or what?" he yelled to his son.

"I'm going for the record," Reggie shouted back.

The boat was about two feet away from the dock. Now it was three feet away. The rope was almost straight in Reggie's hands.

"Okay, hotshot. That's far enough," Peter said. Reggie backed up a little and then ran and leapt off the dock toward the back of the boat. I feared he was going to miss and bash his head against the side of the boat, get knocked out and bloodied, and drown. But his feet landed on the deck. He fell forward into his father's waiting arms. They cheered. Peter smiled at me and shrugged.

"What can I say?" he said. "The kid's got hops."

We sailed until we reached the houseboats on the St. James side of the river. It was nice being on the water. Time rocked gently with the tide. Water whispered that all the trouble waiting for me on shore couldn't touch me as long as I stayed on the river. No Ida, Richmond, student loans, homelessness, cops, credit card companies, unfinished poems, or anything else that wasn't on the boat; everything was fine, there was no trouble at all.

Peter told Reggie to let the sails go slack so we could float along slowly and look at the houseboats. Some were small. Some were massive and angular, with second-floor balconies. Peter opened the cooler next to the captain's chair and took out two cans of beer. He handed me one, and then instead of sitting on the bench across from me like I thought he would, he sat next to me.

Reggie sat back by the wheel and surveyed the river, soda in hand, looking as contented as anyone could ever hope to be. The powerful waterproof sound system played Tom Petty's *Wildflowers*. An album I'd listened to nonstop right after my divorce, and therefore an album that usually brought up unpleasant memories, but on the water, the album was untainted.

We cracked open our beers. Peter looked at me and jabbed his shoulder into mine. "Cheers," he shouted. We took sips of our beers. He said something, but I couldn't really hear him. I tried to tell him I couldn't hear him, but with the wind and the music, I couldn't even hear my own voice. When Peter started talking again, I leaned closer. My life jacket dug into my underarms. His mouth was inches from my ear. "How do you like the boat?" He turned his head to hear my reply.

"It's great," I said.

"Glad you could finally make it, now let's have that chat."

He looked at me and smiled like he saw me putting it together that we were essentially alone. Based on the distance and the loud music, there was no way Reggie could hear us unless we stood up and screamed in his direction.

"So Julian, I'm curious, did you get the letter from Claire and me a few months back?"

"Of course. We stopped playing basketball. Remember?"

"I figured that, but what I can't figure out is why you thought going inside our house and baking a cake would be okay."

"He invited me."

"Yeah well, he's a kid, and you're an adult."

"I figured if he invited me, then it must be cool with you guys."

"Did you ask him if he had permission?"

"I meant no disrespect."

Peter smiled. When he spoke in my ear this time, I got hit with some saliva. "I believe that you meant no disrespect. I do. But you know, something I've learned over the years, in personal matters and in business, is that it often doesn't matter what someone's intention is. If you get bashed on the head with a baseball bat, it doesn't really matter why it happened, now, does it?"

"Of course it does," I said.

"Okay. Maybe I'm not speaking clearly enough. So I'll say this once and then we can put it behind us. Reggie thinks the world of you. If you died in that fire, it would have been hell for us. But if you ever try to tell my son again that my wife and I don't love him or that we're racist—which we are not, and you know that—I'll make your life worse than it already is. Do you understand me?"

"Hey man," I said. I stood up, looked down at him, and yelled,

"Fuck you. You must think you're talking to somebody else. If you want to fight, then we'll fight."

I looked over at Reggie. He didn't seem to notice that me and his father were about to duke it out. And man was I ready to go. *Fuck all the fake shit of life*, that must be what big-time fighters were always thinking.

"Whoa now, Julian. Take a seat." I sat down. "I'm not threatening you, okay? I'm just trying to tell you how I see it. I know you ain't nobody's bitch. But neither am I. And that's all I'm trying to say. I'm a good man and I'll do anything to protect my family. And I think you're a decent guy, I do. Let's try to move past this."

Peter reached out for a handshake. I handed him my empty beer can; he grinned. When he got up to put our cans in the grocery bag next to Reggie, he pushed his elbow into my thigh to lift himself up. I wanted to toss him overboard. But I decided to do what was best for the kid, and this boat, and me having a place to sleep tonight. I let myself relax. The sky was the kind of sky that made you believe there was someone up there who'd painted it. The sun was behind me. Lighting the path for once instead of blinding me. Until we turned back for the shore, and then, even with sunglasses on, it felt like the sun was trying to melt my eyeballs out of their sockets.

PART SIX

39

THE CLOWN ROLLED INTO THE backyard on a unicycle juggling five colorful balls and playing a harmonica. Impressive, but not enough to win over an audience of soon-to-be high school freshmen.

"*Whoa, amazing*," said a kid with an expensive bowl cut. The boys around him snickered. Reggie was among them. The clown stopped his unicycle, rocked back and forth to keep his balance, and added two more balls into his juggling routine.

"*You're so cool*," said the bowl-cut kid. More laughter from the other kids. The clown jerked his head forward to knock off his top hat, caught the brim of the hat with his teeth and tossed the balls inside. He put the hat back on. Still balancing on his unicycle. He produced a trumpet and blew out errant notes. He jumped off the unicycle and raised his arms in triumph. He had a very low and gravelly voice.

"Thank you, thank you. I'm Dupont the Clown!"

"What's wrong with this guy?" the bowl-cut kid whispered loudly.

"We're gathered here today to celebrate Reginald's fourteenth . . .

uh, uh, excuse me, I have the sniffles." Dupont reached into his pocket to pull out a handkerchief. "Oh my goodness, would you look at that." He pulled a rainbow of handkerchiefs from his pocket. Loads and loads of handkerchiefs all tied together. I was almost convinced it would never end. When it finally did, he brought the enormous wad of handkerchiefs to his face and said, "*AHHHHHHH! CHOOOOOO!*"

"Handkerchiefs are unsanitary," the bowl-cut kid yelled.

Not including Reggie, there were ten teens at the party, all white except for an Asian girl who, based on my limited observation, was the ringleader of that pack of girls, and I knew that was no small feat; it was already hard enough being the only minority in a group of friends, but to also push to the top of the social order took real coolness and determination. The teens sat on blankets in the grass, facing the clown and the backyard fence. Claire and Peter and another couple stood on the deck, their drinks and snacks sitting on the railing. I sat on a lounge chair to the left of the blankets, slightly stoned on the last of my weed gummies, sipping a gin and tonic.

The clown was holding a rope with just one hand, but somehow it stayed horizontally straight like it was a yardstick. He frowned and the rope went slack. He smiled and it went straight again. He took an invisible flea out of his hair and placed it on the middle of the rope. The rope sagged slightly from the weight of the flea. Dupont grabbed both ends of the rope and tossed the flea in the air; you could tell it landed back on the rope because the rope sagged a little where it landed. He bounced the flea higher and higher until it got lost in the tree above him. He pulled another invisible flea out of his curly red wig and handed it to Reggie, who was sitting on the front row of blankets. The clown told Reggie to toss the flea toward the rope. It was not a good toss; Dupont had to move out of the way so the flea didn't hit him in the face. He handed Reggie another flea.

"Don't despair," Dupont said. "I have thousands of fleas."

"This is boring. Saw someone in half!" the bowl-cut kid yelled.

"Cut it out, Kevin," Claire yelled from the deck.

Reggie's second flea landed perfectly. I applauded, but no one else did. Maybe it was the weed gummies, but I thought the clown was putting on a great show. I stood up to adjust my shorts, which had ridden up my thighs. At that very same moment, the clown asked for a volunteer from the audience.

"You, sir," Dupont said.

"Yes?"

"Are you volunteering or are you going inside for another refreshment?"

"I guess I'm volunteering," I said.

"Stupendous! Come on up!"

When I reached the clown, he told me to pick a card, any card. He fanned out the deck. I picked the card right under his thumb, thinking he'd never suspect it. He told me to look at the card, remember it, then put it in my pocket. I took off my sunglasses before I looked so he wouldn't be able to see the reflection. It was a three of diamonds. Once the card was in my pocket, he stroked his imaginary beard.

"Ace of spades," he said.

"Nope."

"Unbelievable. I'll be darned. This is the first time I've ever been wrong." Up close, Dupont was older than I'd thought he was. He wore a lot of clown makeup, had rouged-up cheeks.

Dupont guessed again. "Queen of diamonds?"

"Wrong again," I said.

"Okay, okay," Dupont said. "I was just having a little fun. Wouldn't be any fun if I just guessed your card straightaway now, would it? So here you are . . . This is your card."

The clown took off his top hat and produced a jack of hearts. When I told him that wasn't my card, he started to cry a comedic clown cry, a lot of *boo-hoo*s and shoulder bouncing. I thought maybe he wanted me to laugh at him, but I couldn't. Neither could anyone else. His sorrow felt real. Even the bowl-cut kid knew to keep his mouth shut.

While the clown boo-hooed, I saw Richmond walk into the backyard and stand next to my lawn chair. He looked at me quizzically, then smiled and pointed at me with his fingers like they were six-shooters. It had been almost a week since I watched Liesel slap him at the diner.

"Well, I guess my clown days are over," Dupont said. He tore the jack of hearts into tiny little pieces and threw them in the air. "I should just pack up and go."

Take me with you, I wanted to tell him, hide me in your magic top hat, let's get out here; that backstabber by my lawn chair might be here to kill me.

A blond girl sitting next to Reggie was on the verge of tears.

"Don't give up, Dupont!" she said.

"Yeah," Reggie said. "One more try."

"I want to see you do magic," the bowl-cut kid said.

"Winners never quit. You can do it!" the leader of the girls said.

"They're right, man," I said. "Give it one more go."

"Well," Dupont said. "Guess there's one more thing I could try." He picked up the torn-up card and put his hands together. He closed his eyes. He blew into the hole above his thumbs. Looked up to the sky like he hoped someone up there would reveal the card I'd taken from the deck and save his clown career. He closed one of his eyes and fearfully peeked into his hands with the eye that was open. He shook his head sadly. He blew into his hands again. Looked up to the sky and mumbled. He had a pained look on his face like he didn't know if he had the heart to look in his hands again, but he toughened with resolve and looked. He grinned crazily. He looked like the clown from my nightmares. But as he opened his hands, his smile became joyous. The torn-up jack of hearts vanished in a puff of smoke and a fresh three of diamonds appeared in its place.

It was magic. I was standing right next to him and didn't see any tricks. I handed him my card. Dupont held up both cards to show the crowd it was a match. Everyone hollered and clapped their hands. I was so excited I'd forgotten about Richmond, but there he was, clapping with everyone else. The bowl-cut kid lost his shit and ran around the backyard in circles. Reggie and the other boys followed his lead. I almost ran with them, if nothing else to find an escape route, but I decided to play it cool, like nothing had happened between me and Liesel and therefore I had no reason to fear confrontation. I walked over to him.

"That clown's fantastic," Richmond said.

"You should have seen him with his rope," I said.

We were standing about two feet away from each other.

"I've been looking for you."

"Did you come to St. James just to find me?"

"No. I'm meeting William at the bungalow. Grabbing the rest of my gear from the basement."

"Cool."

"But I noticed Liesel's car is parked in your driveway. Is she around?"

He surveyed the backyard like he was half expecting to see her. Claire and Peter waved at him, he waved back and smiled politely.

"She left town," I said.

"Then why is her car here?" He closed the space between us, got in my face. He looked tired and smelled like cigarettes. I took a step back.

"I'm borrowing it while she's gone."

"She let you borrow it, eh?"

"Yeah," I said. "That a problem?"

"I don't know," he said. "Is it? Where did she go?"

"Brooklyn."

"She kept threatening to go."

"Yeah," I said. "She left on Thursday."

"You guys fuck before she left?"

I tried to look offended.

"Are you serious? Of course not."

"Good," Richmond said.

Peter was watching us from the deck.

"This isn't the place for this," I said.

We walked across the street to the bungalow driveway. Richmond crossed his arms and shook his head at Liesel's Jetta.

"I can't believe she left," he said. "I've been calling and texting the both of you for days. Why wouldn't you talk to me?"

"Ida," I said.

"Nothing happened. I promise. But Liesel won't believe me. Last night I sent her an email telling her everyone I've hooked up with since we broke up."

"Why would you do that?" I asked.

"I just can't have her hating me like this."

"You told her about Miranda?"

"Uh-huh."

"Did you tell her about the lady in San Francisco?"

"No. We didn't actually hook up."

"Bullshit, man."

"That was just some shit I told Keith because he's Keith."

"Did Liesel respond to your email?"

He looked at the ground.

"Not yet, man, not yet. She thinks I'm no good. Can you call her and try to convince her to hear me out?"

"You guys are done. Why do you care if she believes you?"

"Because I still want her trust."

"Well, what if *I* don't believe you? You and Ida were holding hands."

"Yeah? So what? I hold people's hands all the time. I've held your hand."

"It was the way you were looking at each other."

"Christ," he said. "I bet you held Liesel's hand when she was complaining about me, didn't you? Probably looked her in the eye so she knew you were listening."

"Fine," I said.

"Exactly. Let's not be children. But bro, if you don't trust me like I trust you, then we're going to have a problem."

"There's no problem. I trust you," I said.

I wasn't all-the-way lying either. I didn't trust him, but I thought he might be telling me the truth. And if everything he said was true, then I was the bad guy, not him.

The front door of the bungalow opened. William ducked under the yellow caution tape that went across the doorframe and stepped onto the porch. "Is that you, Julian? I thought you were dead." We approached each other and met in the middle of our untidy lawn. "I heard you've been hiding out with Liesel."

"We got that squared away," Richmond said.

"Yeah," I said. "Stay out of our business."

"Julian, I would have left you at that IHOP in Sacramento if I knew you were going to come back to Portland and become an abuser."

"What are you talking about?"

He looked at me like he thought I was trash. "You've changed. I heard at the grocery store you got physical with Anne and told her to go fuck herself."

"Man, you can't be serious."

"Those are the facts. You've become abusive."

"You better take that shit back," I said. "You hear this, Richmond? This guy's calling me an abuser over some bullshit he doesn't understand. Talk about trust. I'm happy we don't live together anymore, dude. I'm done with you. I'm done with this band, too."

"Good," William said. "You're out anyway."

"Dudes," Richmond said. "Calm down."

"Nah," I said. "He's a phony fucking friend. A phony all around. A spoiled rich kid who wants to be a rock star. How original, William."

"Fuck you," William said.

"I've seen you in action too. You're so fucking phony, you don't even fuck your girlfriend, you chaste motherfucker."

"Oh yeah?"

"What are you guys even talking about?" Richmond asked.

"We're talking about how he's a shitty friend and a fucking phony fucker," I said.

"I'll show you fucking phony!"

William charged toward me.

"Whoa!" Richmond tried to get between us but didn't move quick enough. William pushed me onto the grass, grabbed my wrists, sat on my stomach, and looked down at me triumphantly. He must have been really mad to try such a thing, so mad that he forgot he had no muscle. I freed my arms from his grasp easily, rolled on top of him, and pinned his arms next to his magnificent face.

"Let go of me," he squealed.

"I'm not an abuser," I said.

"Fuck you, get off me," he said.

Richmond got behind me and put me in a headlock.

"Get off him."

"As soon as he stops struggling," I said.

Richmond tightened his hold around my neck.

"Let him go."

William turned his head and stopped resisting.

"Jesus Christ," he said. "Is that a clown?"

I turned my head. Dupont stood underneath Reggie's basketball hoop. He smiled at us and waved his arms. I let go of William. Richmond let go of my neck. We all stood up and waved hello to the clown. He opened the trunk of the Corolla he was standing next to and pulled out a cardboard box. He put the box on the street, then closed the trunk. He looked over at us and made a megaphone with his hands.

“I’m making balloon animals in the backyard. Would you fellas care to join us?”

“No thanks,” we yelled in unison.

The clown picked up the box and headed toward Reggie’s backyard.

“This band is staying the way it is,” Richmond told us. “Let’s go inside and talk this shit out.”

“I’ll talk, but no promises,” William said.

“Same,” I said.

William walked up to the bungalow and opened the front door. He ducked under the yellow caution tape. Richmond ducked too. I ripped the tape away and balled it up in my hands. I tossed it behind my shoulder onto the porch.

40

IT WAS THE FIRST TIME I'd been inside the bungalow since the fire. The smell was almost suffocating. In the living room, the ceiling beneath my old bedroom was black and sagging. We went to the basement. It had retained its familiar musty aroma. The smell of love and a song taking shape, becoming better than we could have ever imagined when Richmond brought in chords, a guitar riff or maybe a melody and we started figuring things out, deciding that the drums should be rolling with a subtle back beat, and the bass should be grooving but never too busy, that the song should be in a lower key, that the tempo was too fast, or maybe not too fast, it just was that the song was too short, it felt incomplete, it needed a drum fill, a bridge, maybe something arpeggio and syncopated based off the first chord of the song; and we'd keep at it, practice after practice, until the words William sang started to sound important, and then presto, magic had happened, we'd done it again, a new song. The basement smelled like all the hope in the world. I breathed it in lovingly. We all did.

"Okay," Richmond said. "This is official band business, one member in absentia. We've got to hammer this shit out."

We sat on the rug. Our recording equipment was still set up, microphones and wires everywhere, guitar cases, amps, various drum parts, empty bottles.

"If he wants to quit the band, let him quit," William said.

"Well then, how about I quit?"

"But you don't mean that."

"Sure I do."

"I thought you wanted to be serious."

"I'm not playing in this band without Julian."

"Richmond, he accosted our friend."

"She was trying to touch me," I said. "I didn't want to be touched. I knocked her basket over on accident while trying to get away from her."

Richmond put up his hands.

"Now see? There you go," he said. "A big misunderstanding."

"Why was she trying to touch you?" William asked.

"I don't know," I said. "I should have handled it better, but I promise I meant no harm."

"Okay, fine," William said. "But I feel like you hate me now for some reason."

I looked at him sitting cross-legged on the dirty rug in the musty basement. With his secondhand boots and clothing like he was just an average guy. But he didn't need to be slumming it. He could live in a house like Reggie's instead of this dump. But he didn't. It was like he was trying on poverty just for the experience. But how could I blame him for wanting the same things as me? For wanting to make great music with a group of people you respected and believed in. If he was here, it was because he wanted to be here, with me, with this band, and I when I thought about him that way, he was my friend.

"I don't hate you, man," I said.

"I don't hate you either," William said.

"You really want me out of the band?"

"No. Of course not."

The three of us stood up and hugged. Back to being brothers again. Sort of. We sat back down on the rug in the musty basement. The smoke smell was starting to hit my nose and I wanted to get out of there as soon as I could. I had a tough time pretending like me and Richmond were back on old terms. William told us he was close to finalizing a deal for our band with a Seattle-based indie label. They were small but influential. They'd put out Holly's band's debut album and they wanted us to work with the same producer. His studio was in Portland.

"They can get us a practice space, too," William said.

"That's rad," Richmond said.

"And money?" I asked.

"No," William said.

I went back to the birthday party. Dupont made me an elephant balloon animal. He didn't ask me what I wanted; he just gave it to me as soon as I approached him. And then he said the clowniest thing ever: "This is so you won't forget anything about today." And that was the last thing he told me. And to an extent, his magical mind had done it again. If I'd wanted a balloon animal, I would have totally wanted an elephant, that's true, but what was I supposed to do with the thing? Carry it from place to place until it lost all its air? A house-less Black man walking around St. James with a fucking balloon animal? Sorry, Dupont. I put the elephant in the trash bin next to Reggie's garage when no one was looking, and for a little while, in addition to everything else I had going, felt sort of bad for trashing the clown's gift, but got over it due to a confluence of bigger and more immediate issues. I mean, c'mon, I wasn't going to forget about lying to maybe my closest friend about sleeping with his ex. And I had grass stains on my shorts, stains aplenty. I didn't need a balloon to remind me how they'd gotten there.

41

LIESEL'S UNCLE HAD A SPACIOUS ranch house. I was told the large flat-screen television in the living room was to be covered with Pendleton fabric when not in use. When I was introduced to the dog, Walter, I thought maybe she was going to travel through South America for two months with Liesel's uncle and his partner, Manuel, because Liesel never mentioned a dog when she told me about the house-sitting gig. They told me they were leaving in a couple of hours, then I would have the place to myself. Before they left, they showed me around and gave me instructions. Manuel showed me how to dead bolt the side door. It was tricky. You had to put your shoulder into the door and drive your legs forward while turning the key to the left, but the real trick was that the key needed to be inserted just so and turned just so. After his demonstration, I tried it myself and failed. He told me to try again. He said the lock and key needed to be in perfect position to submit to each other's will; he said to close my eyes and feel for the tumblers; that's it, he said, now push harder into the door. When I finally got it locked, he told me I had beautiful calves and the deftness of a safecracker. I didn't know if he was hitting on me or if that was just the way he talked. Liesel's uncle showed me how to work the television, the dryer, the washer, the dishwasher, and the stove. He directed my attention to the important information stuck to the front of the refrigerator. Once I had the Wi-Fi information, I thought I was all set, but no, not in the slightest. They handed me three pages of detailed instructions for keeping Walter the dog happy and alive.

After the homeowners left, I let the dog into the backyard. She ran across the wooden deck and went straight to her favorite tree. I'd never had a dog and had never taken care of one. Walter was a rescue. A boxer. They gave me a ton information about the dog, but I never caught why her name was Walter. Liesel's uncle said she should be kenneled when I went to work or bed or anytime I wasn't in the house because it made her feel safe and ensured there weren't disasters. It had been a long Sunday. I had to work in the morning. I decided to turn in. I followed the instructions and locked Walter in her cage, even though it made me feel like a monster. Cages were no good. I'd watched a scary movie about people in cages with Reggie and his family, so when I locked up the dog I imagined myself being locked up instead, and it made me want to die.

Trenton insisted on going out to lunch. We went to a nearby deli. My jaw hurt. My body ached. The bed in the master bedroom had been the comfiest bed ever, yet still I'd tossed and turned all night. Probably slept for a total of two hours. I'd drifted off just as it was beginning to get light outside and was painfully awoken when the alarm clock blared talk radio at seven in the morning and the dog started howling. At the deli, I was so tired, I ordered the big meat sandwich special and didn't think about how rough it would be to eat that meal and then have to work for four more hours with all those meats working through me, until the person at the counter had already written down my order. I reached for my wallet to pay.

"No you don't," Trenton said. "I got his order, miss."

We sat down to eat at one of the few tables in the small deli. I told him about my dog-sitting situation.

"I don't like living with dogs," he said. "All that hair."

"I don't mind it," I said. "You're not alone, but you're not with a person."

"How are you doing otherwise?"

"If morning prayer had gone on any longer this morning, I would have fallen asleep."

"Another wild night?"

"I wish," I said. "Actually, I was wondering if I could talk to you about something serious."

Trenton raised his eyebrows.

"Are you sure I'm the person to talk to?"

"I got no one else."

"None of your band buddies?"

"Those guys are part of the problem."

"Why haven't you ever invited me to a show?"

"I invited you once and you didn't come."

"I didn't really know you back then."

"Shit, man. I'm sorry. The next show I'll tell you about."

"Okay. I forgive you. Now shoot."

"So, I slept with my bandmate's ex-girlfriend."

"Recently?"

"Pretty recently."

"Multiple times?"

"Yeah."

"Good," he said. "If you're going to do something like that, you might as well make it worthwhile. Still going on?"

"She's in New York now."

Trenton picked up little pieces of sauerkraut that had fallen onto his plate and put them back into his sandwich. He took another bite and scrunched his face. "This Reuben could use a martini."

"Seriously," I said. "What should I do?"

"Nothing."

"Nothing?"

"Does he know about it?"

"No, he doesn't."

"Is she going to tell him?"

"No, she told me she wouldn't."

"Then what's the problem?"

"How can I ever play with him again, knowing I'm such a fucking liar? This could end up breaking up our band. I have to come clean."

"Now listen to me, honesty is not your best policy here. Telling him the truth would be a shit sandwich wrapped in a cute package with a pretty little bow. Trust me. I've been there. Best to keep your mouth shut."

"I just pretend like it never happened?"

"That's right. You eat your shit sandwich."

"I'm confused. Didn't you say not to eat the sandwich?"

"Think about this morning's sales training. Stick to the script until it stops working."

Trenton had eaten everything on his plate. I couldn't take another bite of my barely touched big meat special.

"But I can't sleep," I said.

He smiled. There was sauerkraut in his teeth. "Oh, now I understand. You want to clear your conscience so you can sleep. Now that, my friend, is something I can help you with."

When we got to Trenton's car, he handed me a bottle of unmarked pills.

"Be careful," he said. "This stuff could knock out an elephant."

• • •

Walter went bonkers as soon as she heard me put the key in the door. I walked into the house and went over to her cage in a corner of the kitchen. She panted and barked and spun. I unlatched the gate and she shot like a thoroughbred toward the sliding glass doors that led to the backyard, *clickity-clack*, *clickity-clack*, *screech*, *thud*—she lost her footing on the tile and slid into the tempered glass. She got up and shook it off.

I put on Walter's leash. We went on a walk. Same guy as always was working behind the counter at the St. James liquor store. When I walked in he said, "Hey, Julian, welcome back." I nodded and smiled and said, "Hey man." Any store I frequented in the neighborhood, the people who worked there seemed to know my name. A masked robbery would be impossible for me to get away with. All it would take was a flash of my brown skin, and they'd know it was me, their only Black regular.

The liquor store guy could see Walter through the window. He gave me a dog biscuit when I paid for my gin. When I got outside, the dog knew I had something. She jumped around excitedly. I put the paper sack with booze on the ground and told her to sit. I told her to shake, she put out a paw, we shook. I loved the rough, squishy feel of the pads on her paw. I told her she was a good dog and gave her the biscuit and patted her head. We walked the few blocks to the sushi place.

Ida had ruined the coffee shop for me, but there wasn't anyone in the world who could ruin my Ichiro's sushi craving. Ida, even though she didn't want to see me, and even if she slept with Richmond and lied about it, I missed her. I wrote her long and short text messages, but they never came out right, so I deleted them before I could hit Send.

I'd ordered the sushi ahead so Walter wasn't tied up for long. We took the long way back to her house. Keeping a wide berth from my former home, and Anne's house, and any major streets. I wanted to see no one. I wanted to drink a martini like the salesmen disciple of Trenton that I was and eat sushi and watch television with Walter and not think about anything at all, especially not Richmond, or Liesel, or Ida, or my family, or any part I might have played in messing shit up.

Walter's food station was in the laundry room. I emptied a can of wild Alaskan salmon into her food bowl and topped it with a handful of kibbles as I'd been instructed. Leaving her to chomp in peace, I went off to make a martini. I hadn't tried to make one in years. I found a martini shaker and an unopened dry vermouth bottle in the cupboard where Liesel's uncle kept the booze. I pushed the shaker against the ice dispenser on the refrigerator door. I cracked open the bottle of gin and poured it into the shaker until I counted slowly to eight, then a splash of vermouth. I shook the shit out of the shaker until my hands were freezing. I strained the drink into a martini glass. The glass was almost overflowing but there was still more liquid in the shaker. I took sips from the glass to make room, strained in the rest of the martini, drank more down so I wouldn't lose gin when I plopped in three olives. Trenton would have been proud.

I sat down on the leather couch in the living room and turned on the television. The martini and sushi container were on the coffee table in front of me. I put on *Sister Act 2*. A movie I'd probably seen ten times. Lauryn Hill was my first Black celebrity crush. I tried not to think of Ida. While Whoopi Goldberg was teaching the kids how to sing "Oh Happy Day" with authority, I got a call from Richmond. I ignored it. He didn't leave a voice mail or follow-up text. I thought about calling Liesel to see how she was doing. But getting away from her Portland problems was why she'd left town.

The martini got me drunk, and I was already exhausted, I passed out. I woke up about ten minutes later. The sushi container had been knocked off the coffee table. Raw fish all over the living room rug. Walter was chomping away.

"Goddammit!" I yelled.

She looked up at me quizzically. Put her head down to finish off a shogun roll. It was nine o'clock. I was drunk and groggy and starving.

I let the dog out in the backyard and went back to the living room to clean the rug.

Walter came back into the house and found me in the laundry room eating her premium wild caught salmon straight from the can. She barked. I waved my fork.

"It's only fair," I said.

I locked Walter in her cage and went to bed. And there I was again, same as the night before, racked with lust and guilt and despair. Around midnight I got out of bed and went to the kitchen and took one of the sleeping pills Trenton had given me.

When I woke up, the bedroom was much brighter than it should have been. Right then I knew I was going to be in big trouble. I arrived to work two hours late, ready to get chewed out by the boss before he fired me. But he wasn't there. His daughter was behind his desk doing my former job of answering the phone. But not the newsletter. Until I got fired, that job was still mine. Ailana put a finger to her lips and winked at me. John wasn't at his desk either. I walked over to Trenton, who was on the phone. He told the person to hold on for a second then pressed the mute button on the side of his headset.

"What the hell is wrong with you?"

"Where's the boss?" I asked.

"An in-person sales call in Salem."

"I took one of your sleeping pills and it knocked me the hell out."

"I told you to take half a pill."

"No you didn't," I said.

"You have to build a tolerance."

When the boss came into the office, no one told him a thing. I was safe. Was it God or luck? My mother says you couldn't believe in both.

I sent a quick thank-you to God just in case he'd been the one responsible. During my McDonald's lunch, which I ate alone in Liesel's car, I pulled up my personal email on my phone. I had something from Susan. Presumably, after I'd taken the sleeping pill and fallen asleep, I'd gotten out of bed like a zombie at three in the morning, walked across the bedroom to the armchair where I kept my phone charging, and sent Susan an email detailing my dilemmas. I had no recollection of writing it, but the proof was glowing on my screen. My email to Susan had been long and meandering. Her response was to the point:

Dear Julian,
So good to hear from you. I'm sorry to hear about the fire. Stuff is just stuff. I know that's a strange thing to say from a woman with so many sentimental things in her apartment, but it's true. Ease up on the sauce. Follow your heart. If you need to tell this Richmond everything, then tell him everything and live with the consequences. But do it for you, not for him. And regarding Ida. If you think this could be the kind of love we were talking about after Ilyich, go for her one more time. Tell her how you feel and let her reject you a second time. Rejection is a smaller wound than longing. Call me if you need to. Let me know how everything shakes out.

Your comrade,
Susan

I listened to her advice about the sauce. I pulled it together for the rest of the workweek. Established a nighttime routine: a four-second-pour martini; half a sleeping pill; in bed with a novel by ten; lights out by eleven. By Friday I felt somewhat healthy and responsible. The boss was gone by four, the rest of the guys made follow-up calls, set their game plans for Monday, and left. Sometimes on Fridays the boss would let me leave an hour early and pay me for a full day of work, but he'd made no mention of that before leaving for the day, so I stayed at my desk. The office was empty. I had nothing to do. I put on my headphones and listened to Wire. I was itching to get behind a kit.

When my work phone rang at 4:58, I was already standing with my backpack slung over a shoulder, ready to bolt at five on the dot. I picked up the receiver. I figured it would be a call for someone else. Just a quick transfer to the appropriate voice mail.

"Marketing Monkey, this is Julian."

"Hey, dude, it's Richmond."

I wanted to throw the phone across the room, but the receiver felt glued to my ear. I dropped my backpack on the thinly carpeted floor and fell into my executive office chair.

"You there?" he asked.

"Yeah," I said. "I was just about to leave. Why are you calling me at work?"

"Because I knew you'd answer if you were still there. Can't say the same about your cell."

"What's up?"

"Want to meet for a drink?"

"When?"

"I was thinking in half an hour."

"I would, but Liesel's uncle has that dog."

"Bring Walter along."

"Yeah?"

"Yeah," he said. "We'll meet somewhere you can walk to."

"Alright," I said. "How about the Magpie? It's on Tacoma right after you cross the St. James Bridge."

"I know where it is. See you in half an hour."

He hung up.

42

BEFORE WE LEFT FOR THE Magpie, I got on my knees and had a serious talk with Walter. "Now listen," I said. "Richmond may try to attack me. If he does. I need you to bite the shit out of him. If he doesn't let go of me, find help. Can you do that?"

She barked.

The place was only a few blocks away from the house. When I got there, Richmond was sitting on a bench out front, smoking a cigarette and drinking a beer. He stood up to give me a hug, he put his cigarette in his mouth and bent down to rub Walter's face. She tried to lick him and jump all over him.

"Walter. Oh, Walter, it's so good to see you, girl, yeah, oh yeah, that's a good girl." Richmond looked up at me as he pet the dog. "I got her. Go inside and get a beer. Put it on my tab."

The Magpie served fancy beer but tried to act unpretentious. A bluegrass trio played in a corner. Washtub bass, Liesel would love that. I made my way slowly to the bar. The walkways between tables were narrow and there were people standing in the middle of the room with their beers as they watched and listened to the music being played. Moneyed St. James residents and people across the river liked to come here after work. When I finally got to the bar, Peter sat on a barstool next to where you're supposed to order.

"Hey man," Peter said. "Good to see you. How's the new place working out for you?"

"It's going just fine," I said.

He seemed to be by himself. He was drinking something dark.

"Care to join me? Not any room here, but we might be able to snag a spot out back."

"I'm sorry, I can't. I'm here with someone."

"Nice," he said. "A lady?"

"Nah, just a dude from my band."

The bartender asked what I wanted. He poured the beer then asked how I wanted to pay. I told him to put it on Richmond's tab. He asked if that was the first name or the last name. It took me a second to remember.

"Andrew," I said. "Andrew Richmond."

I got the beers and started to walk away.

"I'll see you soon," Peter said. He patted my back. "Don't be a stranger."

"See you," I said.

I didn't know what I was going to do. Before I saw Richmond, I had it in my mind I was going to tell him about me and Liesel, and I'd been prepared to deal with the consequences, but after seeing him in the flesh, watching him play with the dog, acting like the same old friend as always, I was thinking about eating my own shit sandwich. I mean, finally, finally, I was in control of a situation. And here I was looking to blow things up. Foolish. Maybe Trenton was right. It would be a funny picture if it wasn't me in the middle having to make a decision, but I had a little cartoon Susan whispering in one ear, and a little Trenton whispering in the other.

I sat down on the bench across from Richmond. He offered me a cigarette. I'd been doing a good job not smoking, but needed all the help I could get. Richmond lit a match. He cupped his hand over the flame and reached over the bench to light my cigarette. I thought about Ida, when I'd lit her spliff with ease but had wished for wind in the alley.

He shook out the match. Walter was under the table with her head resting on his lap. Whose side was she on? I hoped she was getting herself ready to chomp. We said cheers to our record deal.

"William's fixing it up as we speak," Richmond said.

"That's great," I said. "Not playing is killing me."

"Same," he said. "This band is my religion. I believe in us so much. I do. When we're all locked in together, I don't know a better feeling."

I didn't want to get beat up, but I loved this dude. Something needed to be done. I needed to be able to play with him for years to come with no big secrets. I couldn't see Walter's eyes, but her face was still in his lap. I hoped she was prepared to bite him if he tried to kill me.

"I need to tell you something," I said. "I stayed with Liesel after we saw you at the diner. We were together until I dropped her at the airport."

Richmond lit a cigarette. He looked sad, but not angry. He scratched Walter's head, then looked me in the eye for a long time.

"Ouch," he said. "Always the people you love."

Walter stayed comfy in his lap. He finished his beer and scratched the dog's head. I was waiting for him to say more, but he just sat there and looked at the cars driving by. A tear slid down his cheek. He wiped the tear away with the back of his hand, and then kept on scratching the dog.

Peter walked out of Magpie holding two full amber-colored beers, I'd never been happier to see him. He set the beers on the table and introduced himself to Richmond.

"You caught some of that clown show last weekend," Peter said.

Richmond perked up and put a fake smile on. "Yes I did," he said. "What a clown."

"My wife was the only one who believed in him. Ask Julian, he knows. Hey, these beers are for you guys."

"Are you sure?" Richmond asked.

"Yeah. A friend of Julian's is a friend of mine."

"Thanks," I said. "Care to join us?"

"I'd love to, but I'm making dinner tonight. You guys take care."

Peter looked both ways before he crossed the street.

"He's a nice guy," Richmond said. "But you."

"I know," I said. "I don't understand why you haven't punched me yet."

"I can't believe she fucked you and still had the nerve to slap me."

"We didn't hook up until after the slap."

"Shut the fuck up before I slap you like she did," Richmond said. "But dude, I need to tell you something about me and Ida."

"What is it?"

"We didn't hook up the night before the diner. But we've hooked up in the past."

Chomp him, Walter, I thought. *Just go ahead and chomp him.*

"You used to hook up? Like how long ago?"

"Last year, we were both each other's person on the side. I'm not going to lie to you. It was intense. But it didn't go on for long because we decided we had to fix our main relationships."

"Hold on," I said. "I have to go to the bathroom."

Inside the Magpie, I waited in line for the restroom and fumed. I could picture the two of them fucking and I didn't like it. Those stupid faces he makes when he plays a guitar solo, did he make those faces in bed? How could Ida take that seriously? How could Liesel? Oh God, I was mad, and I was jealous.

I sat back down at the table with two more beers that I'd put on his tab. Walter was drinking water from a bowl next to the bench.

"How long did it last?" I asked.

"A couple of months," he said. "Nothing has happened recently though. I promise."

"God," I said. "What a mess."

"A big fucking mess," Richmond said.

"I'm sorry," I said.

"Me too, man," Richmond said. "I won't lie and say I'm not hurt about how some of this went down. But a lot of it is my fault."

"Screw that talk, man," I said. "I'm sick of the past. It's a trap."

Richmond smiled big. We reached across the table and shook hands.

"The only looking back I want to do," Richmond said, "is playing in Philadelphia or something and seeing you behind the drums."

"No more lying to each other," I said.

"Never again," he said. "We can lie to the others, but not to me and you."

Everything that needed to be said had been said. We finished our beers. Hugged and parted ways. I still didn't know about God, but I knew the soul existed, and that I had one, and Richmond had one. And it wasn't the beers telling me this. It was the truth. I knew it was some hokey-ass bullshit, but the soul was something I could believe in. I hadn't thought about God or sin at all when I was in despair about betraying the trust of a friend.

43

BRIDGETOWN RECORDING AND PLAYBACK, THE studio our band would soon be recording in, was having a party tonight and we'd been invited. I found out from Richmond that the studio was in a warehouse adjacent to the one Ida's art studio was in. Was that God or luck? If I couldn't know anyway, I guess it didn't matter. I just hoped I'd get to see her.

Reggie came over to the house to watch Walter. After I gave him the spiel about caring for the dog, I showed him how to dead bolt the side door.

"But why would I use the side door if I can just get into the backyard through the patio instead?"

"Hey man, I'm just giving you the rundown, okay? If you don't want to use the side door, then don't use it, but if you do use it, it's going to be tough, so I want you to know how it's done. You can eat and drink whatever you want. Anything except for the booze."

"Very funny," he said. "I don't drink. I promised my dad I wouldn't until college."

I left him in the backyard with the dog and had a shot of whiskey in the kitchen. I went to the bathroom and brushed my teeth so hard my gums bled. When I went back outside, Reggie was sitting on a deck chair waiting for Walter to fetch a tennis ball he'd thrown into the bushes.

"Walter's a girl," he said.

"Yeah."

"Then why's her name Walter?"

"Not sure," I said. "But it suits her, doesn't it?"

Walter came back with the ball. Reggie pretended to throw it one way, and once Walter was on her way toward the phantom ball, he threw it in the other direction. They seemed to be getting along just fine.

"When do you think you're coming home?" Reggie asked. "I have to be home by ten. If you won't be back before then, text me."

"Your formal date isn't coming over, is she? No visitors allowed."

"Natalie? No way."

"The bedrooms are off-limits."

He laughed. "We're virgins. We don't do that kind of stuff."

Reggie made being a virgin sound sophisticated. He had no religious hang-ups as far as I could tell. He seemed to have handled being adopted better than I'd handled anything ever. His family was rich. He took advanced math classes. He was close to six feet tall, almost as tall as I was. He was lanky, but hormones and the weight room would fix that in time. He was a great human being. What good was I to him?

"You're a great guy, did you know that?"

"Yeah, sure," he said. "People tell me that all the time. Want to start playing basketball again?"

"Are you looking to get beat? Now that you're growing up, I'm going to have to start using my post game."

"It doesn't matter what you do," he said. "I'm a walking bucket."

"Oh, for real? You think you that nice?"

"I get better every day," he said.

"Better every day doesn't mean you're at my level."

"You're crazy," he said. "You need to be honest with yourself."

I laughed. "Damn," I said. "That's the truth. But hey man, I should get going."

Reggie got out of the lawn chair to shake my hand. He was a gentleman. I would be in his corner for as long as I lived. I thought about his birth mother being a stranger to him. Anyone like that could use a friend like me. I understood what abandonment felt like. How it could eat at your soul, make you question everything.

44

I CROSSED THE ST. JAMES Bridge and got onto the highway. I hadn't stalled in days, but I still had to think through every step until I got the car in fifth gear. There was a cop car sitting on the highway median. I eased up on the gas. Now that my Illinois license was broken in half and I'd been given a citation for it, I was more afraid than usual about getting pulled over. That cardboard box I'd lost in the fire had held my most important documents. I couldn't get a new license until I called my mother and asked her to send a copy of my birth certificate.

Problem was, I wasn't ready to speak to my parents. They would wonder why I'd taken until now to tell them about the fire, and I wouldn't have a good answer for them aside from avoiding uncomfortable conversations. I was afraid they would inquire about my relationship with Christ. And the past few months had pushed me to the limit. I was sick of lying to the people I loved. Jesus was now a fence that separated us. *Hey, Mom. Yeah, it's really me, Julian, your prodigal son. Listen, I lost all my stuff in a fire. I'm homeless and I don't think I believe in Jesus anymore and I need you to send me certain documents to confirm my identity to the Department of Motor Vehicles.*

I took the Williams Street exit and drove slowly until I found the road that led to the industrial park. The road was no more than an alley that ran between warehouse structures and came to a dead end at a fence. Beyond the fence was a dirt field. As I drove toward the field and the fence, the sun flashed from behind some clouds like God was trying to send me a message in a language that I no longer understood. Did he want me to go full throttle and blast through the chain-link fence? Because it wouldn't surprise me. He only seemed to talk to people with nutty ideas.

Seven o'clock on a Saturday night, but people were still working in some of the warehouses. I heard motors, loud banging, industrial saws, guitars, and crashing symbols. I parked the car. I got out and headed for the thumping bass. The music ended before I made it to the stairs. People came out of a door on the second level of one of the warehouses. They walked partially down a metal staircase, stopped and lit cigarettes. Keith and Richmond were among them. I walked up the stairs.

"Well, well, well," Keith said. "If it isn't the international man of mystery. The thief in the night. The funky drummer. The Benson Bubbler. The Purdie Shuffler. Black Jesus in the flesh."

"Shit," I said. "You that fucked up already?"

"I haven't seen you in weeks."

"Sorry, dude."

Keith gave me a hug.

"Who is she? Do I know her?"

Richmond slapped my shoulder in greeting.

"Julian told me yesterday it had nothing to do with a woman," he said.

"Right," I said. "I was on a spiritual journey."

I took a drag from Richmond's cigarette and a sip from Keith's beer.

"Learn anything while you were away?" Keith asked.

"A man's fate is to die. But life is worth the trouble."

"Sounds like a fortune cookie," Keith said. "Got any drugs?"

"You think I've gotten this far as a Black man, driving around with drugs?"

"Did you drive Liesel's car here?" Richmond asked.

"Yeah," I said.

"Then you're a Black man who drives around with drugs."

We clunked down the metal stairs and walked down the alley until we reached the car. I unlocked it. Richmond sat in the passenger seat, right leg hanging out the car to keep the door open, foot planted on the dusty concrete. He asked me for the key. I handed it to him. He opened the glove box without it.

"This should be locked," he said.

Keith had been peeing on the dead-end fence. He was finished now. He came over and stood at my side. He was wearing button-fly pants and having a hell of a time getting one of the buttons to stay in place, so he kept looking down and fussing. Richmond fished around the glove box until he found a small leather pouch. He tossed it to me. Inside there was a pack of rolling papers and a medicine bottle full of weed.

"Shit," I said.

"Nice, huh? Liesel didn't even know it was there. I got emergency blow taped inside the spare tire in the trunk."

"Let's do the blow," Keith said.

If the cops in the park had found drugs, they would have fucked me up good.

"Later," Richmond said. "We have to make a good impression first."

We found an unused loading dock and sat on the concrete slab. We leaned against the rusty door and passed around a joint. The stretch of warehouses reminded me of the movie I saw the night I stayed at Reggie's house. It was the kind of movie Keith would know.

"Keith," I said. "You like campy movies; you ever see the one where this baseball coach loses his family in a waste dump explosion and then decides to hunt down the people responsible and put them in cages and interrogate them before dumping them in the same toxic waste that killed his wife and kids?"

"Fuck," Richmond said. "Is that a real fucking movie?"

"*Earth Justice*," Keith said. "It sounds stupid and it kind of is. The acting is mostly horrible. They shot it in like two weeks on a shoestring budget in warehouses just like these. But man, I gotta say, some of the writing is pretty fucking good."

"Good writing? We can't be talking about the same movie," I said.

"Dude," Keith said. "Remember when the CEO is in the cage, talking to the baseball coach, but he doesn't know he's talking to the baseball coach, because the baseball coach is disguised as a janitor?"

"Sure, I remember."

"The speech he gives really struck a chord with me. I learned it for an acting class I took a while back. I know it all by heart."

"Prove it," Richmond said.

"Hold on, let me think," Keith said.

He jumped off the loading dock ledge and walked in circles, puffing away at the joint, mumbling to himself. He handed me the joint. He stepped back and furrowed his brow like the CEO did in the movie, put his hands up like he was gripping a cage and pondering the unfairness of life.

"So yeah, I was at the doctor's office the other day because I had a stroke a while back and the doc wanted to run some tests. He loves tests, but I never liked them, especially the ones you can't cheat, you know what I mean? You're a baseball coach, so I know you know what I mean. Most umpires should be hung. So I'm in the waiting room, reading a sports magazine, leafing through while I'm waiting, and uh, there's this advertisement with this gorgeous woman smiling up at me with her perfect tits and white teeth, perfect body in this little red bikini. She's holding a drink like she's offering it just to me, like everything I'm looking at is just for me. Her, the palm trees, the gorgeous beach, not a piece of trash anywhere—"

"What the hell are you talking about?" Richmond said.

"Hey man," I said. "Let him finish."

"I'm sitting at the doctor's office, staring at this picture in the sports magazine. And I got this little grin on my face. This lady sitting next to me sees what I'm looking at and she gives me this look like I'm some kind of scumbag sexual-predator type. Right then they call my name, and I get up to see my doctor, but before I walk away, I toss the lady the magazine and I say, 'Oh, get over yourself, lady. I was just admiring the fantasy. And you know how I know its fantasy? Because I'm part of the machine that keeps the fantasy alive! I get rid of the trash.' And it's the truth too. I told that lady the truth. My wife likes to look at the bikini pictures and point out all the airbrushing, the eating disorders, the fact that no woman, not even the women in these pictures, are actually that perfect. And of course she's right. But you know, that's very similar to waste management. In real life, there's cellulite, and there's stretch marks, and there's poverty, and there's garbage. If you can't get rid of it, you hide it, and people love you for it whether they know it or not."

"Holy shit," I said. "And then the coach is like, 'Your wife left you six months ago and took the kids because she's knows you're a piece of shit.' And then the CEO breaks down and cries. But dude, you sell those lines way better than the actor in the movie."

"You're the only one who gets me," Keith said. "I've missed you a lot."

The entrance to Bridgetown Recording and Playback was a fire marshal's nightmare. We walked up the narrow metal steps onto a small landing. The front door opened into a tiny kitchen packed with partygoers vying for beer in the refrigerator or standing around the snack table, generating so much heat and humidity that walking inside felt like walking into a tropical rain forest. We squeezed into the kitchen. We were baked. Keith went to get us beer. He was a bulldozer. Bumped into someone every time he moved forward. People looked at him with shock or disdain after he knocked over their snack plate or made them spill their drink or when he stomped on their feet or hit them in the solar plexus. He came back with our beers with the sincere belief that he'd hurt no one.

We left the kitchen and squeezed through a vocal booth that led to the main room where most of the recording was done. The room was the size of a basketball court, wood-paneled walls, wooden floors, tasteful rugs, musical instruments everywhere, a grand piano, a Hammond organ. Al Green bumped through a gorgeous sound system. I walked past people I knew, said hello or tilted my head in recognition. I looked around for Ida but didn't see her. I made my way over to William and Skyler, who were standing in the middle of the room talking to a guy named Murray. He was the owner of the studio and the producer we'd be working with.

Murray saw me approaching and put out his hand. He was in his early forties. Tall and bearded and wore a camouflage baseball hat. He had an impressive Wikipedia page. He was born in Alabama, used to be married to a famous actress. After his divorce he sold his recording studio in Los Angeles and moved to Portland for a fresh start. Something I could understand.

"There he is," Murray said. His handshake was firm but not crushing like my boss's. "We were just talking about you." I'd met him once before, but he clearly didn't remember my name.

"Murray wants us to play a few songs before the other guys get started," William said.

There was a band setting up at the back of the room. I didn't recognize the other guys, but I knew the drummer, he was big-time.

He'd played for a lot of big names, and I respected him because he came from a jazz background and had range like Hal Blaine. I was too stoned and hadn't practiced enough lately to play in front of someone like that.

"Look at him," Murray said, pointing at me. "Looks like he's just seen a ghost. No pressure, my friend. But since you guys will be recording here, I thought it would be a good way to introduce y'all to the crowd and some of the people you'll be working with. Got some press here too."

Richmond and Keith came over. Murray shook their hands and asked them if they wanted to play. They were on board immediately. I wondered if I was the only guy who hadn't been practicing. I tapped out rhythms on my desk at work, sometimes hit sticks on my thighs when I was watching television, but I hadn't played a kit since our last show in Los Angeles a few weeks ago. As far as I knew, my set was being stored in the basement of the Woods. In the space where I'd once dreamed my body was hanging on meat hooks.

We went to the studio's control room for a quick band meeting.

"Guys, this is nuts," I said. "I'm not ready for this."

"Then you better get ready fast," Richmond said.

William closed the curtains of the big windows that looked into the main recording room.

"We're going to be great," he said.

"Guys. The music is in our hearts," Keith said. "Don't think, just feel. That's what I do every time. I couldn't tell you the chords to any of our songs. I learned them to forget them."

"Must be nice," Richmond said.

"Fucking bass players," I said.

"We should get up there," William said. "Julian's turn for the pep talk."

"Fine. Let's bring it in," I said. We got in a circle and put our arms around one another's shoulders. "You know. I just gave him shit, but Keith's right. All we can do is our best. And the best comes from the heart."

"Playing with you guys is my favorite thing in the world," Richmond said.

"I've been thinking about Olympia," William said. "We should dedicate this show to her."

"Let's play our best for ourselves and the cat," I said. "Wherever she may roam."

"Alright," Keith said. "Cat on three, then, okay? Ready? Go. One. Two. Three. Cat!"

We forgot to talk about what songs we were going to play during our band meeting. While Murray introduced us to the crowd, William turned around and told us what he thought we should play. As soon as Murray finished talking, I counted off and we got started. The set I was sitting behind was nothing like my 1970s Slingerland—with that kit I sometimes had to be more delicate than I wanted—but the Ludwig I was playing was tight and felt like a tank. The tones were good, but they weren't adjusted to my ear. Richmond had an Epiphone Casino instead of his usual Strat. Keith had a Rickenbacker instead of his Precision Bass. But it didn't matter. We were Plaid fucking Parenthood.

We finished the first song with a crash. William said a few words to the crowd. I looked around and saw Ida standing toward the back of the room. William stepped in my line of vision and told us the next song. The guys waited for me to count off. I counted and we started.

Three songs and we were done. I headed for the kitchen. On the way, the drummer I respected told me I'd killed it. We exchanged phone numbers. He told me he'd let me know about a studio gig he had to pass up on that he thought I'd be good for. He talked to me like I was a professional drummer just like him. A good life was possible, I could see it in this very hazy, dreamlike way.

Ida was in a corner digging around inside a cooler.

"Going for a swim?" I asked.

She stood up and hugged me. Her hands wet and freezing. A

refreshing shock of coldness in the steamy room. The rest of her was warm, and that was nice too, her body against mine, if only for an instant.

"The lack of class in this place. Who the hell drinks Budweiser?"

"I know where we can find whiskey," I said.

We grabbed plastic cups from a bag on the kitchen counter. She followed me down the narrow corridor that connected the kitchen to the control room. It was dark. I turned on the lights. Murray was sitting all alone behind his state-of-the-art console, hands clasped together in his lap.

"Julian, my man," he said. "Holy hell. You were great."

"Thanks. Sorry to bother you."

"Are you kidding? Not a bother at all. I was just taking a moment to think about y'all's music. The first song needed scuzz and more dirt, maybe synth, maybe more distortion, maybe both. The second song could use a more intricate arrangement; I'm thinking some strings. I think you guys are on the verge of psych-rock, shoe-gaze, new-wave perfection. And I'm going to get you there, don't worry. I'm going to whip you guys into shape."

"Sounds great," I said. "Mind if we have some of that whiskey?"

There was a bottle of Blanton's sitting between the computer monitors. I'd seen it earlier when the band had a meeting. Murray rolled his chair closer to the console and picked up the bottle. "You talking this stuff here? I don't drink brown. This was left over from a band that just finished recording here. You can drink as much as you'd like." He wheeled his chair to where Ida was standing and handed her the bottle.

"Thank you," she said.

"No problem, honey. I have to go out there and introduce the next band. Y'all can stay in here as long as you'd like."

I sat on the couch. Ida sat on the office chair and spun around to face me. She was wearing the same white overalls she'd worn when we first met. But the overalls were splattered with more paint than before. Hard work had never looked so good.

"What a fucking weirdo," she said.

I put out my cup and she poured in some bourbon.

"Murray? He's not bad," I said.

"Whip you into shape? That's such a fucked-up thing to say to a Black person."

"I hoped I'd see you here," I said.

"I had no idea. I came in to find something to drink and there you were, playing."

"Do you listen to music when you paint?"

"Sometimes."

"What did you last listen to?"

"Alice Coltrane's *Universal Consciousness*."

"Damn. Compared to that, my band is bullshit. You ever listen to any rock?"

"Nope."

"I think I can get you into it. We'll start with the blues."

"But maybe I already know what I like and don't want to be taught to like anything that doesn't come to me naturally," she said. *Fuck*, I thought. *Slow down, Julian. The last time you saw her was at the diner, and the last time you talked was when she told you to leave her alone.* "I'm just messing with you. Do you know how to draw?"

"No," I said.

"Cool. Then I can teach you how to draw between our music lessons."

"You've seen me play twice," I said. "When can I see your work?"

"Maybe tonight," she said. She poured herself more whiskey. She wheeled over and poured more in my glass before wheeling her chair back to where she'd been before, two feet away. "Do you know about me and Richmond?"

"I do," I said.

"Does he know about you and Liesel?"

Shit, I thought.

"How do you mean?" I asked.

Ida shook her head at me and smiled.

"So silly. See, that's the thing. You kept treating me like you thought I was perfect. And I ate it up. I loved it, but it also scared the shit out of me, because I'm not perfect at all. I'm actually kind of a mess. For a while I thought you might be too good for me. But then when I found out about you and Liesel, I was like, damn, Julian isn't that goody-two-shoes I thought he was. Maybe we can work this out."

She grabbed the bottle from the top of the console and poured herself a little more whiskey. She seemed to enjoy having the upper hand. She had a cute smirk on her face.

"C'mon tell me. How did you find out?"

Ida shook her head again.

"First you answer my question, and then I'll answer yours. Does Richmond know?"

"Yeah, I told him. I thought he might lay a hand on me, but he didn't."

"No surprise there. He told me that's why he couldn't tell you about us, because he loves you too much, he couldn't bear to see your disappointment. But oh my God, Julian. Liesel slapped him so hard it had *me* seeing stars. What a smack. And when she knocked over that coffee mug."

We both cracked up laughing. I wanted to laugh with her about silly shit forever.

"She really did lose it, didn't she?"

"Yes she did. But you must have liked it because you slept with her afterwards. Becky has the studio right next to mine. She can't keep secrets and Liesel knows it. Great revenge on her part; she definitely knew I'd find out. And from what Becky says, you guys were super loud."

"Oh man," I said. "Becky. I should have known."

"No, really, it's okay. I'm not mad, and it isn't even my place to be mad."

"So did I ruin it for us?" I asked.

Ida got up from her chair and sat next to me on the couch. She turned to face me. "How do you mean?"

"Now that we've cleared everything up, can we try again?"

I took her hands in mine.

"Let's see," she said.

Kissing her was like that shooting jacket if I'd slipped it on and the sleeves weren't too short.

"Your lips are lovely," she said.

"C'mon," I said. "I was thinking the same thing. Let's stop playing."

"I want to see what this is," she said. "But I have to warn you, I'm not the most available person. I need a lot of time alone."

"I respect that."

"We'll support each other," she said. "You push me, and I'll push you."

"Girl, I'll push you every night and day."

I leaned in to kiss her. She pushed me away.

"I'm talking about honoring ourselves by being free people."

"Exactly," I said. "Right now?"

"Julian. I'm serious. And I think we owe it to ourselves to take things slow and go on another date."

We poured more whiskey and headed to the music. Richmond and Keith stood at the back of the room. Both said a quick hello to Ida as we walked past them. Nothing seemed strange between Ida and Richmond, but then again, long as I'd known them, they'd been keeping secrets from me. Ida and I walked through a door at the back of the room that led to a hallway. We walked past small rooms partitioned by wood until we got to her tiny studio. There was hardly any room to move around in. The space was taken up by paint supplies and Ida's work. She turned on the lights. Huge canvases. Big, bold abstracts. Blues and greens and whites and browns and oranges and yellows. Often swirled together. She stood behind me as I admired her work.

"Do you ever cry?" she asked.

"I cry all the time," I said.

"I don't think you should ever paint on a subject that doesn't bring you to tears. The best you can hope for is to make the viewer feel what you felt when you were creating it."

I told her I loved her work, and I did. And I could see why Richmond hadn't. He played his guitar as if he were searching for the truth. Ida's paintings weren't interested in answers.

45

WHEN THE MUSIC WAS FINISHED, we all left the warehouse and walked down the stairs to smoke cigarettes and pass a joint. The whole gang was there. Skyler kept waving away cigarette smoke but was willing to make the sacrifice for access to the joint. She was giddy and drunk.

"Let's have a bonfire at the bungalow," she said.

"Babe," William said. "It's been condemned."

"The outside is fine," she said. "It's still your house; you can do whatever you want with it."

"Edgy," Keith said. "A bonfire in the backyard of a house that's been burned. I like this rebellious Skyler. Bring her on tour next time."

"Watch out or I might make us all jump into the swimming pool again," Skyler said.

"I love you," William said.

Richmond looked at me and Ida.

"You guys want to go?" he asked.

"Sure," Ida said. "But I'm too tipsy to drive."

"I'm only a little stoned," I said. "You can ride with me."

"Okay," she said. "But we're taking my truck. Not Liesel's car."

Richmond smiled at me and shrugged. Even when all is forgiven there are ghosts. I couldn't wait until the Liesel shit stopped looming. But the past didn't care what I wanted though, did it? And neither did the future. I had to make it so.

Driving Chuck was fun. The slight grittiness between the changing of gears was the most satisfying interaction I'd ever had with a machine. I stopped at the house to pick up a bottle of bourbon to bring to the bungalow and to tell Reggie he could go home. Ida stayed in the truck. We both knew if we went in there together now, we would probably miss the bonfire, and she was very serious about going on another date before we hooked up.

Walter was in her cage, but it wasn't properly latched. If she pushed on the gate, she'd be free. I didn't see Reggie anywhere. I figured he must have gone home. I opened the cage and the sliding door to let Walter out to pee. I drank some water. When I put the glass in the sink, I noticed there were two white teacups sitting in there, fragile fine China. Out of curiosity, I picked up one of the teacups and took a hard whiff: peppermint schnapps, no doubt about it. Walter followed me as I searched every room. The side door to the house was cracked open. I'd given the guy all those instructions and still he hadn't shut it properly. Classic teenage bullshit.

Reggie and his guest weren't in the house. I called his phone. He didn't answer. I put Walter in her cage and told her goodnight. I got back in the truck and told Ida what was up. The bungalow was less than an eight-minute walk. We walked instead of driving, to see if we could spot him, but we didn't.

There were more people at the bonfire than I'd anticipated. It seemed like anyone who had heard about the bonfire had showed up. A lively group, yet quiet. Everyone spoke in half whispers. It was past ten o'clock, and something about the night vibe of our neighborhood made any decent person lower their voice. Ida and I sat on the stone bench and smoked spliffs. We held hands. The fire blazed. Wood crackled. Voices drifted. My phone buzzed in my pocket.

"Reggie's mom," I said.

"Oh shit," Ida said. "Are you going to take it?"

"I have to, right?"

"Yes," she said. "But don't snitch unless you have to."

"I'm no snitch," I said. "I'll be right back."

I stood up and answered the call, brushing past Richmond, who was sitting on a blanket talking very closely to a woman I didn't recognize. He slapped my butt as I passed him. I answered the phone.

"Hello?"

"Julian? It's Claire. Are you with Reggie? We expected him home half an hour ago."

"I just sent him home," I said. "I'm sure he's on his way." I figured a little lie would give the kid some time to get his peppermint-schnapps-drinking butt home. I walked to the front of the bungalow. Elizabeth Bishop was still locked to the tree. I patted her seat. I looked across the street and saw Claire standing in her driveway.

"Wait, is that you there?" She hung up. We met under the basketball hoop. "He's not answering his phone. Peter walked over to where you're staying to find him. He said he rang the doorbell and the dog started barking, but no one came to the door."

"How long ago was that?"

"Probably fifteen minutes ago. Peter is still out looking for him."

"Yeah, I guess I sent him home about that long ago."

"Huh, will you walk with me a little to see if we can spot him?"

We headed toward the park. Trouble was, I knew Reggie wasn't there. I'd already looked for him at the park.

"So how are you doing?" Claire asked. She wore a long black cardigan that looked loungy and luxurious. *Now that right there is what money is for*, I thought. When I stayed at their house the night before Reggie's birthday party, after they'd found me sleeping in a car, after Peter had threatened me on his beautiful boat, and after eating a phenomenal salmon dinner with white wines that cured my distaste for white wines, we watched that killer coach movie in their basement home theater. Reggie and I had sat on one leather couch, and Peter and Claire had sat on the other; and they kissed and cooed the whole time. They seemed to be truly in love, an apple without a worm like that John Cheever story, real-deal love that was almost like salvation. The kind of love I was after.

"I'm pretty stoned," I said. "How are you?"

"Peter and I weren't stoned, but we were happily tipsy on wine before our son went AWOL."

"Kids, huh? The ultimate buzzkill."

Claire laughed. We passed the public swimming pool. The water glistened. A good night to hop the fence.

"Reggie is forever interfering with my buzz. But he's worth it."

"He's the best," I said. "But I don't think he's as happy as he appears."

"He isn't. He hides a lot of his emotions. He learned that from my husband."

Her phone rang. Peter had found Reggie walking around the neighborhood with Natalie.

"They walked her to her house and now they're heading home."

"At least he's safe," I said.

"Oh no, he's not safe at all, he's in deep, deep shit. He won't be seeing that girl for a very long time. Will you please play basketball with him again? I'm going back to work, and it would be nice to know he's got another adult looking after him."

"Are you for real?" I asked.

"Yes. I know in that letter I asked you to stop, but I understand things better now. You're a good influence on him. You really are."

"So the letter was your idea?"

"Of course," Claire said. "Couldn't you tell by the handwriting? When it comes to our son, the buck stops with me. Oh, there they are."

Peter and Reggie were walking toward us. But there were footsteps behind us as well. It was Ida. She and Claire introduced themselves.

"It's so nice to finally meet you," Claire said. "You and Julian will have to come over for dinner sometime. I wish I had more time to chat right now. But here comes my husband and my troublemaking son."

Claire met up with her family and put her arm around her son. She talked to him quietly as they walked. Peter stayed a few steps behind them. Reggie nodded at me somberly as they walked past us. Peter introduced himself to Ida, and the three of us walked behind Reggie and Claire.

"The poor kid is going to be in a world of trouble," Peter said. "Hopefully not too bad, though. When did this kind of thing happen for you guys? About the same age? I think I was about fourteen myself."

"When did what happen?" Ida asked.

"Messing around. Getting caught by your parents. I figure this happens to everyone."

"Never happened to me," I said.

"That's on account of you being a child bride," Ida said. "Me? My mom caught me kissing a boy behind the school when I was eleven."

"See? Exactly," Peter said. "It's natural. I just hope Claire isn't too tough on him."

Once our parties had split and we were across the street from each other, standing on our respective driveways. Reggie yelled over to me.

"Julian! I'm sorry I disappointed you and betrayed your trust. Walter was really great. I gave her food and water and let her use the bathroom before I left. I'm grounded, but Mom says I can still play basketball. You want to play tomorrow? I have a bunch of chores, but I can play after that."

"I'm busy tomorrow," I said. "But Monday after work I can do."

"That should be fine. I've been grounded. Mom says I won't be going anywhere for a very long time. I won't have my cell phone, so call my house phone if you want to talk. I'll have my mom text you the number. Ida, good to see you again. Julian is a cool guy. If you go out with him, we can all hang out. You can come get frozen yogurt with us after I'm done being grounded."

"Can't wait," Ida said. "It's good to see you again, Reggie."

"The next time it will be ice cream instead of yogurt," I said.

"No. Frozen yogurt all the way."

"Ice cream."

"Yogurt."

"Okay, Reggie, let's go," Claire said. "Goodnight, you two."

Peter shouted goodnight. The family walked into the house.

"I still can't believe it was her idea to write me that letter," I said.

"I love how Reggie gets in trouble and he's still so full of joy," Ida said. "Shows he's got a healthy family situation. And congratulations, they seem to love you now."

"Thanks," I said. "Sometimes I win, look at that. Let's get everyone to hop the fence into the pool."

"We can be rebel kids like Reggie, too," Ida said. "Totally. I'm with you in theory, but tonight I just want to be cozy by the fire."

46

THE NEXT DAY IDA AND I went to the St. James amusement park. The roller rink featured an organist playing a huge Wurlitzer pipe organ. The place shook with soulful vibrations. Ida could really skate. I was no good. Every time I fell, she laughed before she got concerned that I might be seriously injured.

After I'd taken enough abuse, we headed toward the ancient Ferris wheel. The way it moved, you got the feeling it could jam up any moment. I'd only been on it once before. When I first moved to Portland. I'd gotten on it all by myself, and the whole time I'd been afraid of getting stuck in the air, trapped in a cage for hours, needing to pee, and eventually losing my mind. But I braved it for Ida. I acted like I wasn't freaking out.

We were the last to be loaded into a cage. We held hands. It was my kind of weather. Mid-70s. Crisp air, radiant vegetation. The first rotation went smoothly. I spotted the bungalow, my precious old home. I decided I was going to convince William to have it repaired, find the cat, and be roommates again. The second rotation went smoothly as well. I looked at the river. I decided I'd call my parents. Tell them whatever they needed to hear, because I missed them, loved them, and I needed those documents. I'd even tell them I still believed.

On the third rotation, the wheel jerked and stopped, and our car sat suspended above the oak trees. I looked around St. James. Took it all in and waited to see how things shook out. I felt calm. I had Ida next to me. I had a history of thorny situations that I'd managed to find my way out of. I'd climb down the wheel if I had to, steal a sailboat, and take it further west if necessary. Make a real attempt at my own version of happiness. In spite of the rain that had just begun to fall.

ACKNOWLEDGMENTS

My mom and dad have always supported and loved me. No matter what. The older I get the more I appreciate, understand, and love them. I'm honored to be their son.

As the oldest child, I felt it was my duty to make up stories. Thanks for laughing, my brothers. Justen, Joshua, Jonathan, Jordan, and yes, Salomon too. I love you guys. Justen, thanks for encouraging and believing in me and reading my early stuff. Confido.

To all my early encouragers and readers: Michael. Laura. Joey. Danielle. Hannah. Thank you.

I started going to school when I was sixteen years old. What a culture shock for this homeschool kid who didn't know much about the world. My eleventh-grade English teacher, Mr. Kummer, assigned the classics, and he wrote in my writing journal that I could do anything I wanted when I grew up, and I believed him.

Joshua Ferris was my first workshop instructor. Ever since then he's been a mentor of sorts, and I really appreciate him.

The Iowa Writers' Workshop changed my life. Thank you especially to Lan Samantha Chang. A great leader and compassionate teacher. I'd like to thank all my professors, who have made me a better reader, writer, and teacher: Charles D'Ambrosio, Margot Livesey, Ethan Canin, and Frances de Pontes Peebles. Special shout-out to Jess Walter. I hope you find the shape of my novel satisfactory.

I made some good friends during my time in grad school. JJ. Kevin. Ada. Sam. Gemma. Matthew. Santiago. Belinda. Ife. Bobby got me through those first teaching days of rhetoric and I'll never forget. Abigail I can talk to for hours about anything. Thank you, Xochitl, for reading my book a million times and being Xochitl. Thank you, Kiley, for hooking my family up with a sweet Iowa City house next to the cemetery, and for your kind words about this novel. It was a good pandemic house and a good writing house. Thank you to all of the wonderful friends my family made in Iowa.

My band brothers. Brian, Sean, Micah, and Matthew. You've saved me more than once. You've dined me, wined me, let me crash, pulled me off the floor, been my roommates, bandmates, and confidants. Forever grateful and blessed. I can't imagine where I'd be without you three and Rubin from New York.

The Holland family. The Boyd family. The Berger-Ruimy family. The Brown family.

I'd like to thank my amazing agent, Warren Frazier. Thanks for believing in me. To my editor, Sean Manning, thank you for believing in this book, and for those long phone conversations. Shout-out to Tzipora. To Jonathan, Kayley, and Stacey. To everyone at Simon & Schuster!

And finally, Katlin, my most trusted reader. Thanks for being the first person to believe. For encouraging me to follow my heart. Thank you for telling me exactly what you think even when you know it will make me panic and want to toss out the whole manuscript. So many revisions over so many years! Thanks for understanding six years ago when I started to skip out on my CPS sub job sometimes so I could stay in bed all day to read and daydream and write on notecards in that little Pilsen apartment with a great view of the sky.